All the Right Reasons

also by Bethany Mangle

PREPPED

BETHANY MANGLE

MARGARET K. McELDERRY BOOKS
NEW YORK LONDON TORONTO SYDNEY NEW DELHI

MARGARET K. McELDERRY BOOKS
An imprint of Simon & Schuster Children's Publishing Division
1230 Avenue of the Americas, New York, New York 10020

For information about special discounts for bulk purchases, please contact Simon & Schuster Special Sales at 1-866-506-1949 or business@simonandschuster.com.
The Simon & Schuster Speakers Bureau can bring authors to your live event. For more information or to book an event, contact the Simon & Schuster Speakers Bureau at 1-866-248-3049 or visit our website at www.simonspeakers.com.
Interior design by Rebecca Syracuse.
The text for this book was set in ITC Garamond Std.
Manufactured in the United States of America
First Edition
2 4 6 8 10 9 7 5 3 1
Library of Congress Cataloging-in-Publication Data
Names: Mangle, Bethany, author.
Title: All the right reasons / Bethany Mangle.
Description: First edition. | New York : Margaret K. McElderry Books,
[2022] | Audience: Ages 14 up | Audience: Grades 10-12 | Summary: As
cast members of a reality dating show for single parent families Cara
Hawn and her mother go to Key West where Cara meets Connor and now she
must juggle her growing feelings while helping her mom pick a bachelor
they both love.
Identifiers: LCCN 2021031504 (print) | LCCN 2021031505 (ebook) | ISBN
9781534499034 (hardcover) | ISBN 9781534499041 (paperback) | ISBN
9781534499058 (ebook)
Subjects: CYAC: Dating (Social customs)–Fiction. | Reality television
programs–Fiction. | Mothers and daughters–Fiction. | Single-parent
families–Fiction. | Love–Fiction.
Classification: LCC PZ7.1.M364675 All 2022 (print) | LCC PZ7.1.M364675
(ebook) | DDC [Fic]–dc23
LC record available at https://lccn.loc.gov/2021031504
LC ebook record available at https://lccn.loc.gov/2021031505

To James, my second true love after mozzarella cheese.

All the Right Reasons

chapter one

We've been dropped by so many family counselors that I pack snacks for the long drive out to the last therapist willing to referee my parents without demanding hazard pay. I nibble the edge of a homemade potato chip while Mom mutters under her breath, rehearsing whatever opening speech she wants to make.

Our version of family therapy is a lot like court, except for the ways that count. No matter how much Dr. Porter agrees with our side, she can't bang a gavel and fix it. There are no damages here—only damage.

"I'm going to scream if he keeps interrupting me again," Mom mutters, her hand drifting to the envelope tucked beside her, as though it might vanish if she put it in the back seat.

I let another chip sit on my tongue and turn soggy while I think about what happened at last month's session. It feels like I'm trapped in some inescapable time loop where it always goes wrong regardless of what I do. "I'm sorry."

Mom stares ahead with half-seeing eyes, her breath held. The car jerks a fraction as she turns her head to peer at me sidelong. "Did you say something?"

"No." I resume staring out the window, tracking the exits, the towns where Mom and I could start over, if only. If. If. If. The two little letters that have dominated our dinnertime conversations and kept Mom awake at night for weeks, poring over old files and free legal websites.

"Are you okay?" I ask as we turn onto the street of the therapist's office. I keep thinking if I make enough of these openings for her, she'll eventually tell me the truth. But instead, I'm just full of holes.

"Of course," Mom says, pitching her voice higher and smiling automatically, her lips like a curtain drawn along a track. "This stuff is never easy. We'll work it out."

I'd believe in her optimism more if I didn't often hear the involuntary choke of a stifled sob over the sound of the shower or see the gleam of concealer beneath her eyes in the harsh lighting of the kitchen.

She accelerates a little to reach the next open parking spot. Like usual, we've arrived well ahead of Dad and LeAnne, who insists on lording over my mother that she can attend now that she's officially married into the family. Mom opens her door and steps out before I can think of a response.

I follow her inside and hover over her shoulder until Dr. Porter waves us into her office. Unlike the dated waiting room, this room is modern and polished, with glass-top tables and plush carpet that gives away exactly the kind of reputation we have here—I look down at the imprint of where one of the chairs used to be, noting the increased distance between Mom and Dad's usual seats.

Dad and LeAnne arrive five minutes late, which is ten minutes earlier than usual, I guess. He takes off his ball cap and sets it on the table, nodding to Dr. Porter, whose ears move slightly when she clenches her jaw. "Hey, Doc. Sorry. Gym was busy. We had to close late."

"You could just ask people to leave," Mom suggests.

Dr. Porter taps her pen on the top of her knee. "Nice to see all of you again as well. Now, I know that last session there was some discussion about selling Julia's half of the gym. Julia, do you want to open today?"

"Discussion" is a nice way to phrase it. It's not like Dad was finger-in-face screaming at Mom while she batted him in the chest with a copy of their joint owners' contract. No, *that* would be ridiculous.

To my left, Mom takes a deep breath and exhales through her nose. She fixes her gaze on Dad. "I understand that you don't want me to sell my stake to any random person, but don't you think it's a little strict to require mutual approval? That couple who was interested before would have done a great job, and they had a lot of business experience."

"You agreed to the terms when we bought the gym to begin with," Dad retorts, holding up a hand when Mom tries to protest.

"Rick, it's Julia's turn to speak," Dr. Porter reminds him.

"She was finished."

"No, I wasn't. You cut me off." Mom pulls out the envelope she stuffed to bursting this afternoon. "I have another solution. A compromise. You could just buy out my half and take full ownership. That way, it wouldn't matter about the mutual approval clause."

LeAnne scoffs, then covers her mouth and coughs when we look over.

"If I wanted full ownership, I would have suggested that already."

Mom puts a knee down to support herself as she spreads the paperwork out onto the coffee table in a disorganized jumble. "But look at it. I've already done the math." She points to some figure, her hand shaking. "If you just break it up into payments, it wouldn't even be that much per month."

Dad stands and gestures at the documents, his shadow falling over Mom. "I'm not just going to change all my personal plans because you realized that you can't manage your money. You knew all along that we had a prenup."

"Don't act like you'd be doing any better in my shoes without your rental property. We didn't all get college funds so packed that we had money left *for two houses*."

"You obviously should have tried harder for scholarships, then."

Dr. Porter raises her voice. "I'm sensing some hostility. Rick, do you think you could sit back down? We should talk through this from the beginning."

Mom pushes herself up and tilts her head back to glower at Dad. "Oh, I'm sorry that I didn't foresee getting served with divorce papers while you were sitting in the living room acting like everything was fine!"

"Your shortsightedness isn't my emergency."

"Would you just stop?" I call out, shooting a pleading look at Dr. Porter. "Yelling isn't going to fix anything."

But they don't hear me.

"I know you have the money!" Mom swipes at the tears spilling over onto her cheeks, leaving wet streaks through the dark blush of her anger. "This is just another ridiculous power play because you can't stand that we'd leave if we could! You don't own us, Rick."

Dad reaches over to the nearest table to get a box of tissues. While he's turned away from Dr. Porter and he thinks no one else can see, he locks eyes with LeAnne and smiles.

Everyone always talks about how incredible it is to fall in love.

No one ever talks about falling out of it, how lost love sours once-happy memories like some creeping rot that preys only on the past tense.

I could have used software to cut Dad out of all the family photos, but stabbing them with scissors is so much more satisfying. In the middle of the night after therapy, I hack apart everything from my T-ball pictures to the commemorative photograph of that roller coaster ride where Dad barfed pieces of hot dog onto a complete stranger. The only thing I don't defile is Mom's wedding album. She deserves to do that herself.

I thought I was okay with it all. The cheating. The leaving. The loss.

But now, over a year after he left, on this otherwise random Monday, it descends like an avalanche sparked by a single errant step.

Still, making paternal-face confetti is probably not a Dr. Porter–approved coping mechanism.

I stand and stagger to the desk by the front door, kneading my knuckles against the chewed edge of the particleboard. I fire up Mom's laptop and pull up my SeeMe page, opening the screen for a private journal entry. I want a record of this feeling for the next time Dad makes some pathetic attempt to smooth it all over, as if letting me pick the pizza toppings is atonement for destroying our entire life.

I glance at the door leading to Mom's bedroom and tuck a pair of headphones into my ears to minimize the noise. With a shaking breath, I press record, watching as a grainy rendering of me appears on the screen.

"Dear Journal," I say, hesitating as I attempt to translate the burning ache in my chest into actual words. "I feel like I'm stuck. I know it's been a long time, but I still can't believe he's gone. And over what? Why? I mean, Mom is such a badass." Just for emphasis, I lean over and pick up a picture of her crossing the finish line of the Winter Sprinter 100-Mile Relay. I show it to the camera. "Woman ran twenty-five miles in subzero weather!" Even Dad hadn't attempted that race, letting three of mom's friends go with her instead.

Before I came along, there were more pictures of them together, hugging at the finish line or sharing a beer with marathon numbers still pinned to their chests. "Did I not give them enough alone time? I'm not one of those annoying kids, right?"

I sigh and lean back in my chair, groaning. "I wish I knew why Dad was being like this. Working together is so awkward. People are always like, 'It's so cool you have a family business,' but that goes out the window when your dad starts banging some lady from yoga class. And now he's totally different from how he used to be. I don't get it." The most terrifying part is that I can't tell if this is Dad's new persona or if he was this way all along.

I take a deep breath, but it does little to calm the sense of panic I feel sneaking over me. I pull my hair away from my face, twisting it into knots behind my head.

"Hey," Mom calls, emerging into the living room in an over-large T-shirt and old athletic shorts. "What are you doing up at this hour?"

I pick up some of the cutouts, holding them up to the desk lamp for Mom to see. "Just giving Dad a face-lift," I say, tossing our Father-Daughter Dance portrait into the nearby trash can.

"Cara." Mom sighs, leaning her head back until the ridges of her throat bulge against her skin. "This isn't healthy."

"Oh, it's so healthy. You should try it. Watch." I pinch the jagged edge of another picture between my fingers and hold Dad's face in front of mine. "You're a jerk and no one likes you." I crumple it into a ball and move onto another one. "Your 'famous chili' tastes like jalapeño dog crap."

I could do this for hours.

I finally goad Mom into joining me. At first her voice is low, but she gains confidence as she berates the pictures of Dad for every-thing from snoring to standing her up on their third date. She sorts through the various albums, enumerating his worst offenses with an energy that far surpasses the droning, slothlike manner of her second-rate divorce attorney. Maybe she should have represented herself.

"Do you remember that time he left me at a truck stop while I was in the bathroom?" I ask, laughing as I recall his screech of pure shock when he answered the phone. For the next few years, whenever we were going somewhere together, Mom would always say, "Hey, Rick? Did you remember to pack your offspring?"

Mom scoffs. "It was only funny because you were already home safe by the time I found out. Good to know that he's always been clueless."

"Yeah," I say. "He sure is if he left you, Mom."

And just like that, I burst out crying until I can hardly see past the tears blazing down my cheeks, blending with the snot and the spittle and the overall grossness spewing out of my face. "I don't know what's wrong with me. It just hurts all of a sudden." I smack my hands against my cheeks to clear away the tears like a pair of windshield wipers fighting against a downpour.

Mom wraps her arms around me and pulls me from my seat. She squeezes me until I can feel the clasp of her bracelet digging into my shoulder blade. "It's going to be okay. It has to be."

"I don't believe you." I hiccup my way through the words, my forehead bouncing lightly against her collarbone. "I just want to start over, Mom. I don't want to have to see him all the time. He didn't want us."

And he took more from me than he'll know. When two of my classmates asked me to the junior prom this spring, I turned them both down. It's like the magic is gone. What's the point of romance if it's all smoke and mirrors, and when the smoke clears, you can't stand to even look at yourself anymore?

Thanks to Dad, whenever I think of flowers and late-night phone calls, that high-flying rush of love, all I can see is the crater from impact.

"You'll feel better after you get some sleep," Mom says, guiding me back toward the couch. She squints at the laptop. "Are you recording this?"

"Sorry. I was in the middle of a journal entry. I kind of forgot about it." I end the session and turn off the lamp, hoping that the ambient light from the kitchen is enough for Mom to navigate back to her room.

She plants a kiss on my cheek. "I love you. Sleep tight. We can talk more in the morning if you want to, okay?"

"Okay. I love you too."

I don't even bother clearing the photographs off the couch. I fall asleep with them crinkling beneath me, surrounded by soured memories like a bird's nest built of old bread ties and straws and the debris of a different life.

I don't know why people say they slept like the dead. I slept the way only the living can, the exhaustion burrowed into my bones, my eyes gummy with last night's tears. I would have kept sleeping too, if it weren't for the hideous racket coming from outside the door.

I drag myself to a standing position, waving Mom away as she pokes her head out into the living room. "I'll get it." It's too loud to be the mailman, too sporadic to be the police. Maybe Mrs. Abernathy lit her kitchen on fire again in the first-floor apartment below us.

I wrench open the front door, my nose scrunched in annoyance even after I spot my best friend. Vanessa folds her arms as she waits on the open-air walkway outside. "Hey. What gives? I texted you fifty times." She points at the internal wall separating our living rooms. "I even knocked on the wall."

"Oh." I turn back toward the end table that I use as a nightstand. "Sorry, I put my phone on 'do not disturb' before I passed out. What's up?"

Vanessa shoves her cell phone so close to my face that I have to lean my head back to avoid hitting the screen with my eyelashes. "Uh, you're internationally trending right now," she says, her voice a mix of bewilderment and awe. "That's what's up."

I scrub my eyes with the edge of my sleeve and blink until my vision clears. I see my recording from last night, the video paused with Mom hovering over my shoulder in her improvised pajamas. I scan the rest of the page. People are already calling it *Crybaby's Hot Mom*. There's even a dubstep remix where my face has been replaced by a gigantic cartoon baby. "Wait a second. This is really on the internet?"

"Yes!" Vanessa exclaims, shaking her phone for emphasis. "And it's viral!"

"That's impossible," I mutter, trying to remember the previous night, the settings I selected before starting the recording. "It was a private journal entry." This can't be happening. All those personal stories.

But the number at the bottom of the video doesn't lie.

Viewers: 1.3 million.

chapter two

I send Vanessa back to her apartment and delete the video off my page before Mom can get a whiff of this fiasco. I have just enough willpower to keep myself from reading the 3,864 comments or typing my name into a search engine. Judging from what I saw on Vanessa's phone, removing the original post won't do much except make me feel better.

But if I have even a chance of stopping this before it reaches Mom, it's worth a shot.

Between therapy, my meltdown last night, and the ever-increasing stack of unpaid bills on top of the microwave, she has enough to worry about.

I find her standing in front of the mirror in our shared bathroom, her hair dripping in a steady stream onto the tile. She holds a floral blouse against her chest before tossing it away in favor of a black sheath dress. "Do you think I'd look okay in this?"

I close my eyes and clap my palm over my face for added protection as I shuffle around her. "Just once, just once, I want to go an entire week without seeing you in your underwear." We have an unspoken rule that sitting around half-dressed is a perfectly acceptable solution to avoid paying for air conditioning, but Mom is just getting out of control with it now.

"Oh, please. You were *way up in my business* first. Do you know where babies come from?" She drags my arm down to my side. "Answer the question."

"I'm sure it's fine." I keep my eyes trained on the ceiling. "What are you even doing? I thought you were coming to work."

"I can't. I have an interview."

I freeze with a brush pulled halfway through my hair, the bristles keeping it suspended as my grip goes limp. "I thought we talked about this. You can't get a second job. When will you sleep?"

"I don't have much of a choice," she says, shaking her head like a dog in the rain and pelting me with droplets of water. "If I don't find a way to make some extra income, we'll never be able to move."

I give her a half-hearted pat on the shoulder while I rush through my routine. I'm too exhausted to debate this again. "You should wear the dress. It'll match those heels you bought the other day. They were cute."

"You make a good point." She toggles her head back and forth, pretending to weigh my input even though the dress is clearly the victor. Once the shoes have been chosen, the contest is over. "I'm just worried that my triceps aren't as defined and my calves are getting squishy. People kept staring at me at your father's wedding."

A laugh wheezes past the handle of my toothbrush. I'm sure the staring had nothing to do with the fact that Mom couldn't stop compulsively commenting on how gorgeous, and young, and *regal* my stepmother looked in her poufy princess dress. Aside from the fact that Mom even showed up in the first place.

I spit into the sink and rinse out my mouth while I contemplate the total inappropriateness of what I'm about to say. "Mom, you're hot, all right? Like, seriously hot." I almost tell her that apparently

1.3 million people agree with me, but I'm kind of hoping she'll be focused on Dad long enough for this blow over. There's always a new viral video to replace the latest thing, right? Right?

"But do you think I still look, you know, fit? I'm not washed up?"

"No, you're not. It disgusts me how guys look at you." I wave my hand at her toned body, her flawless natural tan. Despite her protests that *everyone can tell*, her waist-length black hair still looks perfect even with the dye to cover up the gray. "On a scale of one to Aphrodite, you're at least a six."

She sighs. "But Aphrodite never won an Ironman Triathlon."

I echo her exasperation. "Okay, then you're . . . halfway to Ares. Is that better? I'm pretty sure it takes, like, five sculptors just to carve one of his butt cheeks."

Her chin bumps against her chest as she looks down at her size-two body and twists her arm into a pose.

I can tell from the curve of her lip that I've said the wrong thing. "What? He's an immortal god. You're just a buff mortal."

She must take the word "buff" as a compliment because she stops using her fingers as fat calipers and turns her attention back to drying her hair.

I don't mention that she never used to be this way before LeAnne. It was about breaking her personal records, even if she didn't top the competitor board. It's like when we moved, she forgot to wrap up her self-confidence in old Chinese takeout menus and newspaper and bring it with us.

I check the time and grumble. "Speaking of business, we're already late. Hurry up."

"You're awfully excited to spend your whole afternoon cleaning exercise mats."

"It beats having to go to school or do another biology project."

"Cleaning exercise mats *is* a biology project."

She has a point. There are a few people in beginners' yoga

class who could use a lesson in Downward-Facing Deodorant.

I speed through an abbreviated breakfast, then return to lurk in the doorway of the bathroom. I do this so often that I'm surprised there isn't a groove worn into the frame. "I get paid by the hour," I shout over the sound of the hair dryer. "Come on."

"It's just your dad. He's not a real boss. It's not like he's going to fire you."

I swipe to the clock on my phone and point to it. I'm over an hour late. "Challenge accepted." He kind of did fire us already. From his life.

It takes a lot of whining and finding the perfect spring scarf to brighten her dark dress before Mom decides that she can leave the house without being reported as an ogre sighting. She climbs into the car and straightens her seat, turning the key with just a little too much force. We're barely on the road for two minutes before her leg starts jittering.

"You look stressed."

"I do?" She lowers the rearview mirror and rubs at the minuscule crease under one eye.

My hand darts out to steady the wheel. "I swear, you're, like, the worst driver on the planet. Maybe you should go to driving school for me."

"Excuse you. I have a perfect record." She pauses. "Unlike a mailbox-smashing someone I happen to know. Hint: she's in this car."

I gawk at her. "Low blow, Mom. That was only one time."

She glances at me in her peripheral vision, her cheeks straining against a smile. "It *was* a low blow. To the fender."

We're still laughing as we pull into one of the angled parking spots in front of our family's studio gym. The café next door has exploded furniture onto their narrow patio in celebration of the warmer weather, the wrought iron chairs dotted with patrons in matching cycling gear. Mom sighs, the levity draining from her voice. "Do you think people will cancel their memberships now that it's nice out?"

"It'll be fine," I say, repeating our unofficial mantra of the past year. "It still rains and stuff."

"Your dad will have to give you a ride home. I'm not sure what time I'll be back. I have a couple of errands to run after my interview."

"Yeah. I'll tell him. Good luck."

I throw the strap of my backpack over one shoulder and push through the glass door into the lobby of the gym. The blenders from the juice bar are making a terrible racket over the upbeat pop music drifting from the speakers in the corners. I hazard a sniff at one of the smoothie samples and shudder. It smells like someone threw spinach into a sewer pipe. "I don't even want to know," I mutter to myself.

Dad turns back toward the front counter, blender in hand, and jolts. "Hey, Cara. I didn't hear you come in." He pours himself a large helping of green goop and takes a sip. "This juice bar was a great idea."

"If you say so." I both envy and resent Dad's ability to always hit the reset button, as though each day isn't accountable for its yesterday. It hasn't even been twenty-four hours since therapy, but here he is, acting like I'm not a goldfish trapped in his fishbowl.

On the bright side, at least he hasn't seen the video yet. There's no way he'd be this calm if he knew I aired his dirty laundry on the global virtual clothesline.

He leans around me to give one of the smoothies to a guy in a neon orange tank top. I sigh as I listen to him explain the health benefits of broccoli for the fiftieth time this week. "And it helps with constipation! It'll be smooth sailing after that shake."

"Dad," I hiss, smacking my hand across my face. "Please stop talking to people about the consistency of their poop. It's seriously not okay."

I think I notice a hint of red on his cheeks. "Is your mom out getting coffee?" he asks as he starts to clean up the vegetable scraps on the counter.

"No, she had something else to do. She said she already talked to Jake about taking over her Zumba class."

"Oh. Bad timing. All this mess about ownership reminded me about getting LeAnne added to the paperwork." His eyes flick over to the receptionist desk, where my new stepmother is making membership cards while her feet pedal a miniature stepper.

I suppress a wave of righteous indignation on behalf of my mother. "You're adding her as an owner?"

"It's only a formality. Your mom will still get half of everything. Well, post-prenup everything, of course. LeAnne just wants to be more involved in the business."

"She has her own job! She doesn't need to keep hanging around here where Mom—" I snatch a protein bar from the display, bite off the corner of the wrapper, and stuff the bar into my mouth to make myself stop talking. I don't even like pistachio, but it tastes better than bullshit. "Forget about it. Is spin class over yet?"

"Yeah," Dad says, picking at the end of a carrot with his thumbnail. "The next one isn't until eleven. You've got time."

"No, that's okay. I'll clean it now." Anything to get away from this conversation.

I trudge toward the exercise rooms and unlock the hallway closet that serves as both a janitorial stockroom and a secret hiding place for all the snacks that the staff members don't want to eat in front of clients. I push aside a bag of Doritos to grab some wipes and a bottle of cleaner. I close the door a little harder than necessary.

The spin studio is the smallest of the rooms, so it only takes about twenty minutes to eliminate the smell of old sweat and a dozen different types of hair products. I scowl at a mystery splotch on the floor, wondering if it's spittle or spilled water.

"There you are," LeAnne calls from behind me in a voice that I'm sure is a few notes higher than her real one. "You can't say hi to your stepmom?"

No, I can't. It would cause me physical pain. "Sorry."

She edges around the room and perches on an exercise bike a row in front of me. "So, I've been thinking," she says, propping one hand on the handlebar.

That's new.

"I know things are kind of tense. Maybe we could hang out and get to know each other better. Why don't you come over for game night on Thursday?"

I narrow my eyes. "*Fortnite* or Monopoly?"

"What?"

"Never mind." There went her one chance of being interesting. "Thanks for the invite, but I think I'll pass."

She follows me back to the closet and hovers in the doorway while I return the cleaning supplies. "Listen, I know this is probably hard for you. Your father was worried about upsetting you by getting remarried so quickly."

Yeah, that's *why I'm upset.*

"I'm fine, okay? And, um, I'm just gonna . . . go . . . now." I slink past her before she can think of a response, and spend the rest of the afternoon doing my best to avoid her in any way possible. It's harder than it sounds in a boutique gym that only has two exercise rooms, a cardio section, and a weight area.

I check my phone throughout the day, but there isn't a peep from Mom. I don't know if that's good news or bad. I ignore the torrent of messages from Vanessa and other friends who have been sending me unflattering screenshots of myself along with incredulous captions. Is this for real????????????

All the screenshots are from secondary sites. So much for my theory that deleting the video off of my page would make any impact whatsoever.

I don't respond to the messages, pained to realize that my old friends from my old neighborhood didn't quite make it to my new life. How could they, when their parents sided with Dad and gave those horrible depositions? *Julia does have a . . . less-than-conservative view about what counts as a single glass of wine. And she curses around Cara. We don't allow that kind of vulgarity in* our *house.*

Whenever any of the customers look at me, I duck my head and turn away. If they've seen the video, they have the decency not to say so, though I do feel more eyes on me than usual as I wipe down the floor-to-ceiling mirrors. Maybe that's just my paranoia.

I accost Dad as soon as it's a respectable time to leave for the day, given that I showed up late in the first place. At least I only work part-time. "Can you give me a ride home and can you please not bring LeAnne and can you please not ask why I don't want you to bring LeAnne?"

"Um, sure." He shrugs and pats the invisible pockets on his athletic shorts. "Damn. Let me get my keys." He heads over to the front desk and reaches around LeAnne, squeezing her knee as he retrieves his key chain from the top drawer.

The only thing that keeps me from vomiting on the floor is the fact that I'd have to clean it up and therefore stay here even longer.

While we drive, Dad tunes in to the radio show we used to listen to as a family on the way home. I let it play for a few seconds before I push the volume button and mute it.

"So, uh, doing anything fun this summer?" Dad asks.

I snort, half of out of derision and half out of pity. With infinite possibilities for topics of discussion, trust dear old Dad to find the biggest conversational land mine every single time. "Not really. Things are kind of . . ." Bleak? A financial dumpster fire? The adult word—stretched?

"Well, you know you're always welcome to move in with us."

I'd rather live in the flaming dumpster. "Thanks."

We pull into the lot of my apartment complex and idle in a strip of sunlight. Dad averts his eyes from the dated facade, settling on the glass enclosure that must have been the reception area back when this was a low-rise motel. "Don't forget to give your mom that copy of the ownership amendment."

"I won't. Thanks for the ride. I'll see you on Saturday." I close the door before he can tell me he loves me. It's funny how it can become a saying without meaning, no different than a Valentine's Day bear parroting phrases.

As I reach the base of the stairwell that leads to the second-story upstairs walkway, Dad rolls down the window, pitching his voice to carry over the hum of the engine. "What about Thursday? Didn't LeAnne ask you about game night?"

"Yeah, she did." The tautness of my smile mirrors the tight ache in my chest. "I'll see you on Saturday."

chapter three

As I run my hand along the rusted banister leading up the outer stairwell of our apartment complex, I pretend that the nausea roiling in my stomach is only from hunger. I don't turn around, even after I notice that Dad's car hasn't moved.

I pause halfway up, knowing that he's waiting for me to come back and apologize like I always do whenever I treat him the way he deserves. Part of me is disappointed that he hasn't seen the video. It would save me from having to tell a truth that has simmered within me all this time—that I haven't forgiven him for his betrayal and I doubt I ever will.

I take a deliberate step, then another, until I hear the sound of his car rolling out onto the street. I reach the landing and inhale sharply as I notice a man in a generic black suit crouched in front of our living room window, a piece of paper clutched in his right hand.

No one tries to sell door-to-door anymore. But I can think of a couple other things that come in colorful paper. Like eviction notices.

He must sense my presence because he straightens abruptly, fixing me with a distinct look of recognition. I take a step back and lift both hands, palms out, as he approaches. "My mom isn't home right now."

"Are you Cara Hawn?"

"Who's asking?"

I hear a hacking cough from behind him, and we both look over to discover Vanessa hanging out of her doorway, her bare foot jammed in the threshold even though it's the middle of the summer and I'm sure the metal is hot. "You okay?" she asks with a characteristically unsubtle flourish of her hand toward our unexpected visitor. "My suit senses were tingling."

"I think so?"

She waves again to silently ask whether she should go away. I gesture that she should stay. We're good at these little unspoken conversations after getting seated apart in every single class for talking too much.

The man's head swivels between us three times before he flattens himself against the railing enough to see both of us at the same time. "Hi. I'm Jon Polk. I'm from Wingfield Productions." He extends a hand in my direction.

I shake it from a distance, the way I might give a treat to a strange animal. "I'm Cara." Any of the questions formulating in my head would come out sounding rude, so I default to my front-desk-at-the-gym voice. "Can I help you?"

"I know this is out of the blue, but I saw your video and I loved it. It's so realistic."

"It *was* real. I left the camera on by accident."

"Right. Of course." Jon nods. "To get to the point, I wanted to let you know that we're casting for a television show, a dating show, and we'd love to have you audition. We're out in Pittsburgh right now at our headquarters."

Well, at least we're not getting evicted. "I don't understand. I'm a minor."

Jon blanches, a rosy tinge bleeding through his cheeks. "I meant for your mother, actually. We're looking for separated, divorced, or single parents with an only child who are looking to find love and get remarried. Think of it as building a new family on camera." He passes me the flyer and a stapled packet. "That's the ad for the original casting call and some extra information with more details. We're in final interviews now, but we can still fit you in if you're interested. It's the first season, so it's going to get a lot of attention."

"When is this?"

"Tomorrow. Sorry, that's so soon, but this was kind of a spur-of-the-moment thing."

Vanessa gapes at him like he's just offered me a seat on the next lunar landing. Meanwhile, I'm sure my expression is more confusion than shock. When Jon mentioned productions, I figured he wanted permission to make GIFs of us or something. "Why us? We're nobodies."

"Not anymore!" Vanessa interjects. "You're *viral* nobodies."

"How'd you find out where we live?" In retrospect, I realize that probably should have been my first question upon discovering a random stranger making hand binoculars against my living room window.

"The city is on your SeeMe profile. We pieced the rest together using your mom's name and one of those online address search things."

That isn't nearly as creepy of an answer as I thought it would be, but I still can't think straight. The silence stretches into awkwardness. I'm suddenly aware of the flyer growing mushy from the sweat on the pads of my fingers. "I should call my mom."

I text and call, but she doesn't answer, hopefully not because she's busy filling out employment paperwork for the second job she shouldn't have to take. I cover my phone and lean closer to Jon. "Quick question. Is there any money if we go on the show?"

21

He takes a breath, then hesitates. "We don't tend to discuss particulars until after we've made a selection, just to guarantee the integrity of the casting process. But I can say that there will be, compensation for whoever we cast as lead."

I hang up in frustration after I get Mom's voice mail again. "Okay. Well, I can't get her to answer, so I guess we can just call you later."

"Great. I'm so glad we could touch base, and I really hope to hear from the both of you. Your story is perfect." In his eagerness to give me his card, Jon accidentally gives me two. I pick at the corner of one with my thumbnail as I watch him retreat down the far stairwell and get into a small white sedan.

Vanessa leans forward into a diagonal plank, her feet still on the threshold with her upper body supported by the railing. Her eyes track Jon's car to the red light at the corner. "Did that just happen?"

Your story is perfect.

I tilt my finger to the side where there's a tiny round scar from the sharp bit of wire on my bridesmaid's bouquet that punctured my skin as we went out for pictures at Dad's wedding. LeAnne didn't want a Band-Aid ruining her photos, so I just clenched my fist harder and harder around those stems, my blood soaking into the rustic burlap ribbon.

Hold it together. That's what I do.

But now that the truth is finally out there, I realize that maybe letting everything fall to pieces is the only way to build something new.

chapter four

I look up at the sound of screeching tires, expecting to see Jon rushing back to tell me something he forgot. But instead of a white sedan, it's Dad's SUV that comes careening back into the lot. He slams the door and runs around the hood, increasing his speed up the stairs as he catches sight of me. "What did you do? I had to hear about this on the radio?"

Busted. My mouth starts speaking before my brain can catch up. "It was an accident! I didn't know the camera was on. I took it down as soon as I realized." I don't mention that it had been viewed over a million times by then.

"Why was the camera even on?" he roars, rubbing his forehead with both palms. "What kind of a stupid—"

Vanessa leaps forward, grabs the back of my T-shirt, and bodily hauls me into her apartment. She stands in the doorway, index finger in the air. "Sorry, Mr. Hawn. Nobody calls my best friend stupid. You can come back when you're not . . . whatever you are right now. Bye." She slams the door in his face.

I pull her into a lopsided hug. "Thank you. I can't deal with him when he's like that."

"I've got you covered."

We stifle laughs as we hear the distinct sound of Dad kicking the door, followed by muffled curses. I sneak a peek past the curtain and see him hobbling toward the stairs, pausing to shake his foot.

It can be actually painful to cram both of us onto the love seat, so I sit across from it on the floor, my legs stretched out before me. "I can't remember the last time I saw him that angry."

"And he doesn't even know about the TV part yet," Vanessa adds.

My groan comes out as some kind of exhausted pig grunt. "I have no idea how I'm supposed to talk to my mom about that."

"Did you tell her about the video yet?"

"No. I wimped out. But maybe she won't murder me." I fill her in about the latest therapy debacle. "If we go on the show, we'll finally have the money to get away from Dad. On the other hand, goodbye to any chance at privacy for the next bazillion years."

Vanessa leans back and exhales hard enough to send her bangs flying upward in a curtain. "It's a tough choice. Do you even want to go on a TV show? Forget about the money part."

"Without it, what's the point in wanting anything else?" I tick off the reasons on my fingers. There's no money to go back to court and tell them I don't want to see him. There's no money to start over. There's no anything except Dad's spite prenup and a child support check that's about to run out in October."

Vanessa nudges me with her foot. "Come on. You know what I mean. Everyone has a plan. I'm just asking if this is messing with what you want."

I shake my head, unable to trust my voice. I'm not like Vanessa, who already has a five-year plan and an obsession with school I will never understand. Even if she has to take out student loans up to her eyeballs, I know she'll be a programmer someday just because she wants it so much.

"Just think of the first thing that pops into your head."

"I don't fucking know, okay?" When I take a breath, the futility hits me again. I pull my shirt up over the lower half of my face, sobbing against the thick ridge of the collar as the frustration rips through me. I press the fabric against my mouth, hearing my rasping breaths overlaid with the echo of the same taunting question asked by every teacher and customer and cousin as though I'm supposed to know by now: *What do you want to be when you grow up?*

Vanessa leans down and wiggles the end of my sneaker. "Don't cry. I'm sorry."

"I just don't want this to be the rest of my life." I can feel the words scraping along my throat like a reluctant gunpoint confession. "Even if nothing else changed, me and Mom would find a way to be happy if we were on our own." Whenever I think of Dad, I feel like a dog banished to the backyard, thankful at least for a bowl, a meal, a pat on the head. Trying to see love in the "at least."

Vanessa tumbles off the couch and knee-walks over to throw her arms around me. She doesn't say anything, but she doesn't have to. I look around her cramped living room with the false wall separating the single bedroom. It's just like mine: too small in all the ways that matter. And people trapped in tiny lives learn not to have dreams bigger than they can carry home.

Once I've calmed down, Vanessa helps me plot the best way to break the news to Mom. But after an hour of talking in circles, we decide there isn't a delicate way to do it. "You just have to spit it out," she says, toying with the drawstring of her sweatshirt.

"I'm not good at that."

"I have faith in you." She points to the floor. "Your phone is ringing."

It's Mom. I answer and hold it away from my ear by a few inches. "Hello?"

"Hey. Are you okay? Your dad left me this bizarre voice mail saying you two got into an argument and he might have broken one of his toes. What's going on?"

"Can I just talk to you when you get home?"

"All right. I'll be there in about fifteen minutes. Try not to antagonize your father anymore. The last thing I need is him following me around tomorrow complaining all day when I finally have an afternoon with no classes."

"What about kickboxing?"

"Tomorrow's Wednesday."

Oh, right. It just feels like it's been eight hundred years since this morning. "I'm not even going to pretend to know what day it is. I'll see you in a few."

I give Vanessa a parting hug and trudge next door, my brain spitting out possible outcomes, almost all of them negative. Mom refusing to speak to me. Losing computer privileges. Being *that girl* for my final year of high school.

I turn the audition flyer and ownership amendment upside down and set them by the laptop, where they won't get swallowed up by the mounds of photographs still covering most of the floor.

My stomach gurgles its unhappiness, the acid rising until I can almost taste it. I make a beeline for the fridge, rearranging containers of health food in search of something more comforting. Finding nothing, I give up and shake the remnants of my homemade chips onto a plate. It only takes a few more minutes to whip up a watery roux with low-fat margarine and add in some of Mom's awful tofu cream cheese. I throw in a pinch of spices for good measure and pour it over the chips. Boom. Nachos.

Between Mom's obsession with healthy eating and the fact that a surprising number of cooking shows are free, I'm getting pretty good at this kind of thing.

I plop onto the couch that doubles as my bed and open the manila envelope containing the ownership amendment. It's only a page and a half, but even to my untrained eyes, the terms are clear. There's no way out, not unless Mom and Dad agree to a sale. The sight of LeAnne's name marring the header makes me want to march back down to the gym and strangle her with an ergonomic jump rope.

I shovel nachos into my mouth faster and faster until I can't hear the throbbing in my ears over the rhythmic crunching. Slowly, the ache in my stomach dissipates, taking some of my frustration with it. I lean back against the lumpy cushions and close my eyes.

The familiar scratch of Mom attempting to fit her key into the lock jars me from my fake-cheese-induced daze. I stuff the ownership amendment down the side of the couch as she steps into the living room. "Cara?"

"I'm right here," I say, patting the cushion beside me after she hangs up her purse and throws the dead bolt.

She sits on the very edge, her thick brows knitted together in concern. "What's going on? When I turned on my phone after the interview, I had all these weird texts from people I haven't talked to in ages."

"Promise you'll let me finish before you say anything."

She closes her eyes, too long for a blink, too short for a wince. "I don't like the sound of that, but okay."

"I accidentally posted that journal entry I recorded last night, and over a million people saw it," I deadpan, a thread of cheese dangling from my lower lip like a spiderweb. I swipe it away and sit up straighter. "Including a producer. How do you feel about being on TV?"

chapter five

*U*nlike the saying goes, it's impossible to talk out of both sides of your mouth at the same time, but Mom really tries. "I can't believe you would be so irresponsible! A million people really saw that video?" The volume of her voice fluctuates depending on whether she's talking more to me or to herself. "But that also means a million people are aware that Rick is an asshole. . . . Definite win there . . . Cara, I taught you to be smarter than that!"

The scream of the train flashing by the apartment complex interrupts my disjointed explanation of the video going viral, the visit from Jon, and the specifics of the show. I embrace the reprieve afforded by the overwhelming noise, savoring any chance to digest Mom's rapid-fire questions before having to answer.

Mom scowls at the window as it rattles in its loose frame. She beckons me into the kitchen, where we sit at the plastic folding table smashed into the corner. I scan the tiny print on the back of the flyer again, comparing it to the meager results from a quick online search. "All I know is that it's a new kind of dating show for divorced parents who are looking to get married again. He said it's like building a new family on camera."

Mom snorts. "Can't be any worse than the one we have now. And you said this is in Pittsburgh?"

"Just the interview. The packet says they're filming somewhere in Florida and that there will be 'fair compensation' if they pick us."

"It's in Florida? And there's money?" She reaches for the paperwork again. "You should have started with that."

"I was trying to tell you before"—I turn around to shout after it—"THE WORLD'S LOUDEST AND MOST ANNOYING TRAIN came through."

Mom reads pages two and three multiple times, flipping back and forth as though it'll change the contents. "Maybe this is our break."

"Really? Isn't it kind of gross to have kids on a dating show?"

"I don't think it's gross. It's not like you're the one falling in love. Do you not want to try out for it?"

I garble something incoherent. Instead of feeling one single emotion, I flash between them like an indecisive child choosing a favorite flavor of ice cream. Confusion. Indecision. I settle on shock. Pure shock that my mother, the woman who wants to see reviews before she changes brands of peas, seems to be seriously considering an audition for a national television show. "I'm not against it. This just seems so random."

Mom covers her mouth, laughing so hard that she can barely get the words out. "On a scale of one to your husband spontaneously divorcing you the day after your twenty-year wedding anniversary, how random would you say it is?"

I smack her arm, giggling. "Stop it."

We sit in silence for a few moments, each of us staring into the space above the other's shoulder, lost in the possibility of having possibilities again. "You know, Mom, these reality TV people can get pretty famous. What if we do this and we have everyone up our butts for the rest of eternity?"

"That's one side of it," she admits, joggling her head. "But on the other hand, maybe there could be opportunities associated with that."

"Like what?" Suddenly, it hits me. I bolt into the living room and retrieve the ownership amendment, reading it as I speed-walk back into the kitchen. "Yes!" I turn it around and place it in front of Mom. "Look! There's nothing in your contract with Dad that says you can't open more gyms!"

I can tell from her face that she doesn't understand. "What does that have to do with anything? And why do you have a copy of this lying around?"

"I'll come back to that part," I reply, my words quickening. "If we go on the show, not only do we get some money to start over, but maybe we'll also get famous enough that we could start our own gym somewhere else. Or, whatever it is you want to do. Athletic-wear line. Perfume. We could become influencers!"

"I think you're putting the truck in front of the strongman. We don't even know if they're going to pick us."

"We should go audition." I tap a drumroll against the table. "Think about it. We'd be free from Dad. You could just walk out on the gym, and he would be stuck running it because he can't tank it without hurting himself, too. And if we had enough money, you wouldn't even care if it went out of business, right?"

"I don't know about that," Mom says. "All my money is invested in that. It's a pretty penny, no matter how much else I might have in the future."

"You know what I mean! We could get a really fast car and drive it up and down Dad's street making lots of noise. Or send him passive-aggressive postcards from, like, Bali with us posing on some rich-people beach."

Mom laughs and scans our kitchen out of the corner of her eye. Her gaze lands on the cracked edge of the laminate countertop that we periodically worsen by trying to fix it before the landlord stops by again. "I was thinking more like a new place to live and buying name-brand oatmeal again."

"Name-brand oatmeal," I say, blowing a whistle over my bottom lip. "High roller."

Mom's smile starts as a shy tug at the corner of her lip, then grows until I can barely glimpse the white of her teeth. It stretches into something almost grotesque before her face crumbles. "I'm such a horrible mother." She stares at the laminate again as tears wobble against the sluice of her eyelids. "It's bad enough that I can't pay for your college or afford driving school. But oatmeal? I can't even get my kid the real oatmeal. Jesus. I'm awful."

"It's okay!" My brain scrabbles to find the right words, but the sight of her tears renders me powerless. A hard knot throbs in my throat. "There's financial aid for college. And I don't need driving school."

Quietly, spoken like a secret, she says, "I don't know why you stay with me."

I run around the table and hug her, mumbling against the top of her shoulder. "Because I love you and you're the best mommy ever."

Mom sniffles and shuffles around the notes she scribbled on the back of a Salvation Army receipt. "I love you too." She leans her head on top of mine. "So, do you want to do it? Go to tryouts?"

I push aside thoughts of Bali and actually think about it. Once I do, I realize there's no harm in giving it a shot. We can back out at any time, assuming they even want us in the first place. "Yeah. I'll audition for the first manned flight to Mars if it gets me away from Dad." My laugh becomes a guffaw. "I can't wait to hear what he's going to say about this if they end up picking us."

"Let me handle that."

"Don't start another big fight," I blurt, loathing that residual urge to smooth it all over, to not rock the boat, to not throw myself on the floor and cling to Dad's ankles and beg him to put back the fucking T-shirts and the suitcase and his Bon Jovi collection. Part of me will always be that girl, ears stopped up with heartbeats and the sound of screams, staring at the empty space where there used to be a toaster. And every morning since, I still listen for the *pop* it used to make, the phantom drip of dark roast, and the father who lied so well that I once believed in happily ever after.

Mom holds Jon's business card up to the light like it might be counterfeit. "I'll guess I'll call this guy and tell him we're in." She rises to her feet, upsetting the balance of the rickety table. "And then we have to pick outfits. Can you look up what to wear to an audition?"

"Do you mind if we do that in a couple of minutes? I need a quick break to process all of this." My brain can't choose what to think about first. My outfit? The money? Dad? Whenever I can't focus, I usually default to journaling aloud on my SeeMe page, but now I'm terrified to even sign in.

With no bedroom of my own, I head for my usual perch on the walkway outside. I must have been making more noise than usual because my phone buzzes a moment later.

> [Va-Ness Monster 3:41 PM] Talk it out or you want alone time?
> [Cara Hawn Solo 3:41 PM] Talk it out. Please.

As Vanessa opens the door, the happy jingle of a talk show intro filters out over the faint roar of a studio audience. She eases it closed behind her, using the knob to steady herself as she clomps over wearing no bra, paint-splattered shorts, and her dad's massive work boots.

I love her complete apathy for whatever the neighbors might think. Covering her car in Pokémon stickers. Checking the mail in fuzzy dreidel pajamas. Throwing her laundry off the balcony because it's easier than carrying it down the stairs, even though the rest of us are too proud to do it.

Mom used to be that way before the custody proceedings, those horrible hours spent listening to friends and relatives pick apart her parenting, spilling her ugliest secrets. Maybe it wouldn't be a bad idea for her to go on television, to hear from someone besides me that she's a good person and smart and beautiful and a million other adjectives, none of which are "worthless."

Vanessa slides her feet through the railing with some difficulty and sits down beside me in a puddle of sun, her wavy brown hair almost golden in the light. "You haven't looked this freaked out since that Health and Family final. How'd it go with your mom?"

The cold fist of embarrassment slams into my gut. "We don't speak of the Health and Family final!"

"It's not my fault that you were the only one who thought apoptosis was a kind of acne."

"I misread the question! Stop reminding me."

She allows me a moment to gather my thoughts before giving her the rundown on Mom's reaction. "I know I shouldn't get my hopes up, but I can't help it. Who knows how many people are on the short list already?"

Vanessa pulls out her ever-present tube of ChapStick and digs a pinkie into the lid to scrape at the remnants squished in the top before smearing a gob across her lips. "True, but they obviously like you already if they're making a special exception. That guy came all the way out from Pittsburgh when he didn't even know if you'd be home."

I draw in a deep breath and hold it until pain nibbles at my chest. Vanessa is right. We've clearly already stood out to the production company. Plus, if anyone can throw together an audition at the last minute and still get the gig, it's Mom. "Okay. Maybe I'm a little doom and gloom. Can you blame me after the way my dad went off?"

Vanessa shakes her head. "I still can't believe your diary went viral."

"Don't call it my diary. That makes it sound even worse."

She leans back to uncover her pocket and extract her cell phone. "Have you read the comments? Some of them are hilarious. The internet has the hots for your mom. Here, I'll read you one."

"Don't you dare," I say. "I will throw you off this balcony."

"Oh, fine. I'll just privately laugh at you behind your back."

"I should head in before Mom comes to check whether I died out here," I say, standing and brushing off dirt from the seat of my pants. "But thanks for listening."

"No problem. Hit me up if you need anything else."

I march into the kitchen, stuffing my hands into my pockets to fidget with the hard pieces of lint at the bottom. Mom is still at the table, sorting through various documents. "Hey. I signed a nondisclosure, and they sent over some extra stuff."

"Like what?"

"It's still not all that in-depth, but it says they're filming in Key West, and the show is called *Second Chance Romance*. The contestants will be 'eligible bachelors and their children, handpicked from all over America in a choose-your-own-family search for a second chance.' We have to pass some tests if we're selected, like a psych exam and a physical. And then there's a bunch of other legal mumbo jumbo about liability and privacy and the contract we'd have to sign."

The mention of the contract reminds me that I still haven't told Mom about the amendment to add LeAnne as co-owner of Dad's half of the gym. While she's distracted by the show, I extricate it from the pile of destroyed photos, chucking the entire thing into the trash as I pass. If that's still his biggest concern after finding out about the video, he needs to reevaluate his priorities.

There's no use worrying about the elephant in the room when the house is on fire.

chapter six

Mom swears that she wants me to drive all the way from northeast Ohio to Pittsburgh for practice on the open road, but I think it really has to do with the fact that her hands won't stop shaking. She sits in the passenger seat with the paperwork fanned out across her thighs, her teeth clicking together like an off-tempo metronome.

As if the audition isn't enough to stress her out, Dad has resumed calling, even though both of our voice mails are full. Finally, Mom gives up and transfers it to come through the stereo system instead of her phone. "Hello?"

"Why weren't you picking up?"

"We're driving."

"Where?"

Mom flails her arms in the direction of the radio. "I texted you and told you we were busy today. It's not like I have any classes."

"You should still be here."

"Last time I checked, you still take about fifty times more days off than I do."

"This isn't about me. This is about Cara and that video that's got me the laughingstock of the whole damn town."

"Okay. Well, Cara is right here. Why don't you just say what you have to say?"

Dad's huff crackles through the speakers. "Fine. First of all, it's abso—"

I can't hear the rest because Mom turns down the volume to almost nothing. She points to the activated microphone icon, then presses her finger to her lips. I nod.

After about three minutes, she turns up the volume again and he's still going. "Hey, Rick? Rick? I just have to butt in here. Sorry. We're about to get where we're going, but Cara says she's sorry and she took the video down already. Bye!" She hangs up before he can get more than half a syllable out. Her phone rings again, but she tosses it into her purse and shrugs.

"You know, if this doesn't work out, maybe you could be, like, a professional Ex-Husband Avoider Counselor."

She rolls her eyes, laughing. "It just makes me want to get picked even more for this show. Get away from here and breathe for five seconds. Can you believe him? God, the nerve. He's lucky I don't set *my* mom on him."

"It's okay. Chill. Don't awaken the Nana." I'm only a little bit joking. It wouldn't be the first time the extended family got involved.

"He better watch out. I'll do it."

The funniest thing about Mom being adopted is that people always judge her by these super-traditional Korean stereotypes or ask if some perfectly normal behavior is a "Chinese thing." Meanwhile, my nana is this tiny little German lady who will give you two black eyes without spilling her merlot.

Culturally, if I were a meal, I'd be kimchi and bratwurst and an ear of Jersey corn. Actually, that sounds…disgusting all together. *Auf Wiedersehen*, my appetite.

"Dad could always counter by summoning the Mommom."

It's weird to think of my only living grandparents as fighters in some kind of divorcé tournament match, but Mommom isn't anything to scoff at either. She'll whoop your butt and make it back in time to glaze the ham.

"Grandmother throwdown," Mom mutters. "You could make a second viral video with that one. But really, I bet even Rick's mom knows how he is sometimes. Just so full of himself. I can't believe I never saw it before."

"Your blood pressure is going to hit eight hundred, and we're not even there yet."

She checks her heart rate on her fitness tracker. "I guess I am a little stressed."

"Oh, just a bit? On a scale of one to Andy in *The Devil Wears Prada*, you're an eight."

"I'm not nearly that bad. Yet."

Her fidgeting grows worse as we reach the city. She consults the driving directions and points to her right. "It says to cross the river and continue east."

I throw my hands up in the air, holding the steering wheel steady with my knee. From the highway, I can see at least *three* stretches of river. "That's not helping! Just pull up the GPS." Navigating by Mom's directions and exit numbers was fine when we were in the middle of nowhere in Ohio. I need a little more specificity for the city.

"It's right here." She points to a spot on the map that I can't see because I'm too busy trying to maintain the perfect speed between two massive trucks. A sedan blares its horn as it cuts me off, then moves into the fast lane.

"Nope," I say, smacking the turn signal and pulling over onto the shoulder. "You're driving, or I'm going to hit someone. Too many cars."

"Are you sure?"

"MOM!"

We switch seats on the side of the road, pausing for a moment as she tries to start the car again, even though I never killed the engine. She exhales once, twice, before we pull back into traffic. I navigate off my phone, giving Mom instructions that are far more precise than "cross the river and continue east."

Eventually, after parking on the roof of an overpriced garage, we manage to find the correct street. Mom verifies the address, peering at a squat office building that lurks in the shadow of the surrounding skyscrapers like an unassuming mushroom growing in the moss between two trees. "This is it." She pats her hair and tugs on the hem of her dress. "How do I look?"

I roll my eyes. "Considering that my video went viral as *Crybaby's Hot Mom*, I don't think you need to ask that question."

We step inside and consult the directory board in the lobby. The building appears to be full of medical offices, law firms, and a real estate company. A sign taped to the wall says WINGFIELD PRODUCTIONS and directs us to the sixth floor.

We take the elevator in silence and step out into an unfurnished hallway. I shrug at the plastic sheeting covering half of the doorways and follow the stanchions directing us to the only finished office space. The woman seated at the reception desk glances up as we approach.

"Hi," Mom says, handing over her stack of paperwork. "We're here for the auditions."

The woman gestures to a clipboard on the counter. "Please sign in. You can have a seat in the waiting area until you're called."

I scope out the area while Mom fights with the cheap pen, scribbling a squiggle on her palm to get the ink flowing. There are over a dozen other kids in the room already, each of them seated next to their mothers.

I choose one of the last available seats, hunching down to avoid the fronds of a particularly broad plastic fern. Mom joins me a moment later, sipping water from a triangular paper cup. She tosses it back like a shot and turns the cup over in the palm of her hand, poking the pointy end. "I'm nervous," she whispers, her eyes tracking a statuesque brunette and her daughter as they disappear around the corner for their audition. "All of these ladies are so gorgeous and put together."

She's not wrong. I appraise the children around the room, some closer to my age while others might not even be in preschool yet. Outwardly, they seem so polished, as though they've always been prepared to go on camera.

I hone in on the girl sitting across from me, her tightly spiraled golden locks and chic outfit. Even her accessories are perfect, down to the way the rose-gold buckles on her purse and her watch match the CHELSEA necklace dangling just below her collarbone. "Somehow I don't think you're going to be the problem," I mutter, the weight of my own inadequacy hanging around my neck instead.

Noticing my attention, Chelsea leans forward, asking, "Hey, aren't you the girl from that video?"

I blanch, wondering whether I'm going to be answering that question for the foreseeable future, regardless of whether we get picked for the show. "We sure are!" To my ears, Mom's voice is too chipper, almost thunderous in the cramped confines of the room. "And we're so excited to be here!"

"What video?" her mom asks.

Chelsea holds her phone closer to her mom to share the screen. Even though the volume must be close to mute, I still hear myself berating one of Dad's pictures as she starts playing my journal entry. I sent angry emails to every website with a copy of the footage asking them to take it down, but to no avail.

"That was supposed to be private," I say, with a little more bite than intended.

Chelsea looks up. "That's what makes it so funny. And I'm sure you got a bunch of likes on it. I wish some of my stuff would go viral like that."

"It definitely had a silver lining," Mom agrees, gesturing around us. "Do you also do those video things? The social media . . . impacting?"

Chelsea laughs, but I get the sense that it isn't as good-natured as Mom's reaction would suggest. "Influencing? Yeah. I'm an actress. I've been in loads of commercials, but my best one is for shampoo. You've definitely seen it."

"Oh, wow." Mom scoots forward in her seat. "So, you've done this auditioning thing before? Do you have any tips?"

"I normally wouldn't help the competition, but . . ."

I text Vanessa a frowny face while half listening to Chelsea tell Mom that her outfit is too dark for spring and she should have opted for something brighter.

> [Cara Hawn Solo 10:03 AM] This girl here thinks she's the best thing since sliced bread. Totally want to punch her in the face. It's like American history class with Jaime all over again.

She must have had her phone in her hand because she writes back immediately.

> [Va-Ness Monster 10:03 AM] Calm down, Andrew Jackson. Just ignore whoever it is and kick their ass in the audition.

I watch as my cell phone battery drains to 30 percent. When it starts to protest its lack of charge, I switch to flipping through a magazine that seems to be made exclusively of advertisements. I rip out the perfume sample and show it to Mom. "Look, a bonus."

She coos over it, sniffing at the edge of the plastic. "And it's *Dior*. Are there more?"

We spend the next ten minutes hunting through the rest of the magazines until we've amassed a respectable collection of makeup and perfume samples. As Mom moves to tear one open, Chelsea makes a tsk sound with her teeth. "Can I give you a bit of advice?" she asks.

> [Cara Hawn Solo 10:29 AM] She wants to give us "a bit of advice."
> [Va-Ness Monster 10:30 AM] Is she that bad or are you just melting down?

"Sure," Mom says, laughing. "I'll take all the help I can get."

"That's really an evening scent. You'd be better off with the citrus for this time of year." As Mom sorts through the samples in her lap, Chelsea quickly clenches her hands into fists, then releases them. "It's the Versace. The citrus."

> [Cara Hawn Solo 10:30 AM] I don't know. She's acting like Mom should know what Versace perfume smells like.
> [Va-Ness Monster 10:30 AM] I take it back. You can duel her if you want to.
> [Cara Hawn Solo 10:31 AM] Hopefully she has stormtrooper aim.
> [Va-Ness Monster 10:32 AM] Girl, you're trying out for reality TV. Better hope they all have stormtrooper aim. Watch your back.

Thankfully, Chelsea and her mom are the next to be called, leaving Mom and me in relative peace, except for my ongoing battle with the fern. Since we were last-minute additions to the schedule, I'm not surprised when the waiting area slowly empties around us.

Finally, just after my stomach is threatening to mutiny, the woman at the front desk calls Mom's name. I grab her hand and squeeze. "Are you ready?"

"No," she says, her hands flitting between her hair and the front of her dress. "Deep breaths. I am taking deep breaths. We are doing this."

The receptionist shows us into a long room with an entire wall of windows, the curtains pulled back to let the natural light in. I follow Mom to the two empty folding chairs set in front of the white backdrop hanging from the ceiling.

The man sitting at the table across from us smiles and offers a wave. "You made it!" he exclaims, pointing between Mom and me with the end of his pen. He bows his elbows out to nudge the people on either side of him, who seem slightly less enthusiastic about our presence.

"That's Jon," I clarify under my breath. "The guy who was creeping through our window."

Mom nods.

"How's it going?" he asks.

I have to pee. Why didn't I pee earlier?

"We're so excited," Mom says, picking at the rough edge of her nail where the polish is lifting. "Thanks for having us."

Jon's laugh is so high that dogs in foreign countries are barking. "Of course. Of course. I'm a big fan of the video, as you know. Crybaby. Hot mom. Absolutely heart-wrenching and *so* funny." He holds up his hands and frames Mom, then me. "I love the whole angle. That's exactly the kind of emotion we're looking for on *Second Chance Romance*."

He gestures to his left, where two women are clustered around a camera tripod. "We're going to be filming this since not everyone can be here. We also have final interviews going on in Houston and Los Angeles."

I gulp. I didn't know that. I thought our odds were bad enough against the people in the waiting room, never mind multiple groups.

"I know you sent in the questionnaire already—thanks for that, by the way. It's such a killer—but I have a couple quick follow-up questions. Nothing too painful, but you might feel a slight pinch." He chortles at his own joke. "Ready?"

"Sounds great," Mom says, folding her hands in her lap and stirring up the faintest whiff of that stupid Versace perfume.

The questions range from simple to ludicrous, invasive to humorous. Mom handles them all with ease, hardly hesitating as she explains her love life and the catastrophic divorce. I try to tune out when she describes her issues with Dad, but my senses are heightened to the point of pain, my heart flailing to its own erratic beat. Separate interviews would have been nice.

"How long have you been divorced?"

"Legally? Nine months."

"Are you currently seeing anyone?

"No."

"Do you believe in true love?"

"Enough that I thought I'd found it once before."

Eventually, Jon wraps up his interview with Mom and turns to me. He consults his paperwork, circling something with a flourish. "So, Cara, let's talk about your father. How would you describe him in your own words?"

My frazzled brain belches up a random list of descriptors and words in no discernible order: *Tall. Manipulative. Business owner.*

Happy. Parent. Chevrolet. Medium rare. Funny. Marathoner. Brown eyes. Acid reflux. Controlling. Science fiction. Lapsed vegetarian. Size twelve. Betrayer. It's impossible to sort through it all. Sweat breaks out along my brow line. "I guess I'd just say . . . which one do you mean?"

Jon consults a piece of paper in front of him. "Your father. Rick Hawn."

"Yeah. Which Rick Hawn do you want to know about?" I sigh. "There are so many to choose from."

chapter seven

*T*he rest of the application process is an endless blur of phone calls and late-night emails. At each stage, we're told that we've advanced again. Our latest task is filling out this bizarre test with three hundred questions while a proctor stares at us over webcam. It's pure nonsense, a test that sounds like it was designed by Willy Wonka.

Once we're finished, I can't stop cracking jokes. "Mommy, would you like to play the saxophone? What is your favorite color? How do you feel about eggplants?"

"I think it's a psych exam," Mom says as she riffles through her file of medical documentation. "They want all kinds of other stuff too. That has to be a good sign, though, right?"

"Probably. I can't imagine they'd waste time asking every single person whether they like flowers or want to be an astronaut."

When we get notified that we're in the final five, we celebrate by going to the store for a special dessert. Mom's definition of a splurge is to buy a container of strawberries. I opt for the half gallon of mint chocolate chip and a bottle of chocolate syrup that I fully intend to drink when she isn't around.

Besides that, things are pretty much the same as always for the next week or so, except quieter now that school is out. Just before summer break started, Vanessa discovered that the door to the roof is unlocked, so we spend a lot of our time up there. She works on scholarship applications or plays video games on her phone while I mostly just stare into space, daydreaming about what it would be like to get the call that we've won. Part of me is afraid that I've built the show up in my head too much. "What if we don't get picked? What are we going to do?"

"We're hiring for a line cook at work soon if you're worried about money," Vanessa says, looking up from her notebook and balancing her pen against the back side of an air-conditioning unit. "I could ask my boss. He's only, like, thirty percent an asshole. Asshole adjacent. And you like cooking."

"I like eating," I clarify.

Vanessa cocks her head to one side. "Did you hear that?"

I listen closer and hear the faint sound of screaming. "Is that my mom?" I bolt for the door, my knees flashing in the bottom of my vision as I hustle to the second floor, leaping the last three stairs. I skid around the corner, fumbling with my key.

Mom opens the door as I'm fighting with the knob. I fall forward against her, pushing her shoulder inadvertently as I try to keep myself standing. She squeals in surprise as we both tip over backward, tumbling onto carpet that is far too thin to provide any cushion.

I smack my hair out of my eyes. "Are you okay? Are you okay?"

Mom breaks into giggles, covers her eyes with both hands, and rolls onto her side. "Knock me over! I don't even care! They picked us! They picked us! We're the stars! We did it!"

I shake her. "We did? Really?"

Vanessa skids around the corner, panting. "You should try out for track." She leans against the door. "I take it you're not being murdered?"

"I'm really touched that you'd draw attention to yourself while there's a nonzero chance that we're being murdered," I tell her as we watch Mom get up and dance across the living room, her bare feet kicking into the air at random.

"I'm taking it you got on the show," Vanessa observes.

"I CAN'T BELIEVE IT!" Mom shrieks, stumbling over the edge of the coffee table as she loses her balance. "TAKE THAT, RICK, YOU CHEATING CHEATER!"

After a largely sleepless night, Mom is up at dawn, clanging the kettle around in a daze, loud enough to wake me, the neighbors, and half of Canada. I crawl off the couch, leaving my feet propped up as I dip into a low feline stretch. "It's so early," I croak.

"We have that conference call with the production guy this morning. I thought we could sit down and make a list of questions beforehand."

"Here's my first question: Why are you doing this to me?" I stand, scrubbing at the crusted edge of one eye with the sleeve of my pajama top. I stick my arms out like a zombie and stagger at Mom. "Cofffeeeeee. Cofffeeeeee."

She pours me a cup from the French press and jerks her chin at the kitchen table, where all of the paperwork about the show is in a messy heap beside her laptop. "I have so many things to ask. I don't even know where to start! And look at this. They call it a stipend. It's *a hundred grand just to show up*." She drags her fingertips down her cheeks. "Is this real life?"

Her version of preparing questions for the call is really just her freaking out and repeating the same worries while I resolve to keep my eyes from drooping closed. I make noncommittal grunting noises at the appropriate intervals.

After an hour of this, I beg to be excused to take a shower. I don't usually lock the door, but I do today, just to ensure a few minutes of peace. I feel more alive once I'm dressed and my hair doesn't look like I just finished a round of Jumanji.

There isn't enough space for us to sit side by side for the call, so we relocate to the couch and tilt the laptop screen back to accommodate the angle. Mom strangles a pen in one hand, leaving tiny ink blots behind as she taps the tip against a legal pad. "Maybe I was supposed to call him instead of waiting for him to call me," she says as the clock ticks one minute past the appointed hour. "What if he thinks I'm late and gets upset?"

Before I can answer, the video chat pops onto the screen with a happy jingle that doesn't suit the tension radiating off Mom. The chat widens to reveal the grainy picture of a middle-aged man in a high-backed computer chair. His face crinkles along well-worn lines, wearing a nervous smile like a favorite shirt. "Hi, there," he says. "I'm Sam. Sam from the show. This is Julia, right? Can you hear me?"

"Yes," Mom replies in the formal, stiff voice she only uses on phone calls. "It's nice to meet you. This is my daughter, Cara."

I wave, freezing the picture for a moment as our ancient computer struggles to keep up.

"Hi. You've both got a busy day today. Do you want to go over the schedule first, or do you have questions for me? Oh, I should introduce myself better than that. Sorry. I'm Sam, your handler."

"Handler?" Mom asks, wagging her shoulders. "Fancy. Makes me feel like a secret agent."

Sam laughs and attempts to smooth a puff of sandy-colored hair, but it bounces back as soon as he lets go. "Uh, yes. I'm a . . . production assistant. I'm going to be coordinating all your activities and meetings and travel and activities."

I suppress a smile at the increasing tempo of his words. It would appear we're not the only ones who are nervous.

"We can do the schedule first," Mom says.

"Okay." He pulls a piece of paper into view and scans it. "First, I saw that you have appointments with your family doctor for early this morning. You have a copy of this, right?"

Mom blanches. "Yes. Somewhere."

"Don't forget the form that we need your doctor to fill out. After that, you both have a sizing at ten thirty." His voice has settled into a smooth, low monotone. "You can buy whatever you like with your clothing allowance, but your first dresses are going to be made locally to your measurements."

"Is there some kind of list about what we're supposed to buy?"

Sam's eyes dart around in random directions as he clicks his mouse and reads something. "There's, uh, there's a checklist. Did you not get the checklist?"

"I don't think so."

His voice grows higher in pitch, the tempo rising. "That's supposed to be its own thing. They were supposed to send that. They didn't send it? I can find it. I'm sure I can find it."

Mom sticks a hand up to the webcam. "Hang on. You're going too fast. Was I supposed to have that already or not?"

"I don't know," he says, tilting his head to mouth a few words at someone off-screen.

Mom peers down at the scramble of notes and improvised shorthand carved into the yellow legal pad. "I don't remember seeing it."

"Sorry." Sam steeples his fingers and blows out a calming breath. "I talk fast sometimes. That's my fault."

When they're finished going over Mom's exhaustive list of questions, I have a couple of my own. "How exactly does this work with, like, me? I'm supposed to help Mom pick the right guy?"

"Sort of," Sam says. "The contestants' kids are all different ages with different family situations. You're not just helping your mom find the right match. You're also choosing a new sibling."

Much to my surprise, I feel better about going on the show after the call is done and Sam has promised me that I will not have to wear a bag over my head for the remainder of my life. My only lingering worry is the doctor's appointment. I pester Mom as we drive to the pediatrician's. "What else could they possibly need? Haven't we already verified that I do not like flowers or want to become an astronaut?"

Mom hesitates, taking a turn a little harder than necessary. "Honestly, I have no clue."

The waiting room at the pediatrician's office stirs up childhood memories of routine vaccinations, fevers, and sprained wrists. The place is a time capsule with peeling mustard-yellow wallpaper and plastic crates of worn children's books. Being a year away from pediatric graduation means that I'm too large for most of the furniture in the play area, so I kneel by the short table in the center of the room to fidget with the animal figurines while we wait.

"Cara?" Dr. Walsh calls, emerging from the door beside the receptionist's desk.

"Hi." I scramble to my feet and dust the carpet fluff off my jeans. "Long time no see."

He consults the clipboard cradled in the bend of his arm. "You know the drill," he says, pointing to the end of the hall where the lone exam room is open, propped against a door-stopper in the shape of a giraffe.

I hop up onto the table with the crinkly paper and hang my feet on either side of the step stool used for little kids. Dr. Walsh scans a form and shrugs, setting it down on the narrow counter by a tub of tongue depressors. "It's a pretty standard physical. Are you signing up for sports?"

After steeling myself for an unpleasant surprise all morning, my shoulders slump with relief. "No, I, uh, I . . . No." I don't know if I'm allowed to say anything about the show. I'll go with awkward silence instead.

The entire physical lasts a mere four minutes. As the doctor prepares to leave, his hand dips into his right coat pocket but stops midway as though it changed its mind.

I frown like a child watching an arcade claw come up empty. "Um, Dr. Walsh?"

He drops my file into a holder outside the door. "Yes?"

I stare at my shoes where one side of the bow in my laces is lopsided. "Do you think I could still get a balloon?"

"Of course." He fishes one out of his pocket with practiced ease and blows it up for me. Green with a smiley face on it. He must buy them by the case. I grab it by the nub on the end and smack it against my thigh while I wait for Mom to finish up at the desk.

"I thought maybe you were too cool for a balloon," she says as she follows me into the parking lot, smirking. "You told me they were stupid when you were fourteen."

"I was being a diva. Whatever."

I text Vanessa from the car to let her know that we're leaving. Mom offers to pick her up on the way, but Vanessa insists that she'd rather ride her bicycle.

A few minutes later, we arrive in the historic downtown, which is little more than a cluster of shops with fancy brick facades centered around a dribbling fountain. Mom eyes the aged storefronts and meticulous landscaping with obvious envy. "I've always loved these old buildings. I wish we could have put the gym here, but none of them were vacant at the time."

Mom guides us along the adjacent sidewalk, swinging her purse from her arm and mooning over the architecture. "This is it," she announces, seizing the handle of a heavy glass door. A burst of crisp air washes over us, smelling of potpourri. "Sam said this is the best place for us to find clothes for the show. We're supposed to video chat with a stylist."

"A bridal shop," I say, reading the frosted letters etched into the glass above the arched doorway. "That isn't super creepy at all."

"It's not creepy. It's a show about finding true love. It makes sense that they would want me to come to a bridal shop. They sell other stuff too."

I reluctantly follow Mom inside, checking the bottoms of my shoes for dirt. "You can get your measurements done anywhere. Actually, I probably could have done them for you at the gym."

She scoffs. "Yeah, but that's boring. Come on, we get an entire new wardrobe paid for *by a television show*. You should be happy!"

"I'd be happier if I could pick out more stuff I'd actually like to wear." I reach into my pocket and unfold the literal laundry list of garments that I'm permitted to purchase. I scowl as I scan through the items, hoping that I overlooked "pajamas" and "three-year-old T-shirts" when I read it this morning. "I love that they specify triangle bikinis as the only acceptable kind of bathing suit."

Mom runs a hand over her flat stomach. "I know. Isn't it great? We won't have to stress over styles."

"You're killing me here. They just don't design bikinis for my body type."

"Nonsense. Your father wore a coconut bra and hula skirt to a Halloween party when we were in college, and he looked awesome. We'll just have to find the right thing."

"Great," I say, sticking a finger in my ear and smacking the side of my head like I'm trying to knock out water. "I can never unhear that."

I linger awkwardly in the foyer while I absorb the extravagance of the decor. The floor is laid out in sectors with dresses hanging beside circular daises and doors marked as individual fitting rooms. Thick rugs are the only splashes of color, tucked underneath coffee tables covered in fake flowers and magazines. Everything is so open, and bright, and clean.

The woman behind the counter bustles over to greet us. She splits us into separate dressing rooms, sending another employee to tend to Mom. I bite my lip the entire time she's taking my measurements to avoid a fit of ticklish giggles. Knowing Mom, she's probably having the same problem.

Vanessa is waiting in the foyer when I'm finished. "Hey," I call out, prompting her to lift her head from her phone. "Were you waiting a long time?"

"Nah. I just got here."

"Thanks for coming to help me shop. You know I'm hopeless with clothes."

She scoffs and tugs at the bottom of her tattered Pokémon sweatshirt. "I don't know how much help I'm going to be."

"There's a stylist for the fashion-y part, but she doesn't know me. You do."

Mom is still being measured, so Vanessa and I spread through the store to admire the magnificent wedding dresses cocooning a procession of mannequins in waves of tulle and silk. "Can you imagine wearing one of these?"

Vanessa shakes her head. "I'd trip and die on that long of a train."

In the attached storefront next door, we find a rainbow of semiformal and formal gowns, sparkling with glitter and sequins beneath the false sun of the fluorescent lighting. A sign at the rear denotes casualwear, but the chic outfits and dramatic cuts are far from my definition of casual.

Vanessa runs her fingers across a tie-neck silk blouse, letting the fabric slide through them like liquid silver. She searches for a tag but doesn't find one. "No price. That's never a good sign."

"Right?" I mumble, glad that someone else understands the constant pressure of clipping coupons, skipping the brand name, and using a little less shampoo every morning. "I can't believe that the show is paying for all of this."

She sighs. "Isn't that the dream?"

"Sorry, I didn't mean to brag or anything."

"No, I get what you were saying." She waves away my apology, but that doesn't stop the shame from nesting in my gut. "Though I don't know where you'd wear half of this stuff again unless you find out you're a long-lost princess or something."

Mom comes over with her phone cradled in one hand. "Cara, this is Angela. She's our stylist."

"Hi." I wave, leaning closer until I can make out the video feed of a young Black woman with oversized baby-blue glasses seated behind an L-shaped desk. "This is my best friend, Vanessa."

"Hey. Nice to e-meet you all. I'm here to help you shop." Angela smiles and holds up a hand. "Not that I'm saying you don't have a good fashion sense. I'm just an informed sounding board for whatever you pick out."

We prop Mom's phone up on a vase while we check out the wares. Mom pauses to examine a green lace top with bell sleeves. She holds it up against the outline of my body. "Will you do me a favor and tell her that's gross?" I say to Vanessa. "She's going to find all this stuff for me and then get upset when I don't like it."

Vanessa hesitates. "From a self-preservation standpoint, your mom has biceps as big as my head, so that's probably a bad idea."

"With the way she freaks out about getting enough protein, you should be more worried about her eating you than hitting you."

I start out trying to be subtle, but after an encounter with a pink sequined tank top and a velvet-covered pair of flats, I end up prying things out of Mom's hands. When I show them to Angela to back me up, she makes a combination groan-whine that causes Mom to suddenly become interested in a clothing rack on the other side of the room.

Finally, we settle on over a dozen outfits, hauling the accessories to the dressing room by the armful and piling them onto the built-in bench.

"Are you sure you have enough?" Mom asks, worrying even as I'm shutting her into the stall. "You barely have three outfits."

"I have a ton!" I've never felt so adventurous, free to buy the shirt that maybe I won't like as much in two days or the shoes that are a bit tight in the toe.

Vanessa holds Mom's phone and chats with Angela while I head into the other stall to change. I normally despise trying on clothes, but these are so far outside my ordinary style that I know I need to do it.

"That's going to be a little warm for Florida," Angela remarks as I show off a long-sleeve baby doll top that only makes me feel a little bit like I'm wearing a bed skirt. "Even if the fabric looks thin."

"Good point. I'm used to Ohio summer, not Florida summer." That revelation leads to swapping out a few other heavier shirts and a thick pair of jeans that feels like it's made at least partially of cardboard.

Angela approves my picks within a few minutes, but Mom can't decide between two evening gowns to meet the quota of formalwear on the list. I sit next to Vanessa on a chaise that feels like concrete covered in pointy buttons designed to stab me in the butt cheeks. "Maybe it's not the cut," Mom says, pointing at the rack behind me. "Do you think the gold would look better?"

"Gold makes us look naked," I deadpan, remembering Mom's horror after donning a bridesmaid's dress for her friend's wedding.

"What do you think, Angela?"

She makes a twirling motion with her finger, and Mom obliges. "It's kind of . . ." She cups her hands in the air in front of her boobs. "I don't think that's a good cut for you."

As soon as I see what she's referring to, my mouth falls open in abject horror, my expression repeated in each of the four mirrors around the fitting station. Mom pokes at one of the seams outlining her cleavage. "I guess you're right. It's too revealing."

"You should just go with the purple dress you had on earlier," Vanessa says, rubbing her thumbnail against a chip in her front tooth. "Don't mess with a good thing."

Mom agrees and backs into the room to change into her street clothes. I pat Vanessa's knee. "I knew I brought you for a reason. If you weren't here, this would go on for another half an hour, and she'd still wind up agonizing over it later."

"No problem. It was fun to see all the dresses."

I almost smack myself in the forehead. I pass the phone over to Mom and pull Vanessa out of earshot of the microphone. "You should pick out a dress for homecoming. We'll both have new dresses!" I don't think either of us can stand the mortification of wearing the same dresses for a third consecutive dance. At the last one, we joked that we were being environmentally friendly and recycling, but it doesn't seem so funny now.

"That's the show's money," Vanessa protests. "I can't commit dress fraud."

"You have to. No one will ever know. We're close enough to the same size that it doesn't matter. There's no way I'm going to be able to wear all these clothes anyway."

She refuses, but I think I see her glance at the navy blue sheath dress slung over my arm. I resolve not to wear it unless it's absolutely necessary.

I bring the rest of my items to the counter where the woman

ringing us up is beaming with a level of delight that can only come from being paid on commission. She gushes over each and every item as it passes beneath her scanning gun.

"We already opened an account," Angela explains. "You shouldn't have to pay anything."

At her words, it starts to sink in that this is really happening. If this works out, we could have a life where we don't have to worry about every penny. Mom can finally go a week without lying to collections about the check that we all know isn't, and never has been, in the mail.

We say goodbye to Angela, who promises us that we haven't seen the last of her, and head outside. "Eighteen hundred dollars." Mom laughs and stares down at the receipt. "What a bargain."

"We got a lot for that price," I say, hefting the bags dangling from each of my arms.

"Quality stuff will last longer too," Vanessa adds.

Mom folds the receipt and tucks it into a compartment in her wallet. "You're right. You're right." Mom looks down at me, the corner of her mouth drooping into a scowl. "We should tell your dad."

"Okay. Do you want to go now?"

"I was kind of hoping you were going to try to talk me out of it. Honestly, I should have talked to him before we spent so much of the show's money on all this stuff. He could make it really tough, legally."

"There's no reason to worry," I say, mostly to convince myself. "It's not up to him. It's not like I'm eleven years old and you want to take me on *Survivor*."

"I guess you're right. What's the worst he can do? Divorce me?" My heart throbs in time with her tinny, bitter laugh. "Let's just go now and get this over with."

chapter eight

*I*t takes less than three minutes for the fighting to start.

"You can't just show up here and 'need to talk' whenever you want," Dad says, pacing the length of the juice bar. "I'm busy."

Mom rips the power cord out of the floor, killing the trio of commercial blenders. "Jake can watch the gym for half an hour while we discuss parenting our daughter. It's important. Very important."

"He's a kid! I'm not leaving him alone with the whole after-work crowd and the juice bar." Dad folds his arms and sticks out his chest in a stance befitting a disgruntled gorilla. "Is she pregnant?"

"Yes," Mom snarls, snatching a piece of fruit from the counter and stuffing it under my shirt. "It's a tangerine. Congratulations."

"I heard that there's something going on with Cara," LeAnne says, swinging under the safety railing from the cardio floor to land next to Dad. She adjusts the turquoise sweatband that she's been wearing to promote our new selection of revolting eighties-inspired athletic wear. "Don't you think I should be involved with that, Julia, since I'm her stepmother now?"

A muscle twitches at the corner of Mom's eye. She still hasn't blinked. "I don't know, *LeAnne*. There's a certain stage at which I would feel it's appropriate to involve an *outside party*, and I'm not sure that's right this second when I haven't even had a chance to talk to Rick."

"Hey!" I yell over them, waving my arms at random like an inflatable at a car dealership. A few of our customers startle at the noise but return to their treadmills and weights at a scathing look from Mom. I slam the tangerine onto the countertop, splitting the skin and spraying all of us with droplets of juice. "Seriously, what is wrong with you guys? Can we not act like this in our own business? Ugh. Why am I the adult right now?"

Mom pinches the bridge of her nose, leaving angry red crescents from her nails. "I'm sorry. I just wanted to go talk somewhere. I figured having a meal together wouldn't kill us."

Dad sighs. "I got a little carried away too. I guess we can go get something to eat." He turns to LeAnne. "You okay with Cheat Day, babe?"

"Yeah. Fine."

I glance between the two of them, waiting for them to pick up on the so-not-funny irony, but they don't. Mom's eyes flare wider by a fraction. Her foam-bottomed sneaker taps faster against the tile. "Let's just go up the street. This way, we'll be close in case the stereo goes haywire again or some other catastrophe happens."

We all wince at the memory of the stereo randomly pinging from inaudible to blasting last week for no discernible reason. It was funny at first, but I bet our customers aren't interested in a long-term subscription to Poltergeist Zumba.

Before we go, Mom swears a lifetime of bodily harm and haunting from the afterlife upon Jake if he doesn't take good care of the gym in our absence. "Don't touch the thermostat. Don't let Henry lift without a spotter. Don't process any coupons. The two-for-one kickboxing class is expired."

"I've got it," Jake promises, sounding like he's negotiating a night home without a babysitter for the first time. "It won't burn to the ground without you."

Mom pats him on the shoulder and makes him recite her cell phone number before we can leave. I walk in front of her by a few paces, serving as a buffer between her and LeAnne. Under different circumstances, this could be relaxing, taking a stroll together under the warm glow of a half-hidden sun. But we aren't those people. When it comes to LeAnne, we never bothered to build a bridge worth burning.

The restaurant is packed, and the only available table for four is in the middle of the room. I tuck in my elbows to avoid bumping any of the waitstaff scurrying back and forth to the nearby beverage station. The crowd only seems to add to LeAnne's growing agitation.

"What is there to talk about?" Dad asks as soon as we're seated.

Mom shakes the menu. "Can we order first?"

"I don't have all day."

I tamp down my annoyance by focusing on the picture of the Wagyu cheeseburger with bacon and truffle aioli. The menu is even laminated. It's like they know I might start drooling on it at any second.

We order our food and drinks at the same time to satisfy Dad's hurry to return to his third wife—the juice bar. Mom wrings her hands in her lap, a habit she's picked up since she can't fiddle with her wedding band anymore. "I have an unexpected opportunity that I'd like to take advantage of, but it involves Cara."

Dad and LeAnne share a look that I can't quite interpret. "I already said I'm not buying you out," he says. "How many times do I have to say no?"

"What? I'm not even talking about the gym."

"This isn't about the contract amendment, is it?"

Mom stares at him, bewildered. "What contract amendment?"

Dad shifts in his chair. I play with the paper from my straw, refusing to acknowledge that his eyes are boring into my forehead. "I gave Cara a copy of an ownership amendment for you to sign," he replies. "I want to add LeAnne since she's part owner of my half."

Mom looks at Dad and LeAnne, closes her eyes a little too long for a blink, and then whispers to our passing waiter, "Can I get a side of fries, please? And a chocolate milkshake."

I lean over and add, "Make it cheese fries. Like, mess that thing up with some cheddar." Mom might be a health freak, but when she snaps, she has the appetite of a champion eater. I'm talking a whole pizza. A box of donuts. Two bags of jelly beans.

"I'm trying to tell you that we're going to be on television!" Mom shouts over Dad's continued murmuring. "We auditioned for a show, and they picked us."

Dad rolls his eyes. "So, what, you drive into Cleveland and pretend to be a soccer mom for twenty seconds in the background? Go ahead. Why would I care about that?"

Mom looks like she's about to catch a felony for homicide with a fork, so I capitalize on her enraged silence to quickly summarize the show for Dad. Mom and I take turns answering his initial questions, which grow more aggressive by the minute. By the time the waiter arrives with our meals, Dad has clearly taken a stand.

"I just don't understand," he says. "What's the appeal of watching a bunch of full-grown men fighting over an engagement ring?"

"They'll be competing to marry Mom. It's supposed to be romantic. You make it sound like Lord of the Rings."

"Romantic?" Dad asks, his voice growing loud enough to disturb the women in the booth beside us. "It's absurd! And you actually want to be a part of something like that? I can't believe people watch this garbage."

"I can't believe people watch Lord of the Rings," LeAnne mutters in between bites of her steak fajitas.

There's a brief moment of cosmic serendipity when the three of us turn in unison to gape at her. My breath hitches as I remember when the entire family came down with the flu just after Christmas one year. We recuperated during an extended-cut, three-movie marathon, taking turns pouring cough medicine into shot glasses and paying the pizza deliveryman. I shake my head, hoping to dislodge the memory and banish it back to my subconscious.

"What?" LeAnne looks between us. "It's boring. I don't like all that elf stuff."

"OKAY. BACK TO THE TOPIC AT HAND, RIGHT?" I say to get Mom's attention before she can digest the fact that LeAnne just insulted Orlando Bloom in her presence. "We need to talk about the show."

Dad puffs out his chest and folds his arms. "I'm not allowing it. I think it's ridiculous, and it's not a good environment for Cara."

"What do you mean, you're 'not allowing it'? If you'll recall, I'm entitled to modify our visitation schedule with advance notice as long as I give you equivalent days. She won't be missing that many of your weekends, and you owe me two of those anyway because of the days she helped with planning your wedding."

"I don't care," Dad says. "She's not going."

Mom crushes a fry between her thumb and index finger. "This isn't a Dad-ocracy. I'm here as a courtesy to you. I could have easily brought this to a legal mediat—"

"Isn't anyone going to ask me whether I want to go?"

They both look at me as though I've suggested settling the dispute with a sword fight.

"I'm seventeen, not seven. I can decide for myself, and I've decided that going on the show is what I'd like to do." I project my voice louder than usual to feign confidence. "There's no obligation for Mom to get married. If she hates everyone, then we ended up getting a cool mother-daughter vacation to Florida for free."

Mom kicks my foot under the table, which I interpret to mean that I shouldn't mention the hundred-thousand-dollar stipend they're offering us. Dad would tie Mom up in a sack and sell her on eBay if he thought he could get more money to renovate the gym.

"You're not old enough to know what you want," Dad says. "You're just a teenage girl."

"I'm eighteen in four months, and I want to go." For emphasis, I add, "The past year has been hard. This will help make up for it." It sounds more spiteful out loud than it did in my head. "And in four months, when I'm eighteen, I get to decide where I want to go and who I want to see." I leave the rest of the threat unspoken.

He sighs. "Whatever. Do what you want. Just don't come crying to me when you're the laughingstock of the town."

"Duly noted," Mom drawls, chugging the remains of her milkshake. "How terrible it would be to have the entire town gossiping about my love life. Oh, wait."

The waiter, perhaps sensing the hostility wafting from our table, drops the check like a live grenade and vanishes. Dad scans the receipt. "Nine bucks for your cheese fries. What a rip-off. I should take this out of your child support, huh?"

Mom's chair screeches against the floor as she slams back from the table, snatching the faux-leather check presenter out of Dad's hand. "Come on, Cara. We're leaving." To Dad, she adds, "You can pay your half at the register."

"What?" Dad scoffs. "Oh, come on, Julia. It was a joke. Why can't you ever take a joke?"

chapter nine

Mom incessantly repeats the question under her breath over the days leading up to our departure. She gripes it to herself while doing the dishes or chopping vegetables with increasing vigor. *"Why can't you ever take a joke?"* After a while, she stops saying the words, but I still recognize the way she wobbles her head when she thinks them.

Her agitation increases the closer we get to our departure date. It seems like her every waking moment is spent haranguing Sam over the details of our travel arrangements and packing lists. It's become automatic to wave at her computer whenever I see the glow of the screen because I know for a surety that Sam is on the other end, talking her through another aspect of the show in his low, rambling monotone.

Finally, it's time to depart, and the only thing Mom can think about is what we're going to forget. "They said not to pack basic toiletries, but what if they don't have toothpaste?"

"We can buy some when we get there if they don't have it."

Mom scrapes her hair back into a messy knot with wisps bulging out in every direction. "I'm just worried."

It takes two trips to load the car with all our luggage. There's an entire suitcase dedicated to just shoes and evening bags to match the gowns that we were instructed to buy. I don't think we even removed the tags yet.

Once we're ready to leave, I clomp up the stairs to check that the lights are off and the door is locked. Vanessa steps out onto the walkway to say goodbye. "Come here," she says, wrapping me in a one-armed hug. "You can't go without a hug."

"Thanks for getting up so early," I say, knowing that Vanessa pretty much keeps the same schedule as Dracula. During the school year, it's basically impossible to speak to her for the first half of the bus ride.

Vanessa hefts the energy drink glued to her right hand. "I've been up since yesterday. I'm pretty wiped, but I couldn't let you go without wishing you good luck."

I squeeze her tighter. "I'll miss you, Va-Ness Monster."

"I'll miss you too. But it's not even for that long. Don't get all mushy on me."

"I'll be back before you know it."

She smiles. "I'll help you move into your new mansion after you're rich and famous."

I replay her words in my head as I return to the car and buckle myself in. Being separated for so long might be tough, but it won't be permanent. Unlike the friends I lost in the fallout of the divorce, Vanessa is more than just some neighbor friend my parents set me up with out of convenience when we were in diapers.

As we drive away, I cling to that half-hearted optimism, excited to see the airport that I've passed a million times before without ever setting foot inside.

For such a major city, the ticketing area is emptier than I expected. There are a few people pecking at kiosks while others file in between the stanchions leading to the check-in counter. I thought it would be as rushed and packed as scenes in the movies.

"Kiosks first?" Mom suggests. "The line is shorter."

We manage to make it past the home screen. "'Enter reservation number or insert booking credit card,'" Mom reads aloud. She thumbs through her email. "Sam sent me so much stuff. Give me a second."

"Maybe we should have gone to the counter since we have no idea what we're doing."

"It's somewhere in here," Mom mumbles, her focus still on her phone. After a few more seconds, she finds the number and pokes the appropriate buttons, unlocking the option to print our documents.

The machine whirs and spits two glossy boarding passes into my hand. Seeing my name printed on the paper makes it real. We're going. I take a deep breath and stuff the passes into the kangaroo pocket of my sweatshirt for safekeeping.

Even though I'm not doing anything wrong, my palms sweat as we approach the security equipment. The agents seem so serious in their uniforms, with grim expressions that are either signs of focus or boredom. Thankfully, there's ample time for me to read the instructions, so I manage to pass through without incident, except for a confiscated tube of hand lotion.

On the far side of the X-ray machine, we grab our bins and hustle to the nearest bench to avoid the swarm of passengers waiting for their belongings. "I didn't think they'd make me take off my flip-flops," Mom says, turning her foot over to examine the black crust of dirt on her heels. "That's disgusting. Is it weird if I go wash my feet in the bathroom?"

"Please don't." All I can imagine is Mom balancing on one leg like a confused flamingo while her foot soaks in the same sink that people probably use to brush their teeth.

"Fine." She begrudgingly stuffs the flip-flops back onto her feet before we melt into the current of travelers flowing toward the nearest intersection. I notice that there isn't a lot of variety in the airport. We pass the same types of stores over and over, giving the impression that we're walking through some kind of time loop.

When we reach a set of stacked screens showing arrivals and departures, Mom compares our flight numbers to the times on the right-hand side. "It says we're on time. Boarding starts in an hour and a half."

"I knew we left too early."

Mom blends back into the walkway, her head tilted up to read the ubiquitous white signs hanging from the ceiling in every crook and corner. "I was just following Sam's directions. It seemed like he had an exact plan for how he wanted us to travel."

"I'm pretty sure Sam had an exact plan for his own birth."

She laughs, shaking her head. "There's nothing wrong with being a detail-oriented person. Especially since you and me are the two least organized people on the planet."

I huff under my breath. "You raised me. I blame you."

The fortunate part of being so early is that we can spare a few minutes to stop for espresso and parfaits while still having our choice of seats in the waiting area at the gate.

I pick a spot next to an outlet where I can charge my phone. "I can't believe we have to give up all our electronics." It's almost cruel that I'm finally having a vacation, a true once-in-a-lifetime adventure, and I can't even tell my friends about it. "Vanessa is melting down about it."

"It'll be a relief for me," Mom grumbles, her fingers closed into a claw around her phone as she swipes out a message. "Your dad won't stop harassing me about how this is stupid and I'm going to humiliate our family on television."

Are we a family anymore? I chew on the idea as more

bleary-eyed passengers assemble around us. They cling to their coffees and kick their feet up on battered suitcases. I'm tired too.

I text back and forth with Vanessa, reassuring her that I'll be all right during our weeks of forced silence. I'm touched that she's too busy worrying about me to get to sleep.

> [Cara Hawn Solo 7:22 AM] You'll be busy with college stuff, anyway.

She answers faster than I thought possible. I can picture her scrunched up on the couch, rambling to her speech-to-text app.

> [Va-Ness Monster 7:22 AM] More like busy with extra shifts at the restaurant to afford the damn college visits. Do you know that they want $47 just for a bus ticket from here to Chicago? And it has four transfers!

I must fall asleep in the middle of our conversation because Mom is nudging me an hour later to get in line for boarding. I've never flown before, so my duckling instinct is strong as I trail Mom down the jet bridge and through the narrow door of the plane. She hooks a right into the main gangway and hunches to slide into the third-row window seat.

> [Cara Hawn Solo 8:39 AM] We just boarded. I'll text you when we get there!

While all the other passengers have the same glazed eyes as a herd of bored cows, I find the takeoff process to be thrilling. I'm about to leave the ground. When it comes time to read the emergency exit instructions, I'm the only one who pulls out the thick placard to follow along with the flight attendant leading the demonstration. "This is so cool," I tell Mom, pointing to the cartoonish figures. "A seat that turns into a life preserver? That's so cool. So cool."

"Are you okay?" she asks. "You sound a little nervous."

I nod as the plane rumbles down the runway. "I'm fine."

"Are you sure?"

"Totally fine. I'm good. Totally cool."

I stick my fingers in my ears as they pop, setting off a splitting headache that throbs in time with the panicked banging of my heart. Mom lays her hand on top of mine on the armrest, either as a comfort or to keep me from running away. Not that there's anywhere to go on an airplane because *we are zooming through the sky held up by things I don't understand because I don't pay attention in physics class.*

Once we're in the air, I drink enough ginger ale to turn my stomach into a churning acid pit. I begin to question my life decisions, starting with the yogurt I ate earlier.

"Hot towel?" the flight attendant offers, holding one out with a pair of tongs.

Mom and I both take them, but neither of us has any idea what to do next. I spy on the couple across the aisle and frown in disgust as I watch the woman scrub her face and hands with it. I have no idea how the airline washes these after use, but I'd like to avoid catching some bizarre Ohioan towel disease before appearing on national television.

Shortly afterward, the flight attendant reappears with an overflowing basket of snacks. I hesitate with my hand stretched over a bag of bite-sized brownies. "Are these free?"

He smiles and gives the basket a reassuring shake. "Of course."

I don't want to seem like a greedy trick-or-treater, but I'm also not going to turn down free food. I take a random handful and drop them into my lap. Maybe more substantial food will improve my nausea. "I didn't know they give you such awesome snacks on airplanes. I thought it was just pretzels or whatever."

"They don't usually," Mom says, popping two almonds into her mouth and depositing the rest onto my tray. "This is way different than coach. These seats must cost over a thousand dollars each."

"Would you eat something?" I give the almonds back. "I don't care if they're salted. You can't drink wine for lunch. You'll die."

She smirks. "Oh, and you're an expert on wine now, are you?"

"You gave me a glass at Dad's wedding."

"Oh, right. Well, everyone needed a drink for that."

The rule that something you're dreading arrives faster holds true. Before long, the downward angle of the plane starts to become disconcerting. I peer out the window and imagine how fast we must be going, how difficult it would be to correct a problem this close to the ground. "Is it already time for landing?"

Mom nods. "What goes up must come down."

All the blood rushes to my head as I lean over with the thick strap of the seat belt cutting into my stomach. Mom rubs a slow pattern on my back, bouncing between the curves of my shoulder blades like a skateboarder on a half-pipe. The noise of the landing conceals the sound of my distressed keening.

"Are you all right?" Mom asks. "We're on the ground now."

"My stomach just fell out of my butt."

Mom mimics dialing and presses her cell phone against her ear. "Yes, hello, 911? My daughter's stomach just fell out of her butt. Please send an ambulance as fast as you can."

I reach out and smack her shin with the flat of my hand. "You're not funny."

"I'm very funny. You're just cranky. On a scale of one to every single Nicolas Cage character, you're a seven."

Maybe there's more truth to that than I want to admit, especially after it occurs to me that we need to do it all again to get to Key West. I was excited about taking *two* planes in one day, but now that I've experienced this Wright-inspired torture, I'm over it. Mom has to threaten to leave me in Atlanta three times before I stop begging her to just rent us a car and drive the rest of the way.

I spend the second leg of our journey with my eyes clamped shut as the tiny air vent above my seat blasts subzero air onto the top of my head. "You don't look so good," Mom comments as we begin our descent. "Tell me if you're going to be sick."

"Don't say the s-word, or I'm about to have a self-fulfilling prophecy on your sandals."

After we disembark, the crowded aisleways and incessant terminal announcements grate on my nerves. The lights are too harsh, like emerging from a dark theater on a sunny day.

The nearby coffee stand is a necessary pit stop before we leave the secured area. I follow Mom down a level to baggage claim, chugging a caramel espresso concoction like a health potion in one of Vanessa's dorky video games. Before long, the fatigue and terror from the plane ride subside, replaced by a jittery curiosity about what I'm going to find when we arrive at the set.

I swipe my tongue over the sugary film on my teeth, tasting the remnants of whipped cream and salt. "I think I can function now." I know Vanessa is definitely asleep at the moment, but I text her anyway. I don't know how much longer I'll be able to keep my phone.

[Cara Hawn Solo 1:27 PM] Made it! Going to get our stuff now.

As we approach the carousel, Mom points at a man in a rumpled white dress shirt, khaki slacks, and muddy work boots. He's dangling a sign with our last name from one hand while poring over a slim tablet held in the other. "I think that's our driver," Mom says, crouching down and tilting her head to read. "Yeah, that's him."

She walks over and stands in front of him, waiting for him to finish whatever he's doing on his tablet. "Sam? Is that you? Oh my gosh!"

Sam glances up and jolts. "You're early! You're Julia. Here. You are here." He shoves the tablet into his messenger bag without bothering to turn off the screen. "Welcome to Florida!" He throws his arms out almost enough for a hug, then jerks his left arm behind his back like it's in time-out. He holds out his right hand, blushing.

Mom laughs and shakes it. "I didn't realize you were coming to get us yourself! I figured you'd just send someone."

His laugh is almost a bark. "I'm the 'someone' who gets sent. Don't be fooled by my fancy email signature. I'm the little guy around here." He pats the slight pooch of fat at his midriff. "Well, figuratively speaking."

I don't know why, but just that small, casual gesture helps lessen my fear that I'm not going to match up with the other kids. After spending so much time around health buffs, it's easy to feel wrong for not being in perfect shape or having to size up.

Despite Mom's outrageous biceps, Sam insists on carrying the bulk of our luggage after he rescues it from a jam at the baggage carousel. We follow him through the maze of the airport to the lower level, where a stretch of taxis are idling on the far side of the concrete median.

The sudden humidity feels like walking through an automatic car wash. "My under-boob is sweating," I hiss to Mom, wishing that I had the foresight to wear shorts and a tank top to this muggy sponge of a state. I wrestle off my sweatshirt and pummel it into a ball.

"A few months ago you were complaining that it was too cold."

She pitches her voice higher and mimics my whining. *"My skin is all red. These leggings aren't warm enough. This heater sucks."*

"Um, excuse me, you judgy judger. It was a polar vortex. My *eyes* were freezing."

Sam jogs over to a Mercedes parked along the curb in a loading area painted with diagonal yellow stripes. He straightens his shoulders and lifts his chin. "I'm not saying that I bribed a maintenance guy to let me park here, but I'm also not denying it."

I exchange disbelieving stares with my reflection in the shine of the sleek silver door. I creep forward and peek through the tinted window. The interior looks like real leather. "They're seriously going all out for this."

Mom sticks her pinkie in the air and mimes drinking out of a teacup. While Sam stows our bags in the trunk, she leans in to whisper, "Just don't tell anyone that we wait for coupons before we buy toilet paper, okay?"

chapter ten

As soon as we start moving, Sam turns the navigation system volume to full blast, either to discourage us from talking or to alleviate his obvious anxiety over extricating our car from the crowded pickup area. He lurches to a stop after only a few feet as a van swerves into the lane. "Left up here," he mumbles, craning forward to read the signs. "Then right."

Once we're free of the congestion, Sam rolls the volume dial back to normal. "Sorry about that. This isn't my car. I didn't want to miss a turn and get into an accident."

I dig my fingers into my temples to massage away the headache that's still spiking across my forehead from both the landing and my ludicrous caffeine intake. "We're used to it. Our stereo back home is haunted. Long story."

We pull out onto the highway adjacent to the water, cruising past a crush of high-rise condominiums, fast food restaurants, and car rental facilities. Even at this distance, the water is the purest blue I've ever seen, though my only real point of comparison is the algae-riddled froth of Lake Erie. I press my face to the warmed glass, angling my legs to avoid the worst of the sun streaking through the window.

[Cara Hawn Solo 1:34 PM] They sent a Mercedes to get us. This place is so cool!

Within a few blocks, the commercial sector of the city bleeds into a narrow network of suburban streets. We pass through rows of single-story houses divided by slices of grass like gaps in a crooked smile. Palm trees interrupt the landscape, casting jagged shadows over the sidewalks.

"Do you know that Key West is also called the Conch Republic?" Sam asks to break the silence. "You'll probably see it on a T-shirt at some point."

I lean forward to hear him better and position my face to get the full effect of the air-conditioning blasting from the vents. "Why's that?"

"They staged a fake secession from the United States in the 1980s. Tourists love that kind of thing, apparently."

"Like a prank?" Mom asks, looking delighted.

I grab both sides of her seat and pull myself closer to her ear. "Don't get any ideas, woman." Our last prank war ended with me getting an emergency haircut and Mom getting soaked head to toe in pickle juice. To Sam, I add, "She loves pranks. Watch yourself."

"You'll fit right in. This town has a sense of humor along with the usual historical stuff." He throws out a few more random facts about the Truman Little White House and the nearby military fort. "It's a shame that we're on such a tight schedule or we could see some of the sights."

I catch a glimpse of the water again as we turn into a gated drive, the apron of which is barely long enough to accommodate the car. Sam opens the window and waves a hand in the direction of a security camera mounted on a white brick post. The gate slides open with a low hum and the rattle of a chain.

"We'll have a meeting later to discuss the opening of the show,"

Sam mentions, stowing his tablet in his waistband as he climbs out of the car and pops the trunk. "But as for right now, your schedule is to get acquainted with the house."

House. He called it a house. It looks like a house that ate another house that ate three mansions and a condominium complex. Between the curved front and the fact that I'm standing in its shadow, the building stretches literally as far as I can see in either direction. The second story sports a massive balcony in front, walled in by white railings that are barely visible against the pale stone facade.

I walk around the edge of the building for a better look. There's no way that this was originally one structure. The front half is built up on short stilts and brick platforms. The rear extends down the side of a gentle slope that I suppose counts for a hill around here in a series of split-level steps. "This thing looks like it was made out of Legos or only the most random clearance building supplies at Home Depot."

Coming up alongside me with our bags, Sam nods. "I can see that."

"What's the deal with it?"

"This used to be a residential neighborhood. This round part was originally a hotel. Then, as the other properties went up for sale, it extended that way." He points diagonally. "And then it went even farther downhill when they added the pool."

That's way more information than I expected. "You know everything."

His cheeks turn a splotchy peach color. "There's a coffee table book about it in one of the sitting rooms…"

"There are multiple sitting rooms?" We catch up with Mom by the massive archway at the apex of the horseshoe driveway. "I'm going to get lost in this house and starve to death."

"They're going to have to give us tracking bracelets," Mom says.

We both stumble when we cross the threshold into the foyer. The space is two stories high, dressed in dark woods and light accents. The staircase to the second floor sweeps dramatically down the curve of the wall with an austere metal railing along its edge. My eyes trace the matching sconces that lead to the upper landing where they flank a half dozen slits that might be windows. Above our heads, a massive chandelier dangles like a grotesque iron spider.

This place is a museum. I pin my arms to my sides, afraid of accidentally damaging the pristine furniture or delicate decorative pieces visible in the adjoining rooms. There are antique porcelain figurines tucked into recessed, backlit alcoves. Crystal that glints like winter ice. Urns. Ferns.

I squint at the wall opposite the staircase, attempting to reconcile the tastefulness of the rest of the house with the hideous heart-shaped lockets hanging in front of me. They must be two feet tall. If a haunted house interior decorator and a Las Vegas wedding chaplain designed a film set together, this would be the result.

I forget my bag and walk over to admire the monstrosities. My fingers reach out for the nearest one, my nose wrinkling at the smell of velvet trimmings left exposed to the summer humidity a bit too long.

"Don't touch that!" Sam shouts. "They can't be opened until the first Sweetheart Ceremony!"

I look to Mom, who appears to be as bewildered as I am. She pivots on the toe of her flip-flop and purses her lips at Sam, revealing a sliver of bright pink on the edge of her lipstick.

He shrinks at the expression on her face and sucks in a deep breath. I can time his pulse by the vein wriggling in his forehead. "Sorry, sorry. I didn't mean to yell. It's just that the first Sweetheart Ceremony is our most important opening event. I'm not exactly top of the food chain around here. If I made a mistake like ruining the surprise, they'd fire me in a heartbeat."

"In a heartbeat?" Mom drawls, peaking an eyebrow. "Seriously?"

I laugh first, then Mom, then poor Sam, who seems to only just realize that she's poking fun. The tension in his jaw breaks into a weak and reluctant smile. "Sorry. I'm sorry. I—" He smiles again. "Tour. Right. You need to see the house. Let's go this way first."

I sidle up to Mom, shielding my mouth with the back of my hand, and whisper, "I think you broke Sam." It wouldn't be the first time that a man became a drooling, dribbling zombie around her, but usually for different reasons.

Her face contorts into an exaggerated wince. "I should be nicer. After all, Sam has apologized to me more in the past five minutes than your father has in his entire stinking life."

Sam keeps a polite distance until we're done. He leads us through the house, tracking the names of the rooms on his fingers like he's reciting the locations in Clue. There's a lounge with a full bar, a formal dining room, two kitchens, and a game room on the lower level with staircases leading to both ends of the house.

It can't, in all fairness, be called just a game room. The entire interior draws to mind the kind of adjectives my sophomore year English teacher had on her word-of-the-day calendar. *Lavish. Opulent. Decadent.* There's even a baby grand piano with sheet music poking out from beneath the tufted bench cushion.

I'm pleased to learn that the contestants are sequestered upstairs until we're all introduced tomorrow night. My head is spinning from trying to adjust to my new surroundings, never mind the dozens of strangers who are actually going to be competing. "I still can't believe there are so many contestants. It seems impossible that we'll get to know them all."

"It won't be so bad after the first vote," Sam replies. "You'll knock out eight pairs of contestants in the first round and then one pair at every ceremony afterward. It's not as rushed as it sounds."

"If you say so."

After the tour of places, we begin the tour of people. Sam introduces each person by name along with their complicated and lengthy titles. I gather that the producers are the most important, even though they're far from the way I imagined them. Instead of expensive suits and Rolexes, they're three ordinary men in scuffed shoes and rolled-up shirtsleeves.

They take turns shaking our hands and introducing themselves. "We're all named Mike, so we go by last names," one of them explains. "None of us are serious enough to be Michael."

I point to the coffees clutched in their left hands. I'm not sure if it's intentional, but the size of each cup seems to match their drastic differences in height. "I'll just call you Tall, Grande, and Venti."

Venti throws his head back in a deep, hearty laugh. He presses his hands against his stomach in a motion that reminds me of Santa Claus or the Pillsbury Doughboy. "I'm the biggest. That means I deserve more caffeine than these two short stuffs. It's a rule."

"I stopped growing from lack of sunlight," Tall says, which isn't far from the truth judging by the vicious sunburn on his otherwise pale skin. "I've spent too many years lurking in edit bays."

"You're in good hands with Sam here," Venti adds. "He's new to our team, but he's got enough energy for all of us put together."

Sam beams beneath the praise. "I'm just taking them to see their rooms now."

We pick up a three-man crew along the way, though they're so intent on filming us that we don't exchange niceties beyond handshakes and first names. The cameraman, Ian, is sporting a faded orange T-shirt that says, B-REEL WITH ME, BRO. Sam claps him on the shoulder as we pass, whispering, "Guess what happened? Mike Wistrand said I was doing a good job!"

"Dude, I'm filming. Would you shut up?" Ian hisses, waving a hand at him.

"Will we always have cameras on us?" Mom asks, surveying the sprawl of the lawn, the pool area, the flat strip of reddish plastic that might be a shuffleboard court.

Sam gestures back at Ian. "You'll have crews like this following you periodically, but there are also cameras distributed throughout the houses and grounds. The producers can, and will, use anything you say on the show. Fair warning."

The Miranda rights flash through my mind.

"What about bathroom stuff?" I ask. I know they wouldn't do anything extreme like put a camera in the toilet, but I don't want the entire country to be able to livestream an audio feed of my farts, either.

"Bathrooms are exempt all the time for you." He turns to Mom. "They're also exempt for you unless you have, uh, a second person—adult—with you, who is part of the show, and you're in there, because, reasons. The cameras can barge in then at any time because . . . reasons."

Mom puts him out of his misery. "I know what you mean."

We skirt the concrete edge of the pool and approach a single-story building that must have fallen straight out of a design magazine. The glass wall facing the pool is actually a set of doors that Sam folds open along a track in the floor. He waits at the threshold and gestures inside. "You'll be living separately from the contestants. This is a guesthouse, but it has all the amenities you could ever want."

I follow Mom into the spacious rectangular structure. We pause to untie our shoes and slip them into wooden cubbies lined with woven matting. I wiggle my toes against the cool stone, skiing forward on my socks with the slightest push.

"What do these people do for a living if this is the *guest*house?"

I wonder aloud, running my fingers over the ridges of the granite countertops, the gleaming stainless steel appliances.

"A lot of these are vacation homes," Sam says. "They picked this one because the former owners added en suite bathrooms when it was used as a wedding venue and hotel. It makes prep time shorter when you don't have to worry about contestants fighting over showers."

"What's this contraption?" Mom leans forward to inspect a short piece of silver grating embedded in the counter beneath a riot of knobs, spigots, and levers. It looks like some kind of dental equipment.

Sam points to the wall where tiny white cups are stacked on wooden shelves with wineglasses dangling from the underside like bats. "Cappuccino machine."

I get the impression that I could spend the next fifty years trying to decipher how to use half of these appliances and still come up empty. Maybe I could manage the toaster.

The rest of the space transitions seamlessly with slight differences in the color of the tile to demarcate boundaries. I glean from the three closed doors that the bedrooms are on opposite sides of the house with the lone bathroom connected to the master suite. And there are cameras. Everywhere. I thought they'd at least try to be subtle about it, but apparently not.

"I'm going to go check out my room." It's not like there's a high standard. I sleep on the couch back at home. It isn't even a nice couch.

I retrieve my bags and haul them over toward the eastern bedroom, using my elbow to work the handle of the door. As I turn around, I realize that everything is white. Not pale, or neutral, or plain. White. The only hint of color is an ivory damask pattern on the wall behind the bed and the stems of the calla lilies on the table by the window. I can't tell if this is supposed to be some kind of edgy minimalist statement or a remodel gone wrong.

"I guess it's cozy," Mom says over my shoulder. "It's nice and bright."

I set my bags on the bed, careful to keep the filthy roller wheels from touching the white duvet. "Yeah. Bright. Like looking into the afterlife."

"I'm nervous," Mom admits. "What about you?"

"I'm excited to get started. This is going to be a whole new life for us, Mom. You just wait." And if it turns out to be awful, we'll just do the same thing that we've been doing for the past year anyway. Stand straight and tall. Smile until our muscles ache. Laugh, the louder the better.

And pretend that neither of us knows the other one is lying.

Once we're settled in and finished exploring, Sam insists that we review his introductory materials. He props his tablet up on the counter and opens a slideshow.

I snicker under my breath. "Did you really make a presentation just for the two of us?"

"No," Sam says, closing the slideshow with a quick stab of his finger. A faint tinge of red spreads across his cheeks. "That would be ridiculous."

Mom pats his shoulder. "It's okay. You can show us. We won't laugh. Much."

Sam glances between the two of us, sighs, and reopens the slideshow. It starts with a basic calendar of events. Since the show is unscripted, most of the time blocks are divided by vague labels instead of actual activities: GROUP/KIDS, GROUP/SUITORS, GROUP/MIXED, INVITATION ONLY. Some of the days end in SWEETHEART CEREMONY, but there aren't any specific breaks earmarked for personal time.

"Okay, so, this is your official introduction to the rules." Sam's fingers jitter against the edge of the laptop as though he's playing an invisible accordion. "In your questionnaires, we asked you some questions. I mean, we asked you to pick out a few activities that you'd like to do with the contestants. We'll space those out throughout the show. If there's anything you want that isn't on the, uh, the schedule, you can check with the producers to see if they can accommodate."

The next few diagrams outline the progression of the elimination process, which looks more like some fantasy football chart than a recipe for love. "This seems very complicated," Mom admits, echoing my own discomfort.

Sam is unfazed. He paraphrases one of the explanatory lines at the bottom of the slide. "It'll be so natural and organic that you won't even notice."

"You hear that, Mom?" I nudge her in the side. "Natural and organic. Your two favorite words in the English language."

"Do I detect a hint of teenage sarcasm?" she drawls.

Sam takes our bickering in stride. "Now, this next part won't apply to the first round when you make the big elimination of eight sets of contestants, but after that, you'll be able to . . . cheat a little." He pulls up a video feed that's currently looking at an empty sofa. "When the show begins, we'll be pulling people in for Confessionals, but with a twist. At any time in between the Sweetheart Ceremonies, which is where you pick who goes home, you can request to see the private Confessional of one contestant from your own group. Cara, that means you can only 'spy' on another child. Julia, that means adults only for you."

"And they don't know we can potentially see their Confessionals?" Mom asks.

"No," Sam says. "This is just for you and Cara. It's basically your personal advantage to see what emotions are really in play."

"At least I won't have to listen to these guys go on and on being gross *about my mom*. I get enough of that at the gym."

Sam scratches at the same spot on his cheek for the ensuing ten seconds of silence. He turns to Mom. "Well, the schedule clearly marks when you will be separated from each other, which is when you and the contestants might want alone time, since you won't have your children around, so I wouldn't worry too much because . . ."

Mom pats Sam on the shoulder. "I think you're just making it worse."

"You're definitely making it worse," I say.

"I'll just stop talking, then."

I turn to Sam, scowling. "Will we also have to do these Confessionals?" I guess I can't be too indignant about it after posting my diary on the internet already.

"The producers will fit in these types of sessions with you during events. They'll toss questions at you as they come up or ask you to talk about how you feel. It's not as structured."

I reach for my phone as it buzzes to protest its dying battery.

Suddenly, Sam smacks his forehead hard enough to leave a faint outline. "I completely blanked on the electronics policy. I hope no one noticed. What is wrong with me?" He stops hitting himself and holds out his hand, his eyes drifting upward toward the nearest camera. "Can I please have your cell phones and any communications devices, including smartwatches? You're not supposed to have any contact with the outside world until after the show is over."

I was hoping he'd forget about that part for a little longer.

[Cara Hawn Solo 4:03 PM] I miss you already. Love love love you. Have to turn in my phone now. You're

going to rock those scholarships and college visits.
Wish me luck. Don't let Mrs. Abernathy burn our
apartment to the ground.

I reluctantly relinquish my phone and watch Sam stash it in his messenger bag along with Mom's phone and fitness tracker. She rubs at the tan line on her wrist, scowling. "How am I supposed to know if I get my steps?"

"Speaking of steps, do we have to go anywhere else?" I ask Sam, hoping that the answer is no. It's been a long day, and I could use a nap, or better yet, actual sleep.

He checks his tablet. "Doesn't look like it. You're all done for today."

"Great. I'm going to bed."

"Don't you want something to eat?" Mom calls after me.

"Definitely not. My stomach still hasn't recovered from the plane."

I speed through an abbreviated version of my usual ritual, not even bothering to comb out the knots in my hair. I change in the sanctuary of the bathroom, knowing that my every move is otherwise on camera. I'm so tired that I don't care if Sam, or whoever is manning the cameras, sees me in my pink plaid pajamas, the fabric far too heavy for the tropical climate.

The firm bed and dense pillows are so different from the lumpy couch back home. My mind wanders farther, settling on the weight of a patchy homemade quilt, the warmth of being sandwiched between my parents as we flipped the pages of a bedtime story.

I snuggle into that memory, holding on to it like a long-forgotten friend as I drift off to a fitful, dreamless sleep.

chapter eleven

A sudden blast of intense light punches me into wakefulness. I flail in the confines of the sheets, almost toppling out of bed in my haste to shield my eyes. After a few moments, I splay my fingers enough to see that the bar of lights mounted above my bed is shining a blinding blue.

I check the nightstand for a remote, but there's nothing in the single drawer except a crumpled pamphlet advertising a guided tour of downtown. I search the fixture itself by standing on the edge of the bed frame for a boost, but there's no switch on the casing, either. Looking for a plug to pull is equally fruitless.

I hop down and hit the switch nearest to the door, which doesn't generate a noticeable change in my surroundings. I listen for the swish of a fan activating or another hidden feature powering on. There's nothing.

Maybe this room is designed to make guests want to leave.

I spend another three minutes rolling around the floor to see underneath the furniture and smacking my palms along the bare walls until I find a tiny screen mounted inside the closet beneath a white cover that renders it nearly invisible. The display shows settings for temperature and humidity as well as a series of environmental features to affect mood. I turn all of them off, stabbing the screen hard enough to make the pixels blur.

"Good morning," Mom calls as soon as I fling open the door to my room and emerge into the shared living space. "You look stressed."

"You'd look stressed too if you thought you were being abducted by aliens." I explain about my abrupt return to consciousness and the ensuing quest to turn off the light fixture before Batman showed up. "It was like one of those serial killer movies where the victim is trying to find the secret way out of the evil lair."

Sam chuckles. "It does have a purpose, if that makes you feel better."

"What do you mean?"

"Exposure to blue light helps suppress melatonin and make you feel more alert," Sam says. He pokes at his tablet, then turns it around to show the off-color, yellowish hue. "That's why you can set your electronics to filter out blue while you're browsing at night. See?"

"I'll have to try it out when I get my phone back."

Mom faces forward and continues staring at the faded square on the wall that used to be a television. I guess the communications ban extends to that, too. "I ate without you, by the way," she calls over her shoulder. "I was starving. Sorry."

"That's okay. I can fend for myself." I search through the kitchen from one side to the other until I find a few dry goods stuffed into a double-wide lower cabinet. Everything is unopened and fresh, making it seem more like the pantry of a play kitchen than an actual home. I pluck a bag of organic flaxseed from the front and hold it over the counter. "Mom, is this really happening?" I shriek, my voice breaking with panic.

I hear the slap of her bare feet on the natural stone floor as she hustles over. "What? What? What's wrong?"

"Are you telling me that we have traveled literally across the country just for me to find *organic flaxseed* for breakfast?" I stab a finger in Sam's direction. *"What have you done?"*

His genuine bafflement is the only thing that keeps me from hitting him with a tub of beetroot powder. "It was part of your questionnaire about eating habits! I practically bought out the local health store!"

"I might have filled out your part too," Mom confesses. "Otherwise, we'd be eating avocado toast and fish tacos for every meal."

I flop down on the ground and pummel the stupid flaxseed with the edge of my fist. "Yes, it's my fault that I like food with taste." I appeal to the camera above my head. "This woman is trying to kill me."

"Come on, now. It can't possibly be that bad. Look." Sam makes a show of opening up a snack bag of dried seaweed and pressing a quarter-sized disc of it onto his tongue. His nostrils flare as he clamps his mouth shut, tilting his head back a fraction like a reluctant child with a pill.

"Famous last words," I choke out as I observe the struggle.

"Seaweed is supposed to be great for your thyroid." He licks his lips twice and consults the nutrition facts. "Maybe a little salt wouldn't have been a bad idea, though."

Mom kneels on my other side to search through the rest of the cabinet. "How about some rice crackers?" She sets the box on the ground. "There's hummus in the fridge."

"Is there anything that isn't made of paste?" I don't mean to be so whiny, but I'm hardly asking for the world here. Plain eggs would be a gourmet smorgasbord.

"Oh! I have an idea!" Mom lurches to her feet and shuffles to her room with as much speed as she can manage on the friction-less tiles. There are a few loud bangs and the sound of a drawer shutting before I hear the telltale crinkle of a junk food wrapper.

Mom returns to the kitchen and places her treasures on the counter. It's only a pack of fruit snacks and the biscotti that I didn't eat on the plane, but I'm not complaining. "You're my hero," I garble at her, dabbing my eyes against my palm. I eat the biscotti in three bites, ignoring the rumble of protest from my stomach. "Thank you. You do love me."

"Sorry," Mom whispers around her hand, laughing. "I didn't realize I was traumatizing you with seaweed."

"I'm just stressed by all the travel," I say as I pull my hair back with my fingers. "You should make everyone eat health food three meals a day. Half of these guys would vote themselves off just to get a cheeseburger."

An hour later, Angela and a team of helpers arrive with rolling black cases and a covered garment rack. They sweep through the house with practiced purpose, commandeering the open living area and transforming it into a workable dressing room.

A harried woman who must be a makeup artist fusses with a boxy container of cosmetics that she sets on top of a stand with stiltlike, robotic legs. A mirror and two panels of lights are affixed to the top. "Do you have an extension cord?" she asks another one of the crew. "Why don't these places *ever* have enough outlets?"

She introduces herself as Val, then points at me. "You. Daughter. Sit."

"Do I get to pick the colors?" I ask, watching her roll out a selection of brushes.

Val laughs as though the idea is ludicrous. "Honey, me and Ange have spent hours studying your face and your skin color. Your palette is already picked."

"Okay." I hold back a sneeze as she works, adjusting the angle of my head according to her pointed taps against my jawline. I look paunchy and haggard under the brilliant lighting, my face marred by dark slashes of contouring makeup.

From my perch on the stool, I can watch Mom getting her hair done. She winces as the stylist adds an impossible number of bobby pins to secure a loose braid that wends across the back of her head. A clip decorated with pale pink and red flowers sits in the center, presiding over a long cascade of black curls.

Val lowers her thin blond brows and clucks her tongue as I move an inch to track Mom's progress. "You're awfully wiggly there, girl." She admonishes me with a jab of her brush handle against my arm.

"Sorry."

Angela watches all from a distance, chatting with Sam or the producers as they filter through to observe. Venti brings over a tray of mimosas and leaves them by Mom, who is more than happy to oblige.

We switch places when we're finished at our respective stations. The makeup artist follows me over to accost the hairstylist, planting one hand on her cocked hip. "Listen, hair man. You better not go too overboard with heat and make her sweat into her makeup. I don't have time for fifty touch-ups."

He peers at her over the edge of his narrow, rimless glasses. "And *you* better not mess up the mom's hair, because *I* don't have time for fifty touch-ups either."

"Don't make me come over there," Angela warns, laughing.

"Fine," the hairstylist says. "We have a deal."

True to his promise, there isn't nearly as much primping and curling as I expected. The braid trailing along the side of my head matches Mom's. The rest of my hair is pinned up, though I can still feel the bottom of it shifting against the back of my neck as I stand.

I thank the stylist before heading over to the garment rack to see what I'll be wearing this evening. I was nervous when they told us that they were custom ordering our dresses for the opening ceremony, but now I'm even more worried that it'll look horrible when there's hardly any time to object before we go on camera. "What do you think?" Angela asks, holding it high enough to keep the hem from dragging on the ground.

"I'm not worthy," I deadpan, taking a step back. The fabric is a silky black that fades in an ombré bleed to a deep crimson along the bottom. A thick band of rhinestones crusts the waistline. "Are you sure that isn't my mom's dress?"

Angela tilts the gown and lays it across my arms. "It's similar. You'll be in complementary colors." I start walking toward the tiny bathroom, but she stops me with a gentle hand on my shoulder. "There's a screen over here for you to change without the cameras seeing you."

"That's a relief. I was wondering how I was going to get into this thing without falling into the toilet."

She sidles around the screen and deposits a pair of black heels on the floor before leaving me to change. The dress is easy to slip on, but I can't quite reach the zipper. When I call for Mom, Sam yells back that she's still busy with her makeup.

"Fine," I grumble, clomping into view with layers of fabric bunched in my fists. "Can someone else zip me up?"

The hairstylist volunteers, tugging the zipper with sure fingers as I hold my breath.

"How's it fit?" Angela asks, looking concerned. "I've got a seamstress on call, and there's extra fabric. We can manage basic alterations."

I let myself settle into the dress like dough that needs time to rise. I wriggle a bit, getting a sense of the stretch of it. After a few minutes, it isn't as constricting. "I think it's okay. It's just on the edge of being too tight."

"Perfect." She claps her hands once, then hurries over to help Mom. In the center of the room, she stops so abruptly that her heel skids on the floor. "Can someone. . ." She gestures at the rolling case to my right. "Accessories for Cara?"

Angela's assistant has a garment bag slung over her outstretched arms, two shoes stuffed in her left armpit, and a piece of paper in her mouth. She makes a helpless mewling noise.

"I'll get it," Sam says, bending to dig through the top drawer. A moment later, he completes my ensemble by pressing a pair of teardrop earrings and a necklace into my palm.

When it's Mom's turn to reveal her dress, the staff forms a semicircle in the middle of the room to watch. I hover off to the side, wishing for the millionth time that I had a camera of my own.

The tips of her toes emerge first, then her lower leg, then her thigh. For a terrifying moment, I think she's naked. But soon I see the rest of the crimson gown forming the plunging split, the way the black beads trace a heart-shaped bodice and trail down the single full-length sleeve.

Mom brushes her hair away from her exposed shoulder and spins in a neat circle. "I love this gown already. It's surprisingly comfortable."

"But . . . ," I stammer. "But your leg."

"What do you mean?"

"If you move the wrong way, everyone's going to see your . . . your . . ." Sam's face grows progressively pinker as I struggle to find the right word. "Your ORIFICES."

Mom slaps one hand onto the nearby vanity and doubles over in an uncontrollable laugh. "My *orifices*? That's the best you could come up with? I'm wearing underwear!"

"You know what I mean! It gets the point across."

Mom rolls her eyes up toward the ceiling and dabs at her makeup. "Stop making me laugh so hard. My eyes are going to tear."

"It's classy and elegant," Angela interjects in her usual matter-of-fact

"It's classy and elegant," Angela interjects in her usual matter-of-fact way. "There's nothing to worry about. My whole team designed this dress for you."

Sam holds out his arm to steady Mom as she adjusts to her new shoes. "We have to head up to the promo shoot, and I think they want a quick interview for sound bites. I'm not sure in which order." He looks around for confirmation, but no one else seems to know the plan. "Well, uh, well, I'm sure someone will tell us if we're not in the right spot."

We spend the rest of the afternoon getting shepherded from one place to the next, taking pictures and posing with the host in various places. Danny Romano is older than I expected for a television personality, with salt-and-pepper hair and a slight frame. He seems used to the camera, and I can't help but mentally sort through past shows I've seen, trying to place him somewhere in my memory. I finally cave while Mom is taking individual shots. "Were you on a different show before this one?"

He laughs. "I get that a lot. I was the host of *The Gavel*. It's the—"

I cut him off by singing the introductory jingle. "Divorce court with Judge O'Malley!"

When I tell Mom, she can't believe it either. She cracks a few jokes about divorcing Dad before we're off again to take sunset pictures. Tall and Grande track our progress, giving us a near-constant stream of feedback.

"Always call Danny Romano by his full name. It's his brand."

"Don't look directly at the camera."

"Stop fiddling with your microphone."

Then, just when I'm about to fall over, Sam hands me a granola bar and breaks the news that we have to go *back* to hair and makeup before the Sweetheart Ceremony.

"Gotta admit," Mom says, sitting on the couch and massaging her heels while we wait for the stylist team to return, "I'm not feeling super sweet right now after all that. More like I could use a nap."

"The other days won't be quite this long," Sam says, wincing. "Are you okay? Do you want an Advil?"

Danny Romano approaches, taking a seat to the right of Mom. Ian shuffles into a better filming position. "You know what's even better than Advil?" Danny Romano asks, shooting Sam a pointed look as he hands Mom some kind of beverage. "Booze."

Mom pushes the garnish aside and takes a long swig, leaving behind the faintest smear of lipstick. Between the two mimosas earlier and this, I worry about how coherent she's going to be.

Danny Romano leans in, smiling. "So, how are you feeling right now, Julia? Is there a lot of pressure? Are you excited?"

"There's a lot of pressure, but I'm super stoked to be here. I can't wait to meet all the guys. I still can't believe this is happening."

Mom's not always the best at reading the room, and I don't think she realizes that this is probably one of those Confessional things Sam told us about, not just Danny—Danny *Romano*—being friendly. "Hey, Mom?" I try to intervene, but Sam and Angela herd me away as Val arrives to touch up my makeup. I keep still, listening as hard as I can to keep track of the conversation.

"What are you looking for in your new love?" Danny Romano asks. "Someone who reminds you of your ex-husband, maybe?"

Mom scoffs. "I'm looking for the *opposite* of Rick. Don't even joke like that." She polishes off her drink.

"And what would this dream man be like? What do you hope to gain from being here?"

"I just want to meet someone who treats me like I'm worth it. Someone funny and smart and nice. I don't care if they're the most handsome person or the most well-off or anything like that. I just want something real."

Danny Romano pats Mom's arm. "Well, Julia, it certainly sounds like you're here for all the right reasons."

chapter twelve

*T*he moment we step inside the foyer, Venti comes over with Danny Romano to review what the Welcome Ceremony is all about. I try to listen, but I'm so exhausted already after such a busy afternoon. "Could I get, like, a cup of coffee or something?" I ask.

Sam takes a step closer. "I can grab you one. How do you take it?"

"With a lot of cream and—"

"Excuse me," Venti says, his tone clipped. "This young lady has had her makeup done already. She can't be drinking something that hot. It'll ruin her lipstick and flush her face."

Sam mutters a string of apologies, looking like his soul just departed his body and entered the reality TV afterlife.

"You have to think about stuff like this," Venti adds. "It's your job."

Maybe it's just because it's television, but it's so disorienting to be around people who are this intense. I can't figure out when they're angry or just annoyed, coaching or condescending. I wonder briefly whether all business is that way.

I stand back and watch as the producers make their final preparations. Tall and Grande move throughout the room, making adjustments and interacting with the crew members as they stage equipment. Venti stands in the corner and observes, leaning against the wall and sweeping his gaze over the entirety of the room.

Grande breaks away after a few minutes and approaches us. He nods at our dresses. "I love that color scheme." He gestures to the curved staircase to our right. "Danny Romano will open the show by welcoming the audience and introducing the two of you. After that, he'll move on to introducing the contestants. You don't have to do anything during that time except for react and interact with others as you normally would."

I don't think he actually means that, since my natural reaction right now would be to run away and hide in an armoire. Mom asks a few questions, enough that I can sense she's nervous as well. "We've got this," she assures him. "Don't worry about us."

Angela herds us into the adjoining lounge and has us practice walking into view of the camera when our names are called. I memorize the number of steps so I won't go too far and ruin the balance of space between us and the contestants. "Hey, you're wearing yellow glasses now," I note. "Weren't they just green?"

"I got a little chilly," she says, lifting the lapel of a jacket that she apparently pulled out of thin air in the past ten minutes. "The green didn't match."

"Oh." That level of coordination makes my head spin. Can everything just stop changing for three seconds?

"What?" Angela strikes a playful pose. "I'm a stylist. I like to accessorize. But thank you for noticing."

Sam hurries over with rolls of tape on either forearm. "If you get confused, your spots are marked on the floor. Just try not to look straight down."

"This is happening." I shuffle in my shoes and adjust a fold in my dress. What if I laugh too hard and pee my pants—well, pee my gown—on camera? I think about the few television scandals I've seen, how the most seemingly minor error can be inflated into a mortal sin. I'd ask Sam if the editors cut out embarrassing mishaps, but I'm not that naive.

The next few minutes are a blur of activity that hardly registers as I struggle to carry out the simplest actions. Breathe oxygen. Blink eyelids. Do not barf.

I almost jump when Danny Romano starts talking. "Good evening. Thank you for joining us on the first episode of *Second Chance Romance*. I'm about to introduce a woman who is so beautiful, so fearless, that she will captivate the hearts of not only these contestants, but also you, America, from the very first moment you meet her. After recovering from a tragic past and a harrowing divorce, she's back here again looking for true love. I am so excited to introduce you to the courageous Julia Hawn."

Mom squeezes my hand, holds her head up, and glides into the lobby looking every bit like a star. Part of me is nervous about what Danny Romano will say about me given his embellishment of Mom's past. Sure, Dad is a jerk, but I don't know that it counts as tragic. Maybe his chili recipe.

"Next," Danny Romano continues, "I'm pleased for you to meet an incredible young lady who has been Julia's rock for so long. Between her late-night tell-all video blogs and secret yearning to become a gourmet chef, we can't wait to see what else we uncover about a mysterious girl who doesn't pull punches. Without further introduction, I give you Cara Hawn."

I like food. That doesn't mean I have a *secret yearning* to become a gourmet chef.

Sam wordlessly shoos me with both hands. I don't know what to do with my face. I plaster on a smile so broad that I can feel it in the muscles of my eyebrows and the tips of my ears. I walk into the foyer, taking careful steps to avoid tripping over Mom's dress.

"Julia," Danny Romano says, laying a hand on Mom's arm. "How are you feeling right now? Are you looking forward to meeting the contestants?"

"I'm so excited to be here, and I can't wait to meet everyone!"

Mom gushes, her words a little faster than normal.

"And you, Cara?"

I think about the money, how we'd be able to move anywhere we wanted. I imagine Mom standing in our new gym, the one she owns by herself, no strings attached. "I'm so excited too. I can't think of anywhere else I'd rather be."

His voice has the perfect, practiced lilt of a television anchor or a motivational speaker. "We're thrilled to have you here with us as well."

I'm so accustomed to seeing television shows that appear to have been filmed in one shot that the first break catches me by surprise. I have the opportunity to blow my nose and check my makeup before we resume the next segment.

Danny Romano announces the first set of contestants by name as they descend the staircase like courtiers arriving at a ball. I was hoping for a full history, but apparently, all we get are names and home states.

AJ and Ella Benton. California.

A tall Black man steps onto the landing, his tie color-coordinated with his daughter's pale pink gown. Halfway down the stairs, I think Ella is about to fall, but she leans forward into an incredible flip and continues through a series of complex gymnastic maneuvers. In an evening gown. And high heels. AJ slides down the banister just in time to catch her.

Part of me is relieved to see another girl my age. The other part is back to feeling inadequate that my greatest talent is being able to fix our toilet with a paper clip and two rubber bands.

They aren't the only ones to put on a show either. Cole Sherwin and his elementary-age son, Grady, break into a square dance in their embroidered matching cowboy boots, earning a suppressed giggle from Mom. It doesn't surprise me to hear that they're from somewhere as sunny as Mississippi, given the pale ring of a sunglasses tan around Cole's eyes and the fact that Grady doesn't seem to mind wearing such a thick jacket in the humidity.

Ray Ortega descends the stairs with great fanfare, holding on to the train of his daughter's massive gown. Sabrina can't be more than six years old, making it so adorable that Mom actually puts a hand over her heart and coos. Ray spins her into a twirl, ending in a synchronized curtsy and bow. It's so cute, I might die.

After each pair reaches the foot of the stairs, the suitors and their kids break into separate groups on either side. There's a split second when the newly arrived pair is still the center of attention, except now they're close enough for us to hear. A few call out greetings or wave.

I start to lose track of names around number fourteen.

Danny Romano waits a moment before announcing the next pair. "From New Jersey, we have Charles and Connor Dingeldein."

I look up to see a dark-haired, broad-shouldered man begin to descend the stairs, casting a bit of a shadow onto his teenage son. I'm about to adjust my stance slightly to see better when Mom bursts out laughing. Venti steps forward from the rear of the room, but Mom waves him away. "I'm sorry. I'm sorry. Can we do that again?"

When Charles and Connor reset, Danny Romano announces them again, and they almost make it to the third step when Mom loses it again. "I'm sorry. It's so rude. I just wasn't expecting *Dingeldein*."

"You gave her alcohol," I tell Danny Romano before he can get cranky about the second interruption. "Look what you did."

We try a third time, but then AJ and Ray both start laughing from the other side of the room. Grande and Venti agree that we need a break, during which time I see Connor take a seat at the top of the stairs. When he looks down and meets my eyes, I can finally see his face, softer than his father's in more than just shape.

He offers a wave with his right hand, and I notice then that his left arm is in a bulky black sling. I wonder what happened.

We regroup a minute later and try again, this time without anyone laughing. I watch Connor as he descends the staircase, trying not to be too obvious about it. But all I can see is his thick brown hair and slender nose, his eyes that I imagine are looking at me with the same level of scrutiny.

Suddenly, I'm aware of a million facts at once. This is a dating show for my mom, not me. He could be my stepbrother if our parents get married. My armpits are sweating. I feel giggly.

Plus, I promised myself after the divorce that the only great love of my life is going to be lox and cream cheese bagels.

Venti is telepathic. That's the only explanation for how quickly he calls a break and pulls me into the lounge, shutting the door behind Ian, who stuffs his camera in my face. "Cara. What a twist. That was a surprising reaction in there. Why don't you tell us about it?"

I sit down on a poufy armchair. "I don't know what you mean."

"Oh, come on, now. I know your true feelings. It was all there on your face."

"What was?"

"You were glowing in there the moment you saw Connor. Do you think he's cute?"

I should have insisted on that cup of coffee. "I don't . . . I don't *not* think he's cute. He's cute. I mean, cute in a not-liking way." Oh God, is this why Sam is always so flustered? What are words? "I guess I'm just naturally going to notice other kids my age."

"You don't believe in love at first sight?"

I don't understand why he's wheedling me like this when I'm not even the one who's supposed to be second chancing or romancing over here. "I don't know. I guess it's real."

"So, would you say there's a chance it's love at first sight with you and Connor?"

"No, that's ridiculous. I haven't even talked to him."

Venti interrogates me in circles for what feels like fifteen minutes. I'm so tired, and I can't sit in the chair without squashing my hair or wrinkling my dress more than necessary. He's relentless. "Cara, we loved the raw emotion in your video. That's why we cast you. We need some more of that. It's okay to admit the truth that you have these strong feelings already for Connor."

I know what he's doing, but I also don't see any way around it. If we want to be successful, to get famous enough that this is worth more than just the compensation for appearing, I have to be Internet Cara, not the real one. The next time Venti asks a question, I tell him whatever I need to keep the cameras rolling:

Confessional: Connor Dingeldein is cute, but I can't have a crush on a contestant's kid. That would be weird. I never expected to meet someone like Connor, though. This could definitely make things more complicated.

Satisfied, Venti lets me go back into the main room, where there's minimal fussing over my makeup before we continue.

The last contestants are Brad and Chelsea Burke from New York, but they don't appear at the top of the staircase when their names are called. There's the sound of raised voices and commotion before the producers head up to investigate the ruckus. Tall returns a few moments later looking exasperated, but in spite of our obvious curiosity, he doesn't volunteer any details. I'm not used to living in a silo like this. It's disorienting to realize that I've only got one hand and no way to see the rest of the deck.

"Maybe they got cold feet," Mom whispers out of the side of her mouth while smiling at all the strangers gawking at us. I marvel at how serene she is amidst the chaos. We're definitely not at the gym's monthly cauliflower pizza social, but you'd never know it from her placid expression.

Meanwhile, I'm struggling to feel like I could possibly belong here. Every way I turn, my gaze falls upon the kind of preternatural beauty that deserves a runway or a toothpaste commercial. The suitors' faces are almost wicked, with sharp angles and shadowed hollows carved into their bones. The children are like a time lapse reminder of my inadequacy. The youngest ones are cute at an age when I was clumsy, the middle bunch poised when I would have thrown a tantrum by now.

And the older girls? Forget it. Any one of them could be a beauty queen when I can't even convince myself to put on pants half the time. My nose wrinkles at the cloying, saccharine sweetness of their perfumes mixed with the harsh tang of hair spray. They stand as still as birds, balanced on needle-thin stilettos like herons waiting for the right time to strike.

That isn't me. I'm just . . . ordinary.

And if this show were really about me, Connor wouldn't be interested anyway. That thought makes it easier to look at him. He's looking back, but I know it's only because he has to. After all, I'm the star, right?

Finally, Brad emerges onto the landing, his arm held out to his daughter. Even from this distance, they're just as stunning as the other contestants. They move with easy grace, their chins tilted up and shoulders pulled back. Their hair is a matching gold, their eyes piercing blue. Cold, and haughty, and *beautiful*.

Brad twirls his daughter toward the other kids, keeping his gaze pinned on Mom like the eyes of a haunted portrait that never seems to be looking away. He stalks forward with sure steps and takes Mom's hand, the first contestant bold enough to touch her. "It's wonderful to meet you, Julia," he says, pressing his left hand over hers. "I can't wait to spend more time together."

Mom is speechless for so long that Brad tips his head and returns to his appointed spot by the time she reacts with a breathless *whoosh* of air. I turn toward her to whisper a joke, but she's already transfixed.

chapter thirteen

As soon as the Welcome Ceremony is over, Danny Romano's features slacken. He scrubs one of his eyes with the back of his knuckle. I wonder how he does it, managing to appear so suave and affable without seeming fake. He removes his tie, slinging it over his shoulder like a hated but necessary burden.

While we wait for someone to direct us to the next activity, I move closer to Mom and whisper, "Any first impressions?" Eliminating contestants this early is completely unfair. I can't even remember their names yet.

Mom takes a long breath and holds it while she contemplates her answer. "Only if I go off of looks." Her eyes flick to Brad. "But a few of them don't really catch my eye."

If I rearrange bits of those sentences in my mind, my mother is basically saying that she only has the hots for *some* of these random men. I squeeze my eyes closed hard enough to feel my mascara-crusted lashes crinkling together. "I don't need to know the details."

Sam hurries over, wringing his hands and consulting his watch with alarming frequency. I want to tell him that his shirt is untucked in the back, but I'm afraid of sending him over the edge.

"We're a bit behind schedule," he says. "The crews are setting up for the next event."

"Which is?" Mom prompts.

"You're going to have short introductory sessions with each contestant. Just a quick way of getting to know a little about everyone."

Mom nods. "Speed dates."

I count the number of people crammed into this room. The thought of meeting all of them is exhausting. "Better be extra speedy with this many contestants."

At a signal from the producers, Sam herds Mom into an adjoining room while I follow another assistant through the front door. She leads me down an ornate stone walkway, hooks a left around the corner of the house, and stops part of the way down the "hill" by the door to the lower level.

"We'll send them out one at a time," she explains, glancing behind her as the camera crew adjusts some portable lighting. "You'll have two minutes with each person."

"Thanks."

Instead of sitting at the table, I settle onto a bench tucked against the wall in the cozy nook formed by the angles of the building. Having two enclosed sides makes me feel less exposed, which is a little ridiculous given the entire team of people assembled around me.

With a pang of shock, I realize that I'm going to be face-to-face with Connor soon.

The first contestant arrives a few moments later, announcing that her name is Madyson. "*M-A-D-Y-S-O-N*," she explains. "I hate it when people spell my name wrong."

"I know what you mean. People always spell my last name wrong." They want it to be 'Han,' then look embarrassed when I say that Dad is white and Mom's maiden name was Werner.

I look around for help, realizing that I don't have a script of any kind, or even a list of canned questions. It reminds me of the first day of high school when everyone is trying to determine whether or not you're going to be a crappy lab partner.

I'm tempted to ask her how old she is, but I'm not sure if that would hurt her feelings. I guess she's about twelve. It's easier to estimate since she's obviously refused any meaningful makeup or hairstyling.

"I like your dress."

She cracks a full-toothed smile and pats the front of her navy blue gown. "You can tell which one is my dad because he's gold with navy accents. We thought it would be so awesome if we matched but were opposites. And in Michigan colors, of course."

"I match my mom, too."

Madyson looks over my dress with focus. I can't help feeling annoyed at the smattering of glitter across the front that I probably dropped all over the floor of the house without realizing. Once there's glitter around, there is no escape. "I get it." She nods like we're sharing a profound secret. "Scarlet. Ohio State. Makes sense."

"I doubt that has anything to do with it. We don't watch, uh, sportsball."

Madyson shrugs, which is better than the rant I was expecting about how meaningless our lives are without football. It's the kind of proselytizing argument LeAnne would make. "Maybe you'd like it more if you got to go to a party," Madyson suggests. "Everybody gets so into it at our house."

It doesn't sound that bad when she puts it that way. For a minute, I can imagine the two of us sitting side by side in a stadium, a bottle of pop in the armrest and corn dogs in either hand. "I guess that could be cool. I know most of the rules from video games."

She sits bolt upright and smacks a palm against the bench. "No way. Do you play *Madden*? *FIFA*?"

"Yeah. Both, actually." I'd play more if I had my own console instead of commandeering Dad's during his custody weekends. Plus, I can always pretend I can't hear him through the headset if he tries to talk to me. "I'm not any good, though."

She bounces on the bench so fervently that her threader earrings rattle below her lobes. "This is so exciting. I was afraid that we wouldn't have anything in common and it would be awkward and awful and you'd hate me."

I'm sad to see Madyson go, especially since my conversations with the next few contestants are so tedious that I feel the two-minute allotments the same way I feel the last two minutes before we're allowed to close the gym for the day. I look up after the fourth session to see Venti approaching, his eyes narrowed into slits as he transitions from the relative darkness to the pool of light surrounding me.

"Hey." He plops on the bench and slides down a bit to keep from towering over me. "You're doing great, but I'm having a little trouble picking up on your emotions."

"Oh. Sorry. They're just not giving me a lot to work with here."

"Can you be a little more expressive? You've got this look on your face."

Yeah, it's called wanting to be asleep in my bed three hours ago.

He brings up Connor again, asking whether I'm excited to meet him, what I might want to know about him. Even though I know this is just a mind game, I can't help but consider the questions. I spend the next minute or two of peace wondering what Connor does for fun and trying to envision him in some kind of daily life.

Chelsea is next. Her walk is more of a stalking prowl than an innocent step into view of the camera. She folds herself onto the bench with care, crossing her legs and tossing her blond hair back from her face where it falls in natural ringlets. "Hi again."

As I contemplate whether I misheard her, I realize that it's

Chelsea, the girl from the audition in Pittsburgh. I didn't even recognize her with her new hairstyle and the gown and the makeup. "Oh, hey. Nice to see you again."

"I feel like I know you way more than you know me," she says. "They've been talking to us about you and your mom for *days*."

I don't really know what to say to that.

"Can I give you a little bit of advice?"

Here we go again. Miss Advice. "Sure."

"You slouch, and it throws off your walk. It'll help you balance better in your heels if you pull your shoulders back. I learned that in my acting class. It helped me land all those commercials."

"Thanks."

I watch her stroll off while I try to calm down. "Can I give you a little bit of advice?" I mutter in a whining tone. It's never a good day when my blood pressure is this much higher than my IQ. I catch a glimpse of Venti standing just beyond the halo of the portable lighting. He's smiling as he watches the red-faced cameraman chew on the knuckle of his index finger to contain a laugh.

Watching them helps me let go of that initial spike of indignation. My temper is more of a lazy river than a tempest, but it still takes several minutes before I'm calm again.

I exchange small talk as best I can, though there's only so much I can engage with the younger children. I've never thought about being an older sibling. Maybe I'll have to get used to it. I keep reminding myself that this could be real. A new family. A stepfather. A sibling.

And as much as Venti has already been nagging me, the only way Connor will be staying a part of my life is as a stepbrother. It'll be easier to remember that later when I don't have all these lights in my face and whispers in my ear. After seeing Mom become a walking, talking human puddle of sadness over Dad,

I'm convinced that love has a BEST BY date. I need to hold on to that before I screw this up for Mom with a stupid crush.

I just wish I knew why the producers are all over this so much already. It's only the first night, but all I've heard about is Connor, Connor, Connor.

But when he finally rounds the corner, the ends of my mouth curl into an involuntary smile that has nothing to do with Venti and everything to do with the tingling warmth in my chest. I almost stand for some reason before I catch myself and lean back. He takes a seat on the bench beside me. "Hi. I'm Connor. I'd say my last name, but I'm afraid the cameraman will murder me if he has to shoot all my scenes over and over like last time."

"Please don't talk about the camera!" Venti calls.

Connor shrinks, looking sheepish. "Hi. I'm Connor. I'd say my last name, but I'm afraid you'll laugh again."

"I'm sorry." I can't tell from his tone whether he's actually hurt by it or not. "It was so rude, but I couldn't help it."

He scoffs. "Please. I went through middle school with the last name Dingeldein. If you can come up with a single original Dingeldein joke, I will quit right now."

"That bad, huh?"

"It was brutal. My dad doesn't think it's very funny, but then again, he doesn't really think anything's that funny."

"What a coincidence. My dad also doesn't think anything's funny."

Connor takes a breath, releases it, then takes another. "I wasn't going to bring it up, but you seem like you've got a sense of humor. I saw your video."

I groan. "Not the video."

He stands at the signal that our time is up. As he turns to leave, he adds, "Hey, it could be worse. Your last name could be Dingeldein."

As soon as he's gone, there's another barrage of questions from the producers.

Confessional: Connor is even more amazing now that we've talked. I love his sense of humor. I feel like we just click, you know?

I can tell by Venti's face that I'm getting better at saying what he wants. I'm so tired that it's hard to keep my true thoughts and feelings separate from what I'm saying to the camera. I do think Connor seems nice, but that simple sentiment doesn't really make for compelling TV.

I almost snort as I imagine Danny Romano's interpretation in his official announcer voice. *Do you hear that, America? She thinks he's nice! Tune in next week to watch Cara staring at a wall for twenty minutes!*

By the time I get to the final contestant, I'm struggling to keep my eyelids from drooping. Luckily, it's Ella, the gymnast, who I've actually been looking forward to meeting.

I sit up straighter, fighting the fatigue dulling my senses. "That whole flipping routine you did was awesome. I don't know how you didn't break your leg or something."

She shrugs and lifts her heels out of the backs of her shoes. "We just thought it would be a cool way to make a first impression. I was a little worried because the stairs curve and I can't see that well upside down."

"It worked." Another few seconds of silence pass, but it doesn't feel uncompanionable. The tightness in my shoulders eases. "So, what made you want to come on the show?"

"I—" She hesitates, as if weighing her answer. "I didn't really, but my dad wanted to. I'm the reason he doesn't have much of a dating life in the first place."

"What do you mean?"

"He's too busy driving me to competitions or helping out with my traveling team."

"Well, can't blame you for telling the truth."

"It's not that I don't think you and your mom are nice," Ella says, wincing. "I don't want to get kicked off. I just thought I'd be able to see more of my friends before it was time to go back to school. That, and I'm missing a ton of practice."

"I know what you mean. About the friends, at least." I feel a sudden pang of longing for Vanessa. As much as we need this money to get as far away from Dad as possible, I hope that I don't regret leaving during our last full summer together. Next year, she'll be cutting it short to go to college; I'm not even sure I want to go to college at all.

Mostly, I don't want us to grow apart, our friendship reduced to occasional text messages. What if we both move super far away? Vanessa would come home for Hanukkah to loudly argue with her parents that applesauce is better than sour cream on latkes; I'd maybe be back for Thanksgiving to loudly argue with Dad that he's a terrible human being. What if we just never cross paths?

"What do you like to do for fun?" Ella asks. "Besides cooking. They told us already that you like cooking."

When I stop to think about it, the question is a sucker punch. This past year has been a flurry of courtrooms and classrooms, shifts at the gym, a moving truck. Family hikes and lunches at the café are past-tense pastimes, and zombifying in front of the television is hardly a hobby. "I don't know?"

It's odd to be sorting people into a discard pile like ill-fitting clothes in a dressing room. I don't remember half of their names, but someone had the foresight to print out a cheat sheet that's taped to the floor like a police lineup. I scrutinize the faces of the kids I just met, mentally pairing them with their fathers.

I try not to linger on Connor too long. I can't tell if it's Venti constantly asking me what I think about Connor every thirty seconds or if I'm just naturally intrigued. I never thought I'd pine for the straightforwardness of romance at school, where at least I know all my classmates and there aren't any surprise introductions to people like . . . well, Connor.

Mom can't nibble at her gelled nails, so she taps the tips over the edges of her teeth like piano keys as she watches the contestants shuffle around. "This is going to be a tough vote. They're all so different."

"What do you mean?" I ask. After spending only a few minutes with each person, I can't tell many of them apart. For me, at least a couple have morphed into a homogenous blob of fun facts and small talk.

"Some are from the west coast. Some from the Deep South. They all look and act different." She points between the two men standing closest to us. "I think I want to keep both of them. The guy on the left is Ray. He's an English teacher. And that's Cole. He's a nuclear something-something."

"Wow, a nuclear something-something. That's supercool. Do you have to go to school a long time to be a nuclear something-something?"

Mom tries to check the time before she realizes that she isn't wearing her watch. "I don't want to take forever doing this. We just have to pick. I'll start." She glances at the photos of suitors on the cheat sheet. "I'd like to get rid of Steve and Elias. We couldn't figure out anything to talk about except the weather."

I guess I'll start with the easy ones too. "I don't really like Chelsea. Do you know that's the same girl who was sitting across from us at the audition?"

"No," Mom says, squinting in Chelsea's direction. "I didn't recognize her this far away."

"José and Bobby don't stick out as big contenders either."

Mom jots down the names. She pauses with the tip of the pen poised over the pad. "Actually, do you mind if Chelsea sticks around for a while? Her father, Brad, was one of my top picks for the night, even if he was late to his own introduction."

I'm literally too tired to care at this point unless she floats getting rid of Connor. "Okay, then. What about Sabrina?" I ask, remembering a shy girl who could hardly manage single-word squeaks with the cameras around. "She's really cute, but she's so shy that I don't know if she's ever going to talk to me." I check the contestant list again. "Oh, wait, she's Ray's daughter. You wanted to keep them."

"Sorry, I don't mean to veto all your choices."

"No. That's okay." I squeeze my hands into fists and try to stuff them into pockets that don't exist on this scratchy ball gown. "You can just pick the rest." If I make too strong of a case to keep Connor and his dad, Mom will sniff that out in a second. Thankfully, it doesn't come up.

When we finish the list, we pass it off to Danny Romano, who holds it in both hands like we've given him the secrets of the universe on a dirty piece of notebook paper. He confers with Tall and Venti for a few seconds before they reach some kind of conclusion. "This is great," he tells us. "No issues from the producers on these picks."

"They can interfere with our voting?" I ask, exchanging a look with Mom. I don't recall that being in the rules, unless it falls under the generic stipulation that the producers make the rules in the first place.

Danny Romano looks to his right and left as if searching for help. He runs a hand over the swell of his stylized hair. "'Interfere' is a strong word. It's more like they'll make some suggestions to keep things interesting."

Before I can figure out what that means, the crew herds us back into our staged positions at the front of the room to make some last-minute lighting adjustments. Danny Romano steps into place beside us, chewing on his lip and fidgeting with his monogrammed pocket square. "You finalize your vote by closing the corresponding picture of the contestants on the Wall of Hearts. I'll explain it for the audience."

Mom nods, eyeing the gaudy oversized lockets hanging on the wall with the picture of a suitor on one side and his kid on the other. I wonder how the owners of this house feel about having so many holes punched into their extravagant foyer.

I keep feeling the weight of a stare that breaks through beyond the dozens of eyes on us already. I want to check whether Connor is watching me, but if I'm wrong, I'll give myself away as a little too intrigued.

As promised, Danny Romano launches into a quick overview of the voting process as soon as we start filming. "Since this is the first Sweetheart Ceremony, Julia and Cara will each choose four pairs of contestants for elimination. We'll start with Julia." He presses a hand against her back. "Which four contestants have you chosen for tonight's elimination?"

The suspense in the room is palpable as Mom approaches the wall and closes the heart for Elias and Becky. Danny Romano recites the names aloud and calls the two of them forward. Becky immediately bursts into tears, glaring at me like I've personally ruined her life. We say a quick goodbye, hugging even though I totally didn't remember anything about our conversation.

When it's my turn, Danny Romano steers me to the center of the foyer, asking, "Cara, which four contestants have *you* chosen for tonight's elimination?"

I'm so nervous that I almost forget who we agreed to vote off. It takes a few seconds to scan the wall and find the correct set of pictures showing Steve and his daughter. It's like playing *Wheel of Fortune* with people instead of letters.

I'm grateful that we'll only have to choose one parent-child pair for elimination during the subsequent rounds. I don't think I can handle this much hugging and crying on a regular basis.

As I watch the losing contestants depart, fathers comforting their kids, the loving way they whisper to each other, I can't shake the pained ache gnawing at my chest. It isn't guilt for their tears or regret that I won't get to know them better after tonight. It's too late for it to be nausea from the plane.

Finally, as we head back to the guesthouse, I realize what it is.

Envy.

chapter fourteen

*T*he next morning starts with an obligatory group breakfast. According to Sam, this is the producers' way of making sure we all have time together each day regardless of what's on the rest of the schedule. Personally, I couldn't care less about interacting with any of the contestants. I just want to interact with some carbohydrates.

According to the rules, we're not supposed to eat on camera, but I guess this must be an exception since it's not an "official activity." I follow my nose to the dining room, where an inordinate amount of food is piled in steaming buffet trays. The French doors are thrown open to the outside and folding tables are arranged on the patio beneath a white pergola. "It's so beautiful," Mom says, her head tilting back to trace the ivy wrapped around the columns.

"I know," I say, but I'm talking about the pancakes and the array of single-serving syrups in a wicker basket beside them. I take a step forward to let Connor pass, pretending not to notice how my eyes keep drifting toward him.

"*You're* so beautiful," Brad calls from the hallway as he saunters inside, wrapping an arm around Mom's waist. He kisses her cheek, lingering with his lips against her skin. "Good morning, gorgeous."

Mom freezes, her shoulders shooting up like hackles. Her gasp becomes a surprised laugh as she looks up at Brad, blushing. "Oh, uh, good morning."

Chelsea sidles around them on her way to the stack of plates. "Dad, you shouldn't touch people without their permission."

He pulls away, nodding. "My daughter is right. I'm so sorry. I was not being much of a gentleman, was I?"

"Oh, you're fine," Mom insists, though she still looks a bit flustered.

As she passes, Chelsea hands Mom a pink tube. "Here. I thought you could use this."

"That's so sweet of you, but we actually have all our lipstick picked out already."

Chelsea tilts her head, her hand pressed over her heart. "Aww. That's not lipstick. It's eye balm. I just noticed that your skin probably needs a little helper." She uses the end of her pinkie to indicate a spot at the edge of her eye. "I fell in love with this stuff when I filmed their commercial. I was their first pick, you know."

"I told you they're awful," I hiss in Mom's ear as soon as we're alone. "Chelsea is a know-it-all, and Brad just drooled on your face without even asking."

Mom eyes Chelsea's babyish face, blond curls, and jean romper. "Don't be so judgmental. She's just being nice."

"If you say so."

"Forget about it. Come on. Let's just eat."

"Don't have to tell me twice."

I start with a bed of hash browns and then build a little nest out of bacon strips to keep the sausages from rolling around. The pancakes are a tight fit after I add a second scoop of scrambled eggs with cheese, but I make it work by folding the edges back with the serving spoon. I douse the whole thing in apple cinnamon syrup until there's a visible pool of it in the slight depression at the center of the plate.

Mom reaches over with a pair of tongs and tries to knock some of the sausages back into the tray. "That's excessive. People are going to think I starve you."

"Stop it." I smack her hand away from my shrine to pork. "Let me have this moment."

Madyson nudges up beside me and slips a bread plate into my hand. It has two thick slabs of ham on it. "Here. You forgot the ham."

My mouth is watering just from the aroma. The breakfast meat trifecta is complete. "Thanks. I can't believe I missed it."

She smiles, revealing the plasticky gleam of a retainer on her top teeth. "Just remember at voting time that no one else hooked you up with the good stuff."

I know that she's joking, but in all honesty, I probably will.

It's jarring to have this many people around when I'm used to it being just Mom and me in the morning. It feels too early to game or scheme, but Tall and Grande are already swooping through, urging people to grab mimosas even as they reinforce that this breakfast is *just* breakfast. As if anything could be purely innocuous with cameras all over.

Connor's dad, Charles, appears across from Mom with a curt nod. He throws his first plate in the trash and grabs a clean one. Their motions mimic each other's as they move across the table like they're performing some secret line dance. They both reach for the napkins at the same time, accidentally giving each other a fist bump.

"Oh, I'm sorry!" Mom says, pulling her hand back. "You go on ahead."

Charles pulls his hand back as well. "No, it's okay. You first."

"Really, it's okay."

"I insist."

It's a little adorable. I balance the plates on the crook of my arm, pick up my orange juice, and waddle over to the seat farthest away from Connor, because I don't care about sitting next to Connor, and I'm not going to let Venti convince me that I do.

Unfortunately, that puts us right by Brad and Chelsea. Mom follows my lead, setting down her plate of fresh fruit and a cup of yogurt.

Before anyone can ask me a question, I unfold the cheat sheet the producers gave me and scan the table, reminding myself of who everyone is. I move it halfway onto Mom's knee and poke her to get her attention. Some of the names are still hazy, but I start to run through what I remember about the standouts from last night.

Brad + Chelsea = Know-it-alls

Cole + Grady = Mississippi and cowboy boots

AJ + Ella = Gymnastics and busy schedules

Ray + Sabrina = English teacher and little girl with a big dress

Edgar + Madyson = Detroit and football

Charles + Connor = Memorable last name and totally nothing else noteworthy. Nope. Definitely not.

"Are you a vegetarian?" Ella asks, jerking her chin at Mom's breakfast selection.

"No, but I like to eat healthy."

Ella beams. "Me too. My gymnastics coach says that diet is super important."

"We can never contradict the gymnastics coach," her dad stage-whispers. "She is all-seeing, all-knowing."

"I'm not complaining." I hold out a piece of bacon on the end of my fork, watching the syrup and grease drip off the tines. "More for me." I stuff the bacon into my mouth in one bite and chew with relish.

"You know," Chelsea begins, leaning forward and holding up her yogurt, "the plain Greek yogurt actually has more protein than the flavored kind."

Mom makes a surprised *hum*. "I didn't know that." She turns around her container, reads the ingredients, then compares it to Chelsea's. "Wow. Would you look at that. Thanks. I'll have to get plain Greek from now on."

I mentally take up a prayer that Vanessa will invent a teleportation machine and come here immediately so that I can complain about Chelsea to someone other than the cameras.

"Miss Julia, where are you?" someone calls from inside the house.

"Out on the patio!" Mom responds.

My head whips around as I hear the sudden pulse of disco music. Cole appears in the doorway with a platter of food balanced on one arm, clad in nothing but blue underwear stamped with OLE MISS ATHLETICS in red letters along the waistband. "Do you need a refill on your breakfast?"

Madyson screeches as her father covers her eyes with a napkin.

"The kids are here?" Cole jumps in surprise, squeals, and dashes back into the relative darkness of the dining room. For a split second, the forgotten platter hovers in midair like a cartoon character who's run off a cliff. Ella stretches out a hopeful arm, but she's so far away that she can only watch as it clatters to the ground in a cacophony of shattering plates.

I eye the hard-boiled egg lolling around on the concrete. There's an entire meal there, not to mention the broken crockery. "What a waste of food."

Cole sticks his head back out, covering his lower body with an unfolded paper napkin. "Hey, any of y'all see my boy around? He wasn't in the room. I think."

Edgar and Madyson offer to go help him track down Grady, but I doubt it'll be a tough search given that the whole property is monitored.

"I want to be mad," Mom says, covering her mouth and laughing. "I really do. But it was just so cute."

Charles starts cleaning up the dropped food and waves Connor over to help. When Connor notices me looking, he smirks. "Look on the bright side. At least he didn't decide to go skinny-dipping."

I smile back.

When I look up, Venti is smiling too. Maybe . . . a little too much.

When it comes to exercise, Mom is the ultimate planner. Despite the team of producers and assistants scrambling around organizing the show, she manages to find a sliver of time that's unaccounted for in the official schedule. "I'm not going far," she tells Sam as she laces up her running shoes. "I just need to clear my head."

"Mom saying she isn't going far is like a doctor telling you to expect some slight discomfort before they chop your arm off."

"Duly noted," Sam says, his eyes flicking to the clock on the microwave. "Either way, we've got a few minutes to kill before it's time for the next event."

He leans out the door and flags down the gaggle of cameramen and assorted crew hovering at the top of the hill near the site of our ill-fated breakfast. They check their watches and phones in unison. One of them cups his hands around his mouth and shouts, "What? Union break!"

"Just come down here!" Sam yells back.

They call instead, and Sam has to reiterate the change to the schedule. By this point, Mom is already bouncing between tile squares and jogging in place. I lunge out of the way of her lashing ponytail and scoot an end table with a delicate blown-glass lamp off to the side.

After a minute, the cameraman is annoyed enough to storm down the path and continue the conversation in person. He smacks his palms along the glass wall like a mime. "How do you open this damn door?"

"Oh, great," Sam mutters as he slides the panels open. "Here we go."

The man fumbles his way through the gap, his chest heaving. He stabs an index finger at Sam. "First of all, I wasn't kidding about the union break. Don't mess with the sanctity of the union break, my man. Bad things will happen. Second of all, you didn't say anything about filming off-site today."

Sam backpedals so quickly that I have to hurl my body in between him and the newly relocated lamp. I shove the table farther into the corner, shaking my head at this poor lamp that seems doomed to die today. "I was just giving you a heads-up in case you wanted to go," Sam says, raising both hands. "She said she's going for a jog. That's within the rules."

"How am I supposed to keep up with her?" He mimics lumbering after someone while filming. "I can't run. It'll look like *The Blair Witch Project*."

"I'm driving. You could come with me."

Instead of defusing the situation, the suggestion only seems to make the cameraman more infuriated. "Yeah, let me just go get my invisible process trailer." He storms off, shouting and waving to his peers. "Fine! Fine! I'll figure it out! I don't get paid enough for this bullshit!"

Sam flaps a hand at his retreating figure. "That's just Ian. We're actually friends, believe it or not. He just hates surprises because he doesn't want to get blamed for delays."

"I can warm up in the driveway," Mom offers, stepping outside and trailing Ian at a distance. She stretches her arms, leaning to the right and left. "That'll save a few minutes."

We look up as Ray hustles down the hill in running shorts and a pink shirt, stuffing a pair of sport sunglasses onto his face. A streak of sunblock stretches across one cheek like a linebacker's eye black. "I happened to see you through the window." He points over his shoulder to one of the windows on the second floor. "Do you mind if I join you? I didn't know we were allowed to leave the property."

Mom has the decency to look a bit sheepish. She smiles at Sam. "I didn't mean to make a big mess for you. I'm sorry."

"No, no, no. Don't worry about it at all. It's important to you. I get it."

"Speak for yourself," Ian grumbles as he passes by with an armful of knotted webbing and a ratchet strap. "Pop the hatch on your car, Sam."

Sam empties the contents of his front pocket into his palm. A folding knife, a tube of unscented ChapStick, a nickel gummed up with some mystery goo. He finds the key fob next, pushing the button and opening the automated rear hatch.

Ian pretends to swoon. "Automatic. How *fan-cy*." He adds a mock posh accent. He and another coworker jump into the back and start weaving the webbing into an elaborate suspension capable of securing them inside the vehicle with the door open.

Meanwhile, Mom works through a quick round of dynamic

stretching, her lips moving along to the count. Ray follows her lead, though he isn't half as graceful. His body type seems more suited to picking up heavy objects than doing prolonged cardio.

"Where's your, um, Sabrina?" I ask, hoping I've gotten her name right.

"Charles said he'd watch her for me."

"Aw, that's so nice of him." Mom hums a couple notes of nonsense under her breath. "Don't tell him I couldn't remember, but who's Charles again?"

"He's the bigger guy with the dark hair." Ray draws a rough outline of wide shoulders with his hands. "Kind of quiet." I can see that he's trying to be nice and not bring up the Dingeldein fiasco again.

"He was across from you getting seconds at breakfast," I say, rescuing Ray.

Mom nods once, the tug of her lips more of a test than a commitment to a smile. "Right. Right. I meant to thank him for cleaning up all that food Cole dropped. You know how I hate wasting food."

"Connor helped too." I suddenly look up at the house, wondering what he's doing during this gap in filming.

"We're ready," Ian calls after a few minutes. He wriggles into a comfortable configuration, dangling his feet dangerously close to the driveway. It reminds me of a toddler's bucket swing at a park, but I'd never tell him that. He hefts the camera to reposition it and swears as he almost loses his grip. "You owe me a beer for this, Sam!"

Sam climbs into the driver's seat and turns off the radio. I scramble onto my knees on the second row of seats and hang my head out the back to keep track of Mom and Ray. "You can go now," I call to Sam. "Her usual pace is, like, ten-minute miles."

"How long can she run?" he asks as we start a slow crawl past the gate and out onto the public street. I watch the nearby roads for any approaching cars, but it's mostly empty, a perk of filming during the workweek.

"If she tried, she could probably run forty or fifty miles. She married my dad at the finish line of this ridiculous ultra-triathlon thing in Hawaii."

"Fifty miles?" Sam chuckles under his breath. "There are some days that I have to talk myself into getting up to put leftover pizza in the fridge. Forget about fifty miles."

"Yeah, moderation is not her strong suit."

Ian punches the ceiling. "Can you two shut up? I'm trying to film here." Despite the annoyance in his voice, he wears a slight smirk.

I exchange guilty glances with Sam in the rearview mirror.

"Do you run any races or with a group?" Mom asks as she settles into a rhythm, one hand keeping her portable microphone from popping off her flimsy waistband.

"Nah, just on my own around my neighborhood." Ray's voice is choppier, easily upset by the bounce of his body. He speaks one word at a time, then breathes. "What about you?"

"I'm a personal trainer, so I run a lot with my clients. I usually do my longer runs alone, though. It gives me time to think."

Mom's intuition for a flagging running buddy kicks in, and she slows, letting Ray recover from his exertion at attempting to match her initial pace. He finds his stride after another quarter of a mile, syncing the swing of his arms. I know what good running looks like, even though I don't do it. I'm more of a sideline supporter, a person to hold the medals and unpin bibs at the end of races.

Sam motions to the footwell behind his seat. I move a sweatshirt and a crumpled fast food cup out of the way, uncovering a half-empty case of water.

I lean out the window and hold a bottle within Mom's line of sight. I'd toss it out the open hatch, but I'm afraid of disturbing Ian and his coworker. Mom throws out a hand and crouches to catch the bottle a few inches above the ground.

"Sorry!" I shout. "Bad throw!"

Ian's lower body doesn't move an inch as his head spins toward me. He doesn't say anything, just widens his eyes until his hazel irises are wholly surrounded by white. A vein writhes in his neck like a burrowing worm. He sticks out his index finger and smacks it against his lips.

I press my palms together and hold them out to him in apology. I somehow keep forgetting that I'm wearing a microphone, even though the little clip stabs me in the back if I sit wrong. Though I guess if that's the only back-stabbing that's happened so far on a reality TV show, I'm probably doing something right.

Mom takes a sip of water and offers the bottle to Ray. Despite the heat, she hasn't broken a sweat yet. "What made you get into running?"

"My wife wanted me to exercise and eat better," he says, sloshing more water onto his shirt than into his mouth. "Ignore me. I'm not too good at this running-while-drinking thing."

"You mean your ex-wife?" Mom clarifies with a nervous laugh. "I hope you aren't still married. We might have to talk about that if you are."

Ray is silent, the bottle crunching inside his fist. His feet fall heavier on the pavement. "My late wife, actually. Breast cancer. Sabrina was—my daughter, Sabrina, was two at the time."

"I'm so sorry," Mom whispers, drifting to a walk. "I didn't know."

Ray pretends to wipe sweat from his brow, catching a stray tear along the way. "No, *I'm* sorry. I didn't mean to get all serious on you." His breath hitches again. "I thought I could talk about this." He shakes his head, angry. "I should be able to talk about this."

"You don't have to if it's too hard."

"I want you to know," he says. "It's part of our lives. I'm always talking to Sabrina about her mother. We volunteer at the Hispanic Breast Cancer Program in Boston so that she can understand. I'm a widower, but I still want my late wife to have a space in my life. And I just wanted to be honest about that."

Instead of continuing their run, they walk the rest of the circuit Mom planned for the morning, only breaking into a jog again when they reach the copse of palm trees that serves as the midpoint. I can read the guilt etched into the lines of her face, the tension in her robotic movements.

I don't know what Ray says to Mom as we approach the house, but it soothes her, the earlier uneasiness giving way to a bubbly laugh. They hug, causing Sam to slam the brakes to avoid leaving them alone in the street.

"You can talk now," Ian grunts as we rumble over the gate tracks and onto the property. "Not that that stopped you before."

I grab a piece of the webbing that's holding him in the vehicle and pull it taut, causing him to involuntarily lift a leg. "Careful, or I'll leave you tied up here."

"Very funny."

We have just enough time for Mom to shower and gobble down a few stalks of celery before it's time for our next session with the contestants. I retrieve the schedule from the coffee table and trace the time slots with my index finger. "It looks like we're separate. You're in the lounge for cocktails, and I'm on the patio for ice-cream sundaes." I turn the paper over. "Who made this? Board games? Come on. There's, like, ninety of us. How are we supposed to play a board game?"

We walk up to the main house together using the winding trail of stepping-stones. I consider our lack of strategy thus far. It would make sense to have a plan now, before things get more complicated closer to the end.

"Hey, instead of picking people to vote off, how about we

make lists of the ones we want to keep?" I remember what Ella said about incorporating her gymnastics into her initial introduction to help her stand out. If I can't even remember some of these contestants, obviously they're not noteworthy enough to keep around. "If neither of us feels strongly about someone, they'll go on a list to be voted off. We can sort out the keepers we disagree on later. How's that sound?"

Mom shrugs, lingering at the junction between the hill and the lower level. The patio is just above us, a white gleam in my peripheral vision. "Sounds good to me. There's no point arguing this early in the show."

Plus, it's a convenient way to keep my favorites around without having to stress that Mom is going to want to send them home because of their parents. I know that means I'll be stuck with Chelsea and her ego, but it seems like a small price to pay to keep Connor. And Ella! And Madyson!

"Just one more thing," I whisper as Sam and another assistant arrive to check on us. "I have a ham-related agreement with Madyson from breakfast this morning. She stays no matter what."

chapter fifteen

*E*ver since we left this morning for Mom's jog, there's been a horrible racket coming from the vicinity of the guesthouse. The whine of power tools and a few profane shouts carry up to the patio where Mom and I linger, sipping our steaming second coffees of the afternoon. It's probably an odd combination after Mom's cocktail hour and my sundae party, but between not being allowed to eat on camera most of the time and our weird meal schedule, I'll take what I can get. Some of the contestants remain with us, helping themselves to another plate or talking at us while we act awake enough to be interested.

We run into Sam at the rear of the house, or at least I think it's Sam. All I can see of him is a mussed shock of sandy-brown hair peeking over the top of an inflatable frosted donut and a tricolored beach ball. Six pool noodles sit across his outstretched arms, giving him the careful gait of a tightrope walker.

"Do you need help?" Mom asks.

He jolts, toppling the beach ball onto the ground. "Oh my. I didn't see you there."

I jog after the ball, noting the new tiki bar installed by the side of the pool. I glare at it with disdain. "Please tell me that we're not having a—"

"Pool party," Sam finishes, not sounding nearly apologetic enough.

"I refuse," I tell Mom as I punt the beach ball into the water. "You know how I feel about pools, pool parties, water parks, water balloons."

"You can't skip it. We're the stars of the show!"

"But I hate water." I moan for emphasis. "I'm an indoor human."

I should have known that water would be involved when I saw that the packing list called for a bathing suit. I hurry and change before Mom commandeers the bathroom, wrapping a thick towel around my body from chest to knees.

Mom steps out a short time later, modeling a white-and-blue striped bikini. She fiddles with the bows at either end of the bottom. "I might like the other one better." She swaps out her original suit for one patterned in shades of gray with a white geometric overlay. The design and coloring are flattering, accentuating her black hair. "What do you think?"

"Definitely stick with that one," I answer.

"I—uh, I—" Sam coughs into the bend of his arm. The color rushes from his face, then floods back. "It is tasteful and fashionable. An excellent choice."

Once the contestants begin arriving at the pool, passing around coconut cups from the tiki bar, Mom and I step outside to join them. I drape my towel on a chair, feeling goose bumps rise on my arms in spite of the oppressive heat.

Clearly, my aversion to water is not shared. Chelsea parks herself at the edge of the pool, dipping her lower legs into the clear blue water. Cole and Grady wade in without hesitation, leaving their belongings behind on a table.

Edgar and Madyson arrive in coordinated outfits again. She's wearing a blue-and-red one-piece swimsuit to match his blue-and-red

Pistons swim trunks. His sandals are Tigers; hers are Lions. It's like Detroit threw up on them.

"You . . . really like Michigan," I say as they pause to slather on sunblock. "A lot."

Edgar laughs and shimmies a pair of goggles over his head. "Born and raised and never leaving."

I file that tidbit of information away to discuss later with Mom. We've spent so much time talking about *how* to get away from Dad and the gym and the awful apartment that we haven't talked about *where* we'd like to go.

I look up as I sense motion at the edge of the pool. With a running start, Madyson springs into the air, grabs her knees, and lands in the deep end with a spectacular splash. Chelsea shrieks and flicks away as much water as she can. She glowers at Madyson. "What the hell is your problem? I just spent all morning straightening my hair!"

"Sorry." Madyson jerks her chin at the wooden lounge chairs positioned around us. "Maybe it'll dry faster if you sit in the sun."

"Whatever. It's ruined." She looks like she might actually cry. When Madyson climbs out and offers her a towel, Chelsea smacks it away. "*You* might be able to look however you want, but I'm an actress in *three* shampoo commercials. I have to show off my hair! God! A towel isn't going to help! Just go away!"

"I said I was sorry," Madyson mumbles.

It's hard to feel bad for Chelsea in general, but especially when she wants to whine about getting splashed right next to the pool. She could have easily sat farther away or chosen a more water-friendly style.

I look around at everyone else. Sabrina has on a little duckling swim cap with a fake beak that is actually the most adorable thing anyone has ever seen in their entire life. Mom's hair is in a messy bun exploding from the top of her head. Ella's is pulled into two flat twists.

Chelsea is the only one complaining, which of course means Ian can't get over to her fast enough with a camera, which is probably what she wanted.

Venti shows up, still in a slightly rumpled dress shirt despite the scorching temperature, and takes a seat across from me. I eye him warily, not wanting another Confessional interrogation. "I noticed you aren't swimming," he says. "Why is that?"

"I don't really like water."

"You know who else isn't swimming?" He twists to look behind us, prompting me to do the same. I spot Connor's distinctive dark hair in the distance, stepping out of the main house with his dad, Charles. "Just letting you know." Venti stands, acting like he's being nonchalant, but I see Ian hustling over with the camera after wrapping up with Mom, who looks like she's getting similar treatment from Tall and Grande.

> **Confessional: I'm not really interested in swimming, but I can tell that Connor isn't either. Maybe this event isn't a lost cause after all if it means we get to spend more time together.**

And it's true. He hesitates, but at a move from Grande, he walks over. I wonder if any of this is real or we're all just pieces getting shoved together to make drama. It is kind of what we signed up for. Though when I look over at Mom, she's by Brad, who she seems to genuinely like, much to my chagrin.

"Hey," Connor says, indicating the lounge chair next to me

while Charles steps into the shallow end, earning a surprisingly enthusiastic wave from Mom. "Is it okay if I sit here?"

I almost laugh at the question. *Is it okay if you sit here? Really? I'm pretty sure Venti will go thermonuclear if you* don't.

"Sure. You're also not a fan of pools?"

He scratches his thumbnail against the Velcro strap of his sling. "Can't get this thing wet. But I'm not crying. I don't like it anyway. The water, I mean."

"What happened, by the way?" It's a bulkier sling than I'm used to seeing, with a little pillow that keeps his arm pushed out from his body. "Fight a bear? Overzealous arm wrestling?"

"I wore it out during my one-armed climbing of Mount Everest. After I fought a bear. A *polar* bear. And then overzealously arm-wrestled it."

I nod, grinning. "I knew it. You look like a polar bear arm wrestling champion." I am genuinely curious, but he's probably sick of people asking, so I don't push it.

Even though I've been grumpy and worn out for the start of the show, Connor makes me see the fun in the freedom of it. I can create shenanigans like never before, flirt with the cute boy, and not have to worry that I'm going to humiliate myself because my first and only kiss was an awkward slobberfest at the Freshman Fling. This is all so temporary, Connor included. Even this early, it doesn't seem like Charles, stands a chance at making it to the end. That means Connor will eventually go home. We'll never *be* anything. And somehow, knowing that it's all completely doomed makes it better somehow.

After a few minutes, Madyson and Ella launch into a chicken-fighting contest with Grady and Sabrina on their shoulders. The younger kids joust with two pool noodles, whacking each other and everyone else within a ten-foot radius.

As Mom swims by, Brad snags her around her waist and lifts her onto his shoulders. She yelps in surprise. "Hang on, Julia! We have to show them how it's done." He struggles to keep his head above the surface until they reach the shallow end where a full-blown contest is breaking out among the adults, too.

"Let's raise the stakes!" Mom whoops and sticks a fist in the air. "Whoever wins is safe from elimination at the next vote!"

At her announcement, the parent-child teams rush to assemble. I hear Ray begging Sabrina to participate over the hooting and splashing. She pushes her father away, and I shoot Brad a dirty look for spoiling the match between the kids by interrupting.

"I like your mom," Connor mentions in an offhand way that seems genuine. "She seems . . . fun."

"She's a total goofy weirdo. It's the best, honestly." I'm suddenly overwhelmed by gratitude that we can be here at all, fighting however odd a battle to finally get away from Dad. "What's your dad like? Not fishing or anything. Just wondering."

Connor tilts his head back and forth. I can't tell if he's searching for the right word or if I've upset him somehow. He shrugs his right shoulder. "We've just got different senses of humor, and we like different stuff. He's all about, like, reading and vacuuming. He's not very adventurous. I probably shouldn't be telling you this."

"It's okay. I wouldn't vote you off anyway." That comes out more serious than I intended. I pretend to watch the chicken fight while internally screaming. Is this flirting? What am I doing? *Mother, why have you not taught me how to not be an awkward little person?*

"Really?"

"Of course. You, Ella, and Chelsea are the only other kids my age." The words are out of my mouth before I can fully contemplate their meaning.

Connor nods, angling his torso toward the pool to watch the game. "Oh, yeah. For sure."

No wonder boys don't want to talk to me back home.

Cole drifts over on the back of an inflatable pink unicorn floaty, his arms wrapped around its neck as it bobs pitifully beneath his weight. "Ray! 'Ey! Over here. You wanna win this thing? My kid don't wanna play anymore either."

I snicker under my breath as Cole sloppily rolls off the side of the unicorn, his foot catching on the plastic handle. Ray is stocky where Cole is rail-thin and lanky, so Cole climbs onto Ray's shoulders and holds out his hands, flapping his fingers against his palms. "Come on, y'all. Bring it."

I admire his confidence, but between Ella's affinity for contorting her body into impossible shapes and AJ's daunting height, they are clearly the ones to beat.

Connor disappears for a moment and returns with something held behind his back. "Anyone in particular you want to get rid of?" he asks as we eye the match. "I've got a secret weapon." He turns to let me see the soggy nylon water ball in his hand.

I'm glad to see he isn't too upset by my less-than-flattering comment. "Let's get my mom. It'll be funny." That seems more diplomatic than outright confessing my distaste for Brad. Since I don't live in the main house, it's tough to figure out whether any of the contestants have developed their own internal allegiances.

Ray and Cole stagger over toward Mom and Brad. Cole bends his fingers into mock claws and grabs for Mom, laughing as she smacks the tops of his hands. She almost topples him with a powerful shove, but Ray lurches forward to compensate.

"Got it covered." Connor sneaks along the edge of the pool, pretending like he's just watching the match. With a flourish not dissimilar from a pitcher, he turns and launches the waterlogged splash ball straight into Brad's face. Brad wobbles, upsetting Mom's balance. She clamps both hands down to try to steady herself, and Ray capitalizes on the attack by bumping into Brad.

Mom screams and backflips into the water, dragging Brad down with her.

"That's cheating!" she gasps as she breaks through the surface of the water. She levels an accusatory finger at Connor. "Oh, you're bad."

Seeing them laughing together makes me realize what I like so much about Connor, and I guess about his dad, Charles, too. They're real people. They don't show up in color-coordinated outfits with rehearsed jokes or painfully transparent grabs for attention to get more freaking shampoo commercials. I don't have to wonder whether the person I'm seeing is a character.

"All's fair in love and television," I shout back as Ella and AJ launch a fresh attack against Cole. Ray dunks lower to grapple beneath the water, but soon Cole is falling over as well.

We relocate to the deep end to avoid interfering in the final battle as Ella and Madyson move into position.

"Mission accomplished," Connor says as he rejoins me.

Suddenly, Madyson screams, whipping her head to the side and smacking a hand against her hair. Chelsea smirks, examining her fingernails with exaggerated casualness. "That hurt!" Madyson shouts at her. She dips her head to tell Edgar. "Dad! She pulled my hair!"

Venti crouches at Ian's feet to stay out of the shot, muttering something to Madyson and gesturing at Chelsea. Screaming breaks out between them a few seconds later.

"What's going on with all that?" Connor asks, frowning, as he returns to the chair beside mine.

"There was some drama earlier because Madyson did a cannonball and got Chelsea's hair all wet while she was sitting on the edge."

This explanation doesn't seem to help ease his confusion. "But it's a pool. . ." Connor says, trailing off.

"You don't have to explain it to me. It's literally the entire reason there's a hole in the ground. To fill it with water."

Ella waits for Madyson and Chelsea's spat to be over before darting forward, but it's clear that Madyson's heart isn't in the match anymore. Not that they were well-matched in the first place, with Ella being at least a few years older. Madyson overextends her arms, making it simple for Ella to grab a wrist and tug.

"Muahaha!" Ella cackles, making silly bodybuilder poses. "Undefeated chicken-fighting champion!"

I turn toward the stairs and the waiting pile of fluffy white towels just in time to see Madyson swipe a tear away against the side of her fist. She grabs a towel and wraps it around her hair, wringing the ends until her forearms shake. It isn't difficult to read the hard set of her shoulders, the muscles feathering along her jawline as she grinds her teeth together.

I nod at her.

Her eyes flash to Chelsea. She nods back.

The battle lines are drawn.

chapter sixteen

*N*ow that it's obvious the producers are intrigued, Chelsea continues her crusade of sabotage against Madyson for the rest of the week. I do my best to stay between them during group events, but there's nothing I can do except feel helpless when Madyson arrives at breakfast with red-rimmed eyes and a University of Michigan ball cap pulled low over her brow. "What's wrong?" I ask, edging up beside her in line.

She sniffles. "I don't want to talk about it." When I press her further, she spins on her heel and leaves, snatching two plain waffles from the last buffet tray as she passes. Her dad, Edgar, sets down his plate and follows her out, his hands balled into fists.

I corner Ella next, figuring she might know. "What happened to Madyson?"

Ella sucks in air through her teeth. "Someone put Nair in her shampoo, and now her hair is falling out."

"But she's, like, little. How old is she? Twelve?" My mouth falls open. I thought it was gum or a bad dye job. My mind scrolls through a list of possible suspects. "And by 'someone,' you mean Chelsea."

Ella shifts from one foot to the other. "I know what you mean, but that's not proof."

"Who else could it be?"

She doesn't answer.

Something inside of me just snaps. I'm reminded of all the cruelties I suffered when my so-called childhood friends couldn't wait to roast Mom, the bullies who never seemed to get caught. A picture flashes through my mind of Vanessa crying in the bathroom last year because someone stabbed a pen through her Pokémon backpack just because they thought it was funny. *Hey, hey, look. I killed Pikachu! Right in the forehead!*

I storm out of the dining room and stalk from room to room until I find Sam arriving with a tray of coffees. "Hey, one sec." He scurries off to deliver the drinks, passing out napkins and sugar from the plastic bag dangling around his wrist. It twists and cuts into his skin, but he doesn't seem to notice. He returns a moment later, munching on a muffin. "What's up?"

"Chelsea put Nair in Madyson's shampoo, and now her hair is falling out. I need help proving it. Can you access the camera footage from upstairs?"

He looks at me like I've just asked him to rob a bank. "I can't interfere, but that sounds, uh, that sounds . . ." He beckons Venti over. "Here. She has a question about the Nair incident."

"You know about it?"

Venti barks a laugh. "Yes, we know. We have the cameras. If you think someone's been wronged, you should do something about it."

I almost scream when I realize Ian's been filming the side of my head. "What am I supposed to do? I can't let her get away with it." Tears well in my eyes, sourced from a spring of frustration and helplessness that sits at the center of my being, depthless and well-fed. "Madyson is a nice person. She doesn't deserve this."

"You could try to investigate," Venti says. "Why don't you ask Connor to help you? You need someone you can count on, after all. Someone reliable."

"That's true," I mutter before shaking my head, realizing I just agreed with him when he's doing that leading, telling-me-what-to-do-without-saying-it thing. I wish I could talk to Mom, but she's always mobbed by the suitors, or the producers find some way to keep us apart. I wonder if that's intentional.

Venti gestures at the camera, nudging me that I should explain the situation in my own words.

> **Confessional: Chelsea put Nair in Madyson's shampoo. I just know it. I have to find some way to prove it to Mom, though. I think I'll ask Connor and Ella to help me. Maybe it's wrong, but it's just easier to connect with the others my age.**

"You have no limitations," Venti says when I'm done giving him his sound bite. "You can do whatever you want. Go wherever you want. If what you're doing is expressly forbidden, someone will stop you. Have fun."

I replay the conversation in my head as I descend to the game room for an hour of forced semistepsibling bonding. Instead of having a designated activity, it seems like we're just free-range kids. Most of the contestants are congregated around the air-hockey and pool tables. A few stragglers walk in after me from the opposite stairwell. I don't see Madyson.

"Hey, do you want to play a game?" Grady asks from the couch, gesturing to the impressive collection of video games on the wall. "I'm really good at racing games."

"There's no television. I bet they took the consoles out too."

His face falls. "How come we can't talk to anybody?"

"It's just part of the show," I say, wishing I had more experiencing talking to younger children. "They want to keep it all, like, a big secret."

I can't say that I'm nearly as disappointed about the lack of tele-visions. In such an enclosed space, having so many people around is a sensory overload. All the conversations blend into a chattering hum, punctuated by the smack of billiard balls and the bass of the music emanating from the gargantuan speakers by the stereo sys-tem. The air is too warm, reeking of hair products and body spray.

"Have you seen Connor?" I ask.

Grady points at the yard. "Lots of people went outside."

"Thanks."

I look over in time to see little Sabrina slide open the door to the patio and slip outside. I follow her, hearing the faint buzz of a shaver before I round the corner to discover Madyson sitting in a metal folding chair as Ray evens out the fuzz on the side of her head.

Ian is only a few inches away, shuffling to get the right angle.

I must look surprised because she immediately hones in on my presence, her mouth drawn downward into a prolonged wince. "Does it look okay?" she asks.

"It looks great, actually."

Connor stands to the side with a mirror, stepping around Madyson in a slow circle to avoid bumping into Ian and Ray, like they're all doing some weird impersonation of an atom with people instead of electrons.

Madyson sighs. "You're just saying that."

I stand back far enough to dodge the tufts of hair rolling across the stone from the slight breeze.

"No, really. You look gorgeous," Connor insists. He notices Sabrina slowly gravitating closer. "What do you think, Sabrina?"

"I like it!"

Connor holds the mirror up as he transitions back into Madyson's line of sight. "Check it out. You just wait until Chelsea sees your kick-ass new hairstyle."

Ray reaches up and bonks Connor on the head with the shaver as he passes, his eyes never leaving Madyson. "Don't curse in front of Sabrina," he says, but his tone is easygoing.

Connor lifts the mirror and pretends to thwap himself on the head in the same spot. "Oops. Sorry."

Once again, my thoughts drift back to what I already know about him, the way he laughed at himself so effortlessly. He's always holding the door for the other contestants or making sure Sabrina and Grady feel included. That effortless kindness . . . Is it genuine? How would I even know when Venti is pulling all our strings?

Ray crouches lower, his nose inches from Madyson's scalp as he works. He adjusts a clip and moves the longer pieces clear of the shaver. "You lucked out that the damage is only on this side," Ray mutters. "Shaving half of your head is in style. The whole thing? Not so much."

Madyson doesn't look convinced. "I stopped putting it on because it burned."

"Luckily for you, my mom owns a hair salon," Ray tells her. "She taught me a few things. Having five sisters helps too." He removes the clips from her hair and brushes the long half into a smooth crest. "There. All done. You look great."

"You don't have your own stylists?" I ask.

Connor shakes his head. "We're on our own."

Madyson pats the shaved part of her head. "I still feel like it's ugly." Tears well in her eyes. "I don't want to be on TV and be ugly."

"It's not." Ray claps his hands against his cheeks and squeals. "Everybody, look! Is that a supermodel? Billie Eilish?" He mimes snapping her picture. "T-Swift? Can I get an autograph?"

Madyson's laugh is more of a throaty groan. "Okay. Okay. I believe you."

Sabrina beams at her dad, earning a reciprocal smile from Ray.

"I can't wait to tell Grammy that you cut hair!"

Madyson takes a deep breath and stands, pulling Ray into a lopsided hug, her face smushed against his stomach. "Thank you for helping me. I'm sure you did a good job." To me, she adds, "Tell your mom that Ray's pretty awesome."

My mind conjures up an image of Mom jogging beside Ray in contented silence, sharing a water bottle and motivating each other. Even when Sam and Ian can't support leaving the grounds, I catch the two of them circling the perimeter of the yard in the early morning. "I think she knows already." A pang of guilt jolts through me when I remember trying to vote off Sabrina the first night for being too introverted.

Connor sets the mirror on one of the tables. I approach him and turn my back to the camera, which is self-defeating since we're both wearing microphones. "I take it you know everything that happened with the Nair," I mutter.

"We thought there was something seriously wrong this morning," he says. "Madyson was *screaming*. She woke us up three rooms away."

"It was totally Chelsea."

I expect him to protest like Ella did, or at least try to be a little diplomatic, but he only nods, saying, "I figured as much."

And there it is again—that honesty. Connor almost reminds me of Sam in that regard, the openness evident on his face even as others are starting to show their teeth.

He scrapes the toe of his sneaker against the concrete before meeting my eyes. "Do you want to play some foosball?"

I point at his sling. "Sure. That won't bother your arm?"

"Nah." Connor wags a finger at me. "For all you know, I could be the one-armed foosball champion of the world."

I burst out laughing. "That . . . is very true. I forgot I was speaking to a Mount Everest–climbing, polar bear arm wrestling champion."

145

"Exactly." He clucks his tongue, lowering his tone in mock seriousness. "Don't you forget it."

As we head back into the basement for the last few minutes of our group activity, it occurs to me that Ray is sacrificing time with Mom to be here with us. He could have been upstairs with the other contestants, drinking and partying or whatever it is they do during their group dates in the lounge.

I can't know if he did it out of goodness or to stay relevant during the Great Nair Debacle, but I like to think it's the first. There has to be someone here who isn't in it for themselves, who really believes in true love. Some people are more transparent than others, like Chelsea's constant references to her acting career. But others aren't as easy to read.

I just have to hope that we're not all here for the chance to be celebrities. That would make us no better than paid actors, just pieces on the producers' game board. And no matter how much I convince myself I'm making decisions on my own, I look at Connor and realize that maybe I'm playing right into what they want.

And when this gets boring, they'll find a way to shuffle the deck.

All anyone can talk about is Chelsea and the Nair.

> **Confessional: If I end up with Chelsea for a stepsister, I wouldn't ever be able to forget what she did to Madyson. And I definitely wouldn't trust her around my stuff. I know it's probably hard to stand out with this many competitors, but this isn't the way to do it.**

By the late afternoon, I'm ready to tie Chelsea in a sack and drop her off a boat in the Gulf of Mexico. Mom and I convene at the kitchen counter in the guesthouse to strategize. I'm tired, and I can tell she is too.

"Wine overload," she mumbles, digging the heel of her palm against her forehead. "The guys kept asking me if I wanted another drink. I think it's their version of an icebreaker."

I get up and fetch her a glass of water. A cursory search of the bathroom yields a travel bottle of painkillers. I shake it at her like a pharmaceutical maraca. "Want one?"

"Want four."

I squint to read the recommended dosage for an adult, then give her two. Her liver is suffering enough as it is. "You're allowed to say no if you don't want more wine."

"I didn't want to be rude."

"It's your show, Mom."

She gives a noncommittal grunt that doesn't exactly fill me with confidence. We didn't come here to find her another crappy relationship. I almost say as much, but the mention of the divorce is enough to give her a headache on a regular day, never mind when she already doesn't feel well. "We should decide who we're kicking off tonight," I point out.

"Good idea."

I find a pen and a printout of the contestant lineup. Mom crosses out the faces and names of contestants who have already been voted off. "Brad and Chelsea, Ray and Sabrina, and Cole and Grady are the big ones on my list to keep." She draws stars around their pictures, adding Edgar and Madyson, then AJ and Ella as I read her my picks.

"What do you think about Charles?" I ask, hoping that I sound nonchalant. "You seemed happy to see him at the pool party."

"Oh." She mashes her index finger against her right temple while she thinks. "Um, yeah, he seems . . . steady. He's not as intense as some of the others. We can keep him if you want."

"It would be way too easy for us to just like the same people, huh?" Looking at the list, the only overlap is Ray and Sabrina, though I don't have anything against Cole and Grady.

"I'm not a fan of Madyson," Mom admits. "Brad told me she started some kind of fight and ruined Chelsea's hair."

"That's totally not what happened. I saw it."

Mom looks baffled, then shrugs. "Maybe he was talking about something else. I just don't believe that girl has a mean bone in her body. All she's ever done is be nice and helpful. She's given me a lot of pointers about being on camera too."

I snuggle up to her, pushing my lip into my best pout. "But you're supposed to worry about the dads. I'm supposed to be worrying about the kids. And Chelsea is bad news."

"I just don't see it that way," she says, her voice rising. "And I . . . I like Brad. He understands that I don't want to be stuck in that gym forever with no prospects."

"Wanting to fix you because she thinks she's better isn't the same thing as being nice."

"It was your idea to vote off the people that neither of us want to keep before we debate the rest," Mom reminds me. "I want to keep Chelsea and Brad. That's it, okay?"

I wave at the camera, our unofficial signal that we would like to talk to Sam or a producer. "Listen, I just want to watch the Confessionals for Brad and Chelsea before the Sweetheart Ceremony. Please, Mom. For me. I'm telling you that she's shady."

Mom sighs, exhaling with force to draw it out. "Fine."

Sam arrives a few minutes later with a light yellow smoothie that gives me flashbacks to Dad's ridiculous juice bar concoctions. He pushes it across the counter to Mom, who eyes the straw with equal suspicion. "What's this?" she asks.

"I made you a, uh, banana thing. Potassium is supposed to

help with hangovers. Thought it might be good for you to get ahead of it." He points to the microphone dangling haphazardly from her waistband. "Sorry. I just happened to be back with the producers while you were talking."

Mom takes a hesitant sip before apparently deciding it's good. "Thanks. I'm normally not this heavy of a drinker. I lost track."

Before she can fall asleep or fall over, I nudge Sam about showing us the Confessionals. Sam shows Brad's to Mom in her bedroom, then shows me Chelsea's at the kitchen counter. "You don't get to see them all, just the one filmed from this segment," he explains.

"Okay."

[Confessional, Chelsea 2]: I don't hold any hard feelings about what happened at the pool party. I was just upset because I put a lot of time and effort into my appearance. I'm an actress, you know. I can't have my hair getting soaked for no reason. It's very finicky to treat. I use a ton of product. Though not Nair. That's some next-level commitment to being bold. You go, Madyson, girl. Points for originality.

I take a deep breath and let out a frustrated squeal of anger that makes me sound like a disgruntled farm animal. Sam edges his tablet away as I slam my fist on the countertop.

"I told you there wasn't anything wrong," Mom insists after we reconvene to share the salient points. "Brad's was really recent, and he has no idea what this Nair thing is about."

"Chelsea practically confessed! She was gloating." I beckon Sam closer. "Show her!"

"I can't," he replies, holding his tablet to his chest like I might try to steal it. "I can only show it to you. Those are the rules."

149

Mom reclaims her seat, propping one elbow on the counter and leaning her forehead into her palm. "Did Chelsea outright admit that she did it, or is that just your interpretation?"

"She didn't say it exactly, but she—"

"Then it's possible you misunderstood. I don't want to talk about this anymore, Cara."

I wish I could keep the video to show Connor later. But unlike Mom, I think he'll believe me without it. With a pang in my stomach that for once isn't about how infrequently we eat a real meal here, I wonder when my word stopped being enough for Mom, too.

"Fine. They can stay. I reserve the right to complain about it, though."

My tirade against Chelsea extends through hair and makeup, getting dressed, and the short walk to the main house. I grouse and grumble until the exact millisecond that Danny Romano arrives to prepare for the Sweetheart Ceremony.

We still have to run our selections by the producers, but they appear pleased with our instincts thus far. Our victim for today is Nicolas, who refers to himself in the third person and only wants to talk about politics. He's a less smooth version of Brad, who at least pretends to be interested in whatever Mom has to say. I'm embarrassed to admit I don't know a single thing about his daughter.

By now, I'm used to having cameras following my every move, at least enough to feel bored as Danny Romano recites his canned lines. "Julia and Cara, who have you chosen for tonight's elimination?"

Not Brad and Chelsea. That's the answer. Not Brad and Chelsea.

chapter seventeen

*A*fter our last conversation on the subject, it's become increasingly clear that I'm not going to sway Mom's opinion about those two without concrete evidence that they're skeevy. I bide my time, hoping to catch Connor without an audience to tell him about what I've learned since the last time we talked. It's easier said than done with so many contestants in the house.

I finally corner him when he excuses himself to go to the bathroom. I signal that he should follow, then lead him to a random door at the opposite side of the house. We step into a small library lined with built-in shelves and musty encyclopedia collections.

I try not to think about how I'm alone with Connor for the first time. That he's *right here.*

He sneezes, wrinkles his nose, and then sneezes three more times in quick succession. "Sorry, I have allergies. I'm apparently terrible at sneaking around." He glances in the direction of the dining room, where it's still free-range contestants, then at the nearest camera. "They probably all heard that."

I scowl at the layer of dust and dead bugs crusted on the windowsills. "I'll talk fast." I give him a rambling overview of Chelsea's Confessional. "I have an idea of how to finally prove she's guilty."

"I'm in," he says, just like I thought he would. "I don't want to live in the same house as someone who puts Nair in shampoo bottles."

"We have these invite-only activities scheduled today where we can pick who we want to hang out with. I'll invite you to mine. I know Mom will invite Brad to hers." I rub my palms together. "I've been trying to convince my mom to vote them off, but she likes Brad a lot. I just need something to change her mind. If we can get into their room, we can snoop on them both."

"How are we going to get in if the door's locked?" Connor asks. "And what if Chelsea is hanging out in there? We'll need a distraction." He fiddles with a plastic buckle on the sling supporting his left arm, clicking his nail against it. "I'm not doubting your scheming skills—"

"Good," I interject. "You shouldn't. I'm a Scorpio."

"—but aren't there a lot of moving parts for just the two of us?"

"You have a point." I think back to what Venti said about not having any rules or restrictions on my behavior. I assume that breaking a door lock is within the realm of what I'm allowed to do. But maybe I don't have to. "Let me test a theory. The invite-only activity starts in two hours. Meet me downstairs?"

I cross my fingers, knowing there are a thousand ways this could go wrong. But I can't stand by and let Mom fall for more of Brad and Chelsea's nonsense. As I scurry down the hallway in search of Venti, I increasingly begin to understand that this isn't just a game.

Cara Hawn's Secret Plan That Will Probably Backfire Somehow

Step 1: Get cute partner in crime.

Step 2: Convince the producers that I'm about to do something awesome that involves breaking and entering, snooping, and payback.

Step 3: Ask Venti to keep Chelsea occupied.

Step 4: Get the key to Brad and Chelsea's room from Venti.

Step 5: Break in.

Step 6: Find incriminating evidence.

Step 7: Show to Mom and then laugh as Chelsea gets kicked out of the house forever.

I wasn't even sure I could get past Step 2, but Venti was fascinated to hear that I was willing to stir the pot. Though, truthfully, I don't know if I'd have the courage to spy on Brad and Chelsea without Connor accompanying me. There's something about him that just makes me feel steadier somehow.

Confessional: Chelsea thinks she's so smart. Let's see how she likes it when someone else starts playing dirty.

Ten minutes before I'm supposed to rendezvous with Connor, I attempt to subtly rush Mom out of the guesthouse. I fix her a bottle of water and leave it on the counter after verifying that Brad is going to be there. "Have fun!"

I wait until she's halfway up the trail before I take the long way up to the house, popping into the dining room through the patio doors where we usually have breakfast. From there, it's a tight turn and down the stairs to the game room, where I find Connor already waiting in an armchair. "Hey," I say, plopping onto the couch. "Thanks for coming."

"What'd you figure out after breakfast?"

"I talked to Venti and—"

Connor cuts me off. "Wait. Back up. Who's Venti?"

"Oh. Um. The producer. I just gave them nicknames because they're all Mike. He's just the most vertical Mike. Hence, Venti." I shake my head before I can get distracted. "Anyway, he said he was going to pull some strings to keep Chelsea occupied while we investigate."

"Nice job. Was I supposed to wear a black turtleneck and an eye mask or something?" Connor asks, humming a mock secret agent theme song. "Top secret Nair investigators."

I laugh. "I'm imagining you robbing a bank or something singing that corny song and getting yourself busted."

"Yeah, and who knows? You could be stuck with my corniness forever."

My laugh becomes a panicked giggle until I realize he's talking about our parents getting married. Not, you know, us. Isn't he? "Me and Mom are, like, the queens of corny."

"I can live with that."

Suddenly, I'm aware that we're alone together again. My thoughts start pinging around in random directions, like building some Venn diagram of Connor Dingeldein. His hair is freshly combed. Was that because he knew we'd be meeting up? Did he pick the chair so he wouldn't have to sit next to me? Is he only playing along with Venti? Does he actually like me?

I take a deep breath to refocus. "Okay. We're on a bit of a time crunch. Here's the short version." I lay it out as quickly as I can. "Mom's yoga date is supposed to take an hour. That should give us at least twenty minutes to scope out Brad and Chelsea's room and cover our tracks."

"Sounds good. Ready when you are." Connor rises to his feet and holds out a hand to help me up. I press my fingers against the smooth skin of his palm as I stand, our toes only inches apart. "When my dad told me about coming on the show, this isn't exactly what I expected."

He hasn't let go of my hand, as though he's deciding whether to lean down and kiss it. Or me. Maybe. But I don't want him to kiss me if it's all just an act. "Is it better or worse?"

"Better. I was worried I wouldn't have anything in common with you. They told us all about you, but it never seemed real until . . . there you were that first night."

"And then?" I ask, hoping my voice sounds sultry and not like I'm heavily mouth-breathing.

"You looked beautiful and perfect, just like I thought you would. But I had no idea if any of it was real. I was afraid you'd be some bullshit person they made up."

I heave a sigh of relief. "That's exactly what I've been thinking. How much of this is real when there's so much meddling? I can't even tell what my own thoughts are sometimes because they're always poking and poking and poking."

"Exactly!" Connor's fingers grip mine a little tighter with emphasis. "Same here. They ask me about you all the time."

"While it's validating to know you worry about this kind of stuff too, let's go back to how I'm beautiful and perfect." I add on a goofy guffaw to show that I'm joking. A little bit. "But we should really get going before we waste any more time."

"It wasn't a waste," he says, hooking his pinkie through mine for a heartbeat as our hands drift apart. "I'm glad to know it's not all for show, even if they are starting to get in our heads."

I bite my lip, gesturing in the vague direction of the upstairs. "I wish I could tune everyone out sometimes."

"It's not your fault."

It's such a relief to know that Connor understands what it's like to live with the producers' constant meddling and doesn't blame me for getting lost in it sometimes. Maybe this is all their doing. Maybe it's real. Maybe it doesn't matter. All I know is that he makes me feel like a princess and a puppet and a fool, and I absolutely fucking love it.

chapter eighteen

We emerge from the lower level a moment later, trying to act as normal as possible. Once it's clear no one else is milling around the foyer, we casually jaunt up the main staircase, turning into the shorter half of the hallway. Cameras are plastered all over the place, but I have to admit that I'm a bit surprised Ian and his crew haven't popped up to follow us. I'm not complaining, though. Nothing in this house draws attention like seeing Ian tracking whoever is in the spotlight at the moment.

I pause at the corner, checking both ways before moving on. I rap my knuckles against the third door on the left, waiting. No one answers. "This is it."

I remember Sam mentioning that this house used to be a small hotel, which makes sense with the general layout. I just wish we were a little more secluded. I reach out to swipe the key, but before we can enter, I hear voices from the staircase.

Venti reassured me that most of the other contestants are by the pool or drinking in the lounge, but maybe someone slipped away. There's nowhere else to go in a dead-end hallway.

"Hey," Ella calls out as she rounds the corner. "What are you two doing up here?"

Sabrina appears at her side a moment later, a broken flip-flop in one hand, the other still on her right foot.

"We're, uh, we're . . ." I think Sabrina is adorable, but I know that little kids like to repeat stuff. I jerk my head at Brad's door and give Ella a pointed look. "Looking into . . . situations."

"Oh!" Ella nods and ushers Sabrina past us to the neighboring room. While Sabrina goes in to get new shoes, Ella hovers in the doorway. "I just saw Chelsea outside. You want us to keep a lookout for you? We can hang around for a bit."

I'm momentarily speechless at the offer. I've always liked Ella, but I didn't get the impression that she was taking Madyson's side in all of this when we talked about it earlier.

She must understand my confusion because she adds, "Sorry for blowing you off a little. I didn't want to get dragged into some drama, but now I see exactly what you're talking about with Chelsea."

I mull it over for a moment. "Yeah, actually, it would probably be a big help to have a lookout." I glance at Connor to see if he objects. He shrugs. "We'll be fast."

I leave the door propped open in case Ella or Sabrina has to shout a warning as I step inside Brad and Chelsea's room with Connor following on my heels. It's fairly spacious, but nothing like my accommodations in the guesthouse. I start with the dresser, discovering rows of folded clothing items in each drawer. I eyeball them from a distance, not wanting to paw through Chelsea's underwear.

"If Chelsea has the whole dresser, that probably means that Brad is hogging the closet," Connor says, sliding open one of the mirrored doors. "I'll start there."

I squat to check underneath the furniture, but the bed frames sit directly on the floor. Brad's side of the room is organized with a precision that I imagine is only matched by his own daughter. His shoes are color coded and lined along the wall by size, the coins on the end table stacked by type. When I pull open the single drawer, I am unsurprised to discover a bag of toiletries and a copy of his flight itinerary folded into a neat square.

I update Connor with a quiet whisper over my shoulder. "I haven't found anything yet."

"Me either," he calls back. "There's nothing personal in here at all. Just clothes."

He moves into the bathroom, taking a knee while he scrutinizes the contents of their bath caddy. I hear the water start running in the sink.

I pat down Chelsea's comforter and shake out her shoes, but there's nothing.

"I don't know what Nair looks like," Connor admits, emerging a moment later, "but all I found was regular shampoo. I tested some on my skin and everything."

"Looks like this was a bust." I don't know what I hoped to find when I hatched this plan. Maybe an incriminating picture or a journal, some proof to sway Mom away from Brad or prove that Chelsea is the villain behind the Great Nair Debacle. That might be easier if Brad's cell phone wasn't locked away with the rest of our electronics.

The sudden creak of the floor outside is the only indication that someone is approaching. Sabrina and Ella barrel through the door a moment later, waving frantically. "They're coming!" They try to run back out, but it must be too late. Sabrina dives into the sliver of space where the closet door is open despite not knowing what she's even going to land on.

The rest of us exchange wide-eyed, panicked glances. We scramble for the bathroom, but I only make it two steps before the door opens and Brad walks inside, looking confused. "What are you doing in here?" he asks as he spots us.

I hear a giggle behind him. "Who are you talking to?" A pair of slender hands wraps around Brad's neck from behind, pressing into his shoulders.

Brad steps forward, and the horror story just gets worse. The hands disappear, and Mom steps into view. "Mom? What are *you* doing here?"

"Cara?"

"This is Brad's room!"

She grabs the sleeve of his moisture-wicking polo shirt and shakes it. *"And this is Brad."*

"Why are you in here?" I ask again, my voice rising to a shrieking pitch. "Do I want to know why you're in here?" I turn toward Connor and close my eyes, muttering, "Oh God. Oh, gross. Someone, please kill me. This is not happening."

Despite there being six of us in the room already, Ian manages to shove himself through the door. He kneels on Chelsea's bed while the rest of his crew tries to get a boom mic into the room without stabbing any of us in the eye.

Mom stomps forward, and I can tell from the set of her mouth that she is in a full-blown parenting rage, the sort of expression that would send me scurrying to Vanessa's if we were back home. "Cara Laraine Hawn. I know that you did not violate this man's privacy by breaking into his personal space and going through his personal belongings to support your ridiculous conspiracy theories!"

"What conspiracy theories?" Brad asks.

"She thinks Chelsea put Nair in that other girl's shampoo. We can talk about it later." Unlike Dad, Mom never makes me feel afraid, but she does make me feel about two inches tall. She sticks her index finger almost against the tip of my nose and then draws a line to Brad in the air. "You . . . will . . . apologize . . . RIGHT NOW, YOUNG LADY, AND I HOPE THIS GOES ON TELEVISION SO THAT EVERYONE CAN SEE HOW PETTY YOU ARE!"

"You're not allowed to talk about being on television!" someone shouts from the hallway. I lean to my left and see Tall and Grande just arriving from the direction of the main stairwell, both wearing identical smirks.

And then it hits me. Mom and Brad coming back here. Ian being on standby. Tall and Grande looking so smug. Even Sam is there, his eyes lolling all over as he avoids looking at me.

Venti set us up.

Connor must draw the same conclusion—or else he's just terrified of Mom—because he takes a step behind me, whispering, "Oh, shit."

Mom whirls around to face Tall and Grande, her breaths puffing from her nose like an incensed dragon. "I DO NOT NEED YOUR PRODUCTION INPUT INTO MY PARENTING AT THIS TIME. THANK YOU, MIKE AND OTHER MIKE."

"Sorry!"

"Other sorry!"

I try to take a step forward, but Connor grabs the back of my shirt and pulls me against him. He holds onto my wrist, sending shivers up my arm that are either from the warmth of his hand or my fear of imminent death or both. "Wait," he whispers through his teeth, so quietly it could have been my imagination. But it isn't.

Because a moment later, I see what he must have noticed before: Sabrina's head wriggling through the gap in the closet. "Why's everyone yelling?" She starts crying, the tears swelling in her eyes before plunking against her cheeks like fat summer raindrops. "Is the game over?"

"What game?" Mom asks, spinning in a circle.

"We were playing a game," Ella blurts, the smartest of us. "Hide-and-seek."

Mom turns her all-knowing, telepathic, mind-reading mom stare on me. "Is this true?"

I don't have time to think about what this moment means. I can only follow my gut. And my gut says: "Yes."

"How'd you get in here?" Brad asks, sounding less convinced.

I hold up the key card, keeping my hand over most of it so they can't see it isn't labeled. "I stole the master key out of the production room when they left the door open." I internally wince, knowing it's a weak cover at best.

At my answer, everyone freezes, not quite sure what to do next. Ian swivels between us. Mom continues scrutinizing me. "In that case, I'm sorry I yelled at you about Chelsea. But you still can't break into people's rooms."

The only thing that matters is that Tall and Grande are silent. They know they can't rat me out without incriminating themselves.

Eventually, Mom decides not to fling me into the sun. I pick up Sabrina and pretend to comfort her, even though she's way too heavy to carry for too long. As I pass Brad, he leans in close enough that I can smell the wintergreen of his aftershave. His blue eyes flash with suspicion. "The next time you decide to go through my things," he hisses in my ear in singsong, "remember to push harder on the nightstand drawer when you close it."

My head whips around to see what I could have possibly missed while being so careful. The drawer is closed. But I looked.

I looked.

chapter nineteen

*A*s if today wasn't already a complete disaster, we have to start talking about the Sweetheart Ceremony tomorrow. I've had a lifetime maximum of looking at Brad and Chelsea, but of course, Mom keeps pointing out that there are others we barely pay attention to who should go first.

Even after Angela and Val clock out with the rest of the stylists and half of the contestants go upstairs, I still can't go hide in my bed because Venti wants to talk. When he gets in my face about my feelings, it doesn't take a lot of deep soul-searching to figure out what I want to say.

Confessional: The producers on this show are back-stabbing backstabbers, and I'm not saying a damn thing else today, so don't even try me right now.

Confessional: I'm so grateful Connor was there to help me play it cool. And if it hadn't been for Sabrina and Ella's quick thinking, I could have blown it that I really was spying on Brad and Chelsea. It's annoying that I didn't find any evidence of Chelsea putting the Nair in Madyson's shampoo, but I know it's out

there. I don't trust her. Brad doesn't trust me. This is getting so overwhelming. But on the bright side, Connor held my hand today, so it wasn't a complete train wreck.

I return to find my room in shambles. The decorative pillows are strewn across the floor, their protective coverings unzipped and peeled back. My dresser is close to tipping from the weight of the open drawers. The rest of the guesthouse is untouched, sending the clear message that this was intended as retribution for me.

"How long have you been here?" I ask Mom as I step back out into the living room, my head throbbing hard enough that I swear my eyeballs are growing in their sockets.

She glances up from a magazine she bought in the airport and has read six hundred times already, the one concession the producers were willing to make about outside media. "The past half an hour or so. I stopped by the lounge to have a drink with Cole and Edgar and then went to an interview with Danny Romano. Why?"

"Were Brad and Chelsea around?"

"I don't know. Why? What's wrong?"

I turn toward the kitchen counter where Sam is seated, scribbling something on his tablet with a stylus that doesn't appear to be cooperating. "What about you, Sam?"

He opens and closes his mouth several times. "I can't, uh, I can't . . . I'm not here. I mean, I'm here, but I'm not *here*."

I want to be annoyed with him for not warning me that Venti was setting me up for that humiliating argument with Mom, but I know he's limited in what he can do. Figures that one of the only people I trust to give me a straight answer can't even talk to me half the time. "See for yourself." I direct Mom to my room, following as she surveys the destruction. She can't even fully enter without treading on debris tossed about like the last vestiges of a wild house party.

"Oh my God. Look at this mess. What happened?"

I crouch to pick up the iron from the closet, winding its cord around the handle. "Brad and Chelsea happened! They're pissed at me. I'm telling you!"

Mom lifts an eyebrow. "Sounds like there's more to that story. Anything you want to tell me about what went on today?"

I sigh. There's no point in stalling. Mom is a master interrogator when she gets a whiff of mischief. "I broke into their room to snoop, okay? I just had to find something to prove that they're not as perfect as you think they are."

"Well, then, this is what you get for violating their personal privacy," Mom snaps, rushing to straighten my shower caddy before the soap can spill. "If they did this, then they were perfectly justified in giving you a taste of your own medicine."

"What do you mean? Spying is part of the show. That's why we can hear their Confessionals!"

"Then we'll just have to hear what they have to say, won't we?"

She stomps out into the kitchen and almost rips the tablet out of Sam's hands. "I would like to see the Confessional for Brad! And you can show it to Cara, too!"

"I can't," Sam reminds us for what must be the fifth time. "It's against the rules. I can only show you. It could be, uh, inappropriate for a minor, uh, child."

Mom rolls her eyes up into her head and leaves them there for a second, giving her the appearance of some demonic maternal creature who's come to smite me with her motherly wrath.

When she's done viewing the video in the other room, Mom comes out with a piece of paper in her hand. "You can't watch it directly, so I'll read it to you instead."

[Confessional, Brad 5]: I have to admit I was startled to discover that Cara had gone through my personal possessions without my permission. That's not the kind of behavior I would want in a stepdaughter. It makes me wonder whether Julia is the right woman for me. I think the world of her, but would she support me being a stronger disciplinarian? I just wouldn't be able to allow that kind of behavior. Chelsea would never.

"Chelsea would never, MY ASS!" I flail both arms and a foot in the direction of my bedroom. "SHE LITERALLY DID!"

We pause as the glass door slides open and all three producers slip inside, followed by Ian's crew.

Mom is on her feet, chest heaving. She fixes me with her withering I'm-not-playing-around, I-will-cancel-Christmas stare. "Don't you make this about them! They've done nothing wrong. You went out with your little friends and did this! I should vote them all off!"

"It's not just up to you!" She has another thing coming if she thinks she's throwing off Connor, Ella, or Sabrina without a fight. Plus, I know she's bluffing, at least about Sabrina. I've seen how often she works out with Ray. "Would you let me watch mine now?"

Mom goes back into her bedroom while Sam pulls up the tablet with Chelsea's Confessional. "I don't want to see that," I snap at him. "I want to see Connor's."

Sam yelps and makes the adjustment. I dig the heels of my palms against my eyes, feeling the burn of pressure and tears.

"I'm sorry, Sam. It's not your fault."

"It's okay. It's okay. I get it."

I just need to know whether Connor's mad at me about how

far south our snooping went. Even though he doesn't know I tattled on us to Mom, it was pretty clear she had doubts about our hide-and-seek excuse.

[Confessional, Connor 4]: I told my dad the truth about what happened earlier. He's not mad or anything. I almost wish he'd be more like Cara's mom. She's all in your face with her feelings. I like that. And I really like Cara. Her mom probably hates me.

Mom emerges a minute later. "What did she say?"

I shrug. "I watched someone else's Confessional."

"Instead of trying to understand how Chelsea is feeling?" Mom bites her lower lip, her nostrils flaring. "I can't believe you don't see what's wrong with your actions."

"I'm just trying to show you that they're not right for us."

"You can't make that call when you haven't spent any time with them, especially with Brad. Why can't you just take my word for it?"

"They're know-it-alls!" I sashay my hips and rub my hands all over my torso. "Brad is always rubbing up on you and being disgusting, and it's—"

"WHAT IF I WANT HIM TO?" Mom thunders. "BECAUSE HE'S CHARMING AND HANDSOME AND HE WANTS ME TO THINK BIGGER FOR MY LIFE? WHAT IF I'M TIRED OF BEING ORDINARY? WHAT IF I'M LONELY BECAUSE I CAN'T EVEN GO ON REAL DATES BECAUSE I HAVE TO SPEND ALL MY TIME WORRYING ABOUT TAKING CARE OF YOU?"

I stumble back, the tears already blurring my vision. "Well," I say, my voice cracking, "if I'm so much trouble, I'll just go and let you hang out with your new family. Dad did it. Why can't you?

I guess I'm just batting oh for two." I run out of the house as she calls after me, ignoring the painful smack of my microphone against my hip.

Once again, I'm the leftover girl. I barely make it into the main house before I'm sobbing, a searing ache burning across my chest. I stagger into the lounge, startling a group of contestants, who scurry off, drinks in hand. I sit on the floor behind the bar, knees pulled close, and cry against the fabric of my literally fancy pants that cost too much money and I only bought to go on this horrible show.

Crammed in the corner like this, I don't think any of the cameras in the main room can see me. I've only ever had beer, but I reach over and grab a random bottle of something brown. I unscrew the lid before anyone can come stop me, pouring a tiny bit of liquid into my mouth and the rest down the front of my shirt. I don't even care.

"Cara? Are you okay? My dad said you were crying."

I wipe my eyes and look up at Connor. I shake my head. It's too late to pretend that I'm fine. "I got in a fight with my mom."

He takes a seat, brushing at his athletic shorts where he sat in spilled liquor by accident. "Do you want to talk about it?"

It's such a refreshing question after being forced to talk about my feelings numerous times so far. "I don't know." I take another swig and grimace. The taste is horrible, but it's worth the calming warmth spreading through me. I was so focused on the lack of cameras that I almost forgot about my microphone. "Want some . . . pop?"

"No, thanks," Connor says, taking the bottle and capping it.

"Don't be a party pooper."

"I'm taking medicine, so I can't have . . . sugar . . . from soda. But you shouldn't be drinking it either. It'll just make you feel worse later."

I stick both middle fingers up toward the back of the bar, even though I know they can't see me. "Yeah, you're probably right."

"Sit tight." He puts the bottle out of reach, as though I don't have two dozen others I could grab without moving more than an inch. "I know just the thing that'll cheer you up."

chapter twenty

*C*onnor returns with a bulging trash bag twisted shut at the top. "You brought me the trash?"

He steps through the saloon-style doors into the galley kitchen off the side of the lounge. "You just wait," he says. It's a little funny because I can see him standing on his tiptoes and half his face appearing above the doors, but nothing in the middle. "I know how much you want to be a chef and all, but—"

"I don't want to be a chef!" I yell, more at the producers listening in than at him. "They made it up. I just like food. I cook in order to eat the food."

The refrigerator door opens and closes. "Good. Less pressure for me, then."

I replay the conversation in my head and try to tune out the clanging and cursing from the kitchen. I don't know how difficult it is to cook with only his right arm. "Do you want help in there?"

"I've got it!"

The burning smell begs to differ. I scan the ceiling for smoke alarms, thankful that they're high in the vaulted space as wisps of smoke float into the lounge. Connor appears a few minutes later with napkins and a plate, setting them on the counter. He goes back for cups of orange juice, and then what my nose tells me are the world's saddest grilled cheese sandwiches.

Instead of asking me to move, he just transfers everything to the floor like it's normal to have a picnic on the floor behind a bar while you're covered in some kind of whiskey. I wish I could tell him that I know how he feels about what happened earlier, but then I'd have to admit to snooping on his Confessional. "What did you make me?"

He smiles and pokes me in the cheek with the tip of his pinkie. "I made you stop crying."

"Only because I was worried you'd light the mansion on fire by the way it smelled." I take the proffered sandwich. "But thanks. I do feel better."

"Don't judge a sandwich by its smell."

I'm surprised that the bread is a golden color, not blackened to a crisp. I take a hesitant bite, letting the flavor bloom on my tongue. It's unusual, but not bad, and the burning smell must have been from the bacon in the center. "This is delicious. What kind of cheese is this?"

"Gru . . . Gru . . ."

"Gruyère? That's an odd choice."

Connor chuckles and takes a bite of his sandwich. "It is a little weird. I don't know. I'm not a foodie. I just opened the fridge in the big kitchen and picked whatever sounded the fanciest."

"I'm sorry I doubted you." I clink our glasses together. "But why orange juice?"

"You always have it at breakfast." He takes two bites in a row, chewing longer than necessary. "Not that I'm juice-stalking you or something."

"Total juice-stalker. I bet you know what kind of utensils I use too."

"I saw you with a fork this morning. *And* a knife. So scandalous."

I throw the crust of my sandwich at him, hitting him just below his throat. "See? I knew you were a creeper." I hate doing this, using banter and jokes to keep him away from what hurts when he's trying to be here for me. "Tell me something." I sound desperate even to my own ears. "Something real. I feel like I'm in some kind of fantasy world where no one means what they say and there are tricks and games and it's just . . . I just want something. Anything. Please."

Connor's head dips a fraction as he thinks. "When I was a kid, I had this little wooden toy shaped like a puppy. It was on wheels, and I could pull it around by a string. I named it Pup Pup and basically took it everywhere with me." He laughs, but just once. "Okay. That's not completely true. I never stopped taking Pup Pup everywhere. He's upstairs. He's my good-luck charm. Don't judge me."

"Is he really? That's adorable. I'll have to meet this famous Pup Pup sometime."

I think he's going to nudge me, but he just places his hand on my shoulder for a heartbeat. "Your turn. Tell me something real."

"Okay." I skip over the dark memories, searching for a story in the same vein as Connor's. "My family loves Lord of the Rings. We've seen all the movies a million times. One Halloween, I decided to carve my jack-o'-lantern to look like Gollum. But I'm terrible at arts and crafts, so when my grandfather came over to visit, he thought it was him. And he was so proud of it. He made us take a picture of him with it next to his head."

"Did you tell him the truth?"

"No! It would have broken his heart."

We keep swapping stories long after I know I should have gone back to make up with Mom. But I can't tear myself away from Connor, how easy this is. I tell him about my childhood and my life, and before I know it, we're not talking about childish things anymore.

"When my dad walked out, my mom kept insisting he was going to come back because he only took a suitcase and one box of stuff." I even remember which box it was because I'd tried to throw it away. He said he was saving it. I didn't ask why. "And she just didn't realize that he took everything he wanted. And it all fit in that box."

Connor nods, chasing a few crumbs around a plate with his index finger. "I don't know if my parents were ever in love to fall out of it. They just accepted each other like it had to be that way. I wish they would hate each other. I can't stand how nice they are."

Six Real Things about Connor Dingeldein

Pup Pup is upstairs on his dresser right now.

His family hides a pickle ornament on their Christmas tree as a game.

He wants to be an architect. Too much school for me, but kudos.

RIP to his pet gerbil, who definitely did not go to live with Santa.

Doritos are not a favorite food, but he's cute, so I'll forgive him.

His parents are the wrong kind of nice to each other.

In between, I tell him about my high school and Vanessa, the way my old friends stabbed me in the back, and LeAnne. I explain how my parents met in college and fell in love and got married in Hawaii in a destination wedding that my aunt still complains about. I've never told anyone this stuff before, but it's like giving

173

each other pieces of ourselves and hoping that the other person will care enough to assemble the puzzle.

Just as it's my turn to tell another story, Ray pokes his head in the back door right beside us, Sabrina riding along on his shoulders. "Everything all right? I would say it smells good in here, but my parents taught me not to tell lies."

Connor's mouth falls open. "It's not that bad. I made us something to eat."

"It smells like burning. And liquor." Ray gives us a pointed look. "It might be a good time to wrap it up."

We mumble our agreement. He flips Sabrina upside down, swinging her by her legs as he jogs back out into the hallway, her squeals resonating the length of the building. I stand and start clearing the floor, stacking our cups and tossing the napkins on top of the dirty plates. Connor moves to rise, but halfway to standing, his knee buckles. He catches himself on the lip of the bar, blowing out a relieved sigh.

"Are you okay?"

"Yeah," he mutters, reaching down to massage his knee. "I just lost my balance."

"Oh. I do that all the time." I press a finger to my chest. "Coffee-table-bashing expert right here. I sleep on the couch, so whenever I have to go to the bathroom, it's a nice obstacle course in the dark."

I pick up the plates and start heading toward the kitchen, where I think there's a dishwasher. Connor stops me with a hand on my shoulder. "Wait. I don't want to lie to you." His eyes flash up to the cameras. "If I tell you something, will you promise to just . . . remember who I am? You know, the things I just told you. Pup Pup and the Christmas pickle and architecture school. And not replace me with some picture you have in your head from a movie."

"Yeah?" I say, not really sure where he's going with this or what

174

it has to do with losing your balance. But I can tell from the wobble of his eyebrows that it's important somehow, maybe even more so than everything else he's already shared with me. "I promise."

He takes a deep breath. "I'm disabled. I have something called Ehlers-Danlos syndrome. It basically means that the stuff that holds my body together doesn't work super great."

I'm not sure what to say. "I'm sorry. Is that why you have a sling?"

"Don't be sorry. It's just who I am. And yeah. I tore some stuff after casting. Bad luck." He wriggles the fingers of his left hand, the tips peeking out from the end of his sling. "You know what's funny? I used to complain about all the physical therapy, but I only realized I want to go to school for architecture because the physical therapy place always has design shows on."

"And now *you're* on a reality show."

Connor quirks his head, thinking. "True. I never thought about it like that before."

"I'm glad you decided to try out." I suddenly realize that I feel better despite the fact that we never really talked about my fight with Mom in detail. It was enough to just be here together, to feel like I mattered.

I wrap my arms around him before I change my mind, careful not to hurt his shoulder. He leans his head on top of mine, and I almost make a short joke, but I don't want to spoil it. Before we broke into Brad's room, I'd wondered what it would be like to kiss Connor, but all of that's gone now. I've kissed a boy before, and it didn't mean a damn thing. But I've never stood like this, feeling a heartbeat against my cheek.

Connor twists a ring of my hair around one finger. "I'm glad I decided to try out too."

chapter twenty-one

I walk straight through the house and into my room, ignoring Mom completely despite her fervent attempts to get my attention. After I've had a much-needed shower, I work on cleaning my room, thankful to have a reason not to talk to her. Much to my relief, the owners' throw pillows, knickknacks, and furniture are unscathed. My clothing is rumpled, but not permanently damaged. In fact, the only thing that's unaccounted for is one of the knee socks that Vanessa gave me for my birthday last year. I set the unmatched sock aside for later.

Mom knocks on the door as the sky darkens, and I momentarily panic, thinking that I've forgotten to choose an outfit for the next Sweetheart Ceremony. But that isn't until tomorrow. "What?" I ask, the question coming out sharper than intended.

She opens the door, her eyebrows rising slightly as she sees how much I've picked up. "First of all, I'm sorry for what I said earlier. I got caught up in how upset I was, and I didn't mean to throw that on you."

I know she didn't mean it, but it still stung. "Okay."

"I don't want things to be so hostile. I just spoke to the producers, and they approved my request for a redo on my invite-only date that got interrupted by the hide-and-seek thing. You're coming too, and we're eating in twenty minutes."

"I had a sandwich not too long ago. What are we having?"

"Lemon chicken and sides. They're ordering out since there are only four of us."

"Four of us?"

"I invited Brad and Chelsea. I want you guys to make up. This is getting messy."

I shake my head, all the calm contentedness from my conversation with Connor evaporating on the spot. "Not happening. I'd rather have a spa day with LeAnne, the Balrog, and Satan than eat dinner with those two after they trashed my room."

Mom rushes closer in a flurry of anger, ripping a paisley summer dress off a hanger. She tosses it onto my bed, seething. "Put this on. We're going to dinner." Her front teeth click together. "Don't argue with me."

"Why are you so obsessed with Brad? Is it the producers? Are they pushing you together?" My questions come out as a whine, probably because I'm secretly hoping that's the case. If Venti is haranguing Mom about spending time with Brad, at least it isn't all real. There's still some hope that I can break through to her.

"Why do you have to act like there's some kind of scheme? I just like Brad. He's ambitious and smart, and he cares about my dreams."

"Fine."

I stomp to the bathroom with my toiletries, throwing my clothes onto the floor and changing into the dress. I tear a brush through my hair and nearly poke out my own eyeball as I try to apply my makeup with shaking hands.

It wasn't supposed to be like this. We were supposed to be a team. And now? I can't even look at her. I'd rather spend time with

Connor than with my own mother. What's happening to us, and how do I stop it?

I compose myself and dab more foundation over my splotchy complexion. Mom is ready when I emerge, pacing the length of the living room in her peep-toe pumps. I walk right by her and up the world's most pathetic hill to the main house without waiting to see if she's following. I don't care.

Sam stumbles across the foyer a few minutes later, his arms laden with double-bagged containers of food. He strains to lift his hand high enough to wave. "Hey, Cara. Is your mom ready?"

"Don't know. Don't care."

He snaps both hands back to his chest like a startled tyrannosaurus. "I, um, I thought things were better now."

"We got into a fight again. I don't want to talk about it."

Ian and his crew must realize I'm not above biting because they hover at a safe distance, watching as Brad and Chelsea descend the staircase. Of course, they look absolutely stunning, with all the allure of a pair of poisonous frogs. I glower at Brad and his stupid golden hair and blue eyes and perfectly fitted vest with an actual pocket watch. Chelsea isn't any better with her gray sheath dress and her finery and her flawless, doll-like curls.

Our greetings are terse.

"Chelsea."

"Cara."

"Brad."

"Cara."

Mom swoops in to save the day. "I'm so glad that you were able to join us," she tells them, as though there are a lot of other options when you're on televised house arrest. "I thought we could eat in the dining room."

Brad sits at the head of the table with Mom on his left and

Chelsea on his right. A flicker of annoyance runs through me at the lack of symmetry. I take the chair next to Mom, an uncomfortable, slat-backed chunk of walnut.

Ian and his crew reenter from the patio side, flanking the French doors like sentries. They whisper for a few moments and fiddle with their earpieces. Their T-shirts and cargo shorts are in glaring contrast to our stuffy formal outfits.

"Thank you for inviting us to dinner," Brad simpers. "There's nothing I love more than a good meal with family."

Well, Brad, there's a reason that "family" is an f-word.

I suck in a calming breath as workers parade through to serve our meal. The first woman arrives with wine and water, the second with silverware and cloth napkins. Sam bustles in last, his knuckles white on the edges of an overloaded serving platter. He stares at the center of it, taking cautious steps.

His features break into relief when he places it down on the table with a clatter. I lean back in my chair as he sets out bread plates with soft rolls and palettes of butter in the shape of flowers. The main course is a chicken dish in some kind of light sauce, paired with steamed broccoli and a mound of garlic mashed potatoes.

"Do you need anything else?" Sam asks, studying the spread before us.

Mom smiles at him. "No, thank you, Sam."

Ian pretends to cover his mouth and laugh as he passes. Sam doesn't acknowledge him except for a joking kick against his steel-toed boots as he wedges open the patio doors to circulate the cool outdoor air.

"Oh." Brad lifts his right hand and snaps. "There's no pepper."

Before I can stop myself, I slam my fist against the table. Mom's wine splatters onto the white tablecloth and pools against the wood. "This is exactly what I'm talking about! Don't snap at him. He's not a dog."

Brad lays a hand over his heart. He turns to Sam, who is clutching the empty serving platter like he's considering the many ways to weaponize it. "I hope you didn't take offense."

"Of course not." Sam vanishes into the kitchen and returns with a wooden pepper mill. *I hope he peed in it.* "Enjoy."

I chew my broccoli into a pulp, locking eyes with Chelsea across the table. "Who chose the menu?" she asks, sniffing a strip of chicken with distaste.

"I did," Mom replies. "Sorry if it's bland. I tend to avoid red meat."

Brad waves away her concern. "No worries. We love all sorts of food."

"Do you have a favorite?"

"I like French," Chelsea says, drawing the last syllable into a faint hiss. She waggles her eyebrows at me. "It's Daddy's favorite, too. What about you?" Her tone makes it into a dare.

Mom smiles, either oblivious to or ignoring my rising temper. "Nothing exotic like French food. If we're going to splurge, we usually go to this little restaurant by the gym I own. They have old-fashioned malts, and burgers, and fries. It's good."

"Oh, Julia." Brad's laugh is a mirthless condescension. "You need to broaden your horizons. Greek. Thai. Ethiopian." He slides a hand over hers. "There's nothing more incredible than seeing a new country and tasting the local cuisine. I'll take you wherever you want to go for our honeymoon."

Mom makes goo-goo eyes at him like a puppy seeing snow for the first time. "That sounds lovely. I've always wanted to visit South America. My sister studied abroad in Peru when we were younger, and I was so jealous."

Venti sticks his head through a gap between the film crew.

"Quick note here. We can't hear you when you're eating, so just cut up your food and move it around a little. Pretend."

"We're not even allowed to eat?" This is too much. I've reached my emotional limit.

"Just pretend," Venti repeats, making a circular motion with one hand. "Don't even talk about the food. You're here to talk about breaking into each other's rooms and what happened with the Nair and Madyson. The rumors. Chelsea, why don't you talk about your feelings concerning that whole situation?"

I look at my meal. It's a shame that someone put so much effort into plating our food in an appealing arrangement when all I want to do is barf.

"I do actually have a problem with everything about the Nair and Madyson," Chelsea says. "I think it's really juvenile and high school of you to be spreading rumors about me."

"I am literally a high school juvenile."

Mom snorts.

Brad leans away from her, his eyes narrowing. "See, Julia, this is what gives me pause. Your daughter is rude and unladylike, and you think it's funny. That doesn't set a good example for her, and it's not the kind of influence I want around Chelsea."

Chelsea puts on an angelic smile that makes me wonder if jumpsuit orange might be my color after all.

"You weren't such a perfect influence when you went and destroyed my room and threw stuff all over the place," I interject, since Mom appears to be speechless at the moment.

Brad purses his lips. "I had nothing to do with that."

"Oh, that's convenient. I'm supposed to apologize for everything, and they won't even admit they did the same thing! They're hypocrites." Mom reaches for me as I stand, shoving back from the table. "I'm not apologizing. I'm done here."

I storm out of the room and head back to the house to wait for the next Sweetheart Ceremony, when I will, again, not be able to get rid of these people.

Confessional: I wanted to come on this show to start a new life with my mom, but now I'm starting to think I don't like the life she has in mind.

chapter twenty·two

*M*ost people would be alarmed by screaming in the middle of the night, especially after a day of so much tension with Brad and Chelsea. I am not most people. When Mom resumes her second bout of earsplitting howls, I run through three possibilities: spider, animal in the house, or genuine emergency.

I snatch a handful of napkins from the kitchen as I jog to her room, skidding on the cold tile. "Where is it?" I ask, my eyes on the ceiling. "Wolf spider? Daddy longlegs?"

"In here," she calls from the bathroom.

I follow the sound of her voice, shrinking as I see the bulbous swell of the wall behind the toilet. Mom is frantically sopping up the leaking water with all our bath towels, her pajama bottoms drenched to the knee. "What happened?" I ask, horrified.

She throws her hands up. "I don't know! I heard this noise, so I got up to check and found all this water on the floor."

"What should I do?" In my daze, I pat my imaginary pockets, looking for my cell phone to call the apartment supervisor. It takes a moment for my surroundings to congeal into a concrete place, a time. "You shouldn't stand there, Mom. If that breaks, you're going to get soaked. I'll go get Sam."

Unfortunately, my lack of cellular devices makes the latter complicated as well. I pull on Mom's shoes, not caring that they're a size too big, and flop my feet up the incline to the main house. I knock on the door where the producers often go, but no one answers. Next, I try waving at the cameras, jumping up and down with urgency. "Come on, you camera-watching, stalky weirdos. I need help!"

I finally hunt down a member of production, but he has no idea how to get a plumber at this hour. I hover outside the office, eavesdropping on his phone conversation with someone from the day shift. When he sees me watching, he hangs up and says, "That was Mike Wistrand. They're trying to get a contractor out here, and they're coming in now to deal with it."

"I'm not an expert, but this thing looks like it's going to straight up explode. So, like, maybe you could turn off the water or something?"

I get a lot of blinks and confused looks and not a lot of confidence that all my possessions are going to remain free of sewage for the foreseeable future. I know that there has to be someone in this building who can do something *now*. I jog up the stairs and start pounding on doors with my fist. "Hello? It's Cara." I move down the row, knocking. "Anybody?"

Finally, a door cracks open. Cole appears in the hallway, donning a black-and-gold windbreaker with a fleur-de-lis on each arm. "What's wrong?" he croaks, pawing his hair out of his eyes.

"There's water leaking all over our bathroom, and there's no one on set who can fix it right now."

"Uh, I can fix that." He vanishes inside for a moment and returns with a pair of untied sneakers on his feet. "After you."

On our way out the side door, Cole asks production to keep an eye on Grady, then raids the utility room, finding a meager supply of hand tools and a sad mop. I take the mop while he riffles through the toolbox. "Do you know what you're doing?" I ask, not meaning to sound insulting. "Not that it matters."

"Miss Cara," Cole says, burping against the side of his fist, "I might look young, and I might be a little drunk still, and I might have flunked the ninth grade two times, but I'm a nuclear non-licensed operator. I can handle me a toilet."

We're doomed.

I show Cole to the bathroom, where Mom shares my skepticism. "Shouldn't we wait for a professional?" she worries aloud. "This isn't our house. I'm not sure about insurance."

"There's some guy up there who's, like . . . Night-Shift Mike . . . and he has no idea what's going on except that Day-Shift Mike is coming in right now and they're 'trying to get a contractor out here.'"

"I can dooo it," Cole answers. He fiddles around in the bathroom, walks the perimeter of the house, and then comes back inside. "I shut off all the water for now. Looks like a pipe burst inside the wall, but hard to tell. Did ya touch anything before it started?"

Mom repeats her story about waking to the sound of rushing water.

"Guess we'll have to wait 'til the pros get here," Cole says, opening the cabinets and pulling out the spare set of towels.

"That iced tea is going to come back to haunt me," I mutter as I think of how long it will take to get dressed in real clothes and trek up to the main house every time we have to pee.

Mom reaches over and plucks a washcloth from the top of the pile. Cole snatches it away.

"Miss Julia, you do not clean a thing. It is two o'clock in the mornin', and a lady as beautiful as you needs a lot of beauty sleep." He kisses her on the cheek, careful to keep his dirty hands clear. "Now you sleep tight, and I will clean this up."

"No, no, I couldn't. This isn't even your mess."

"Go," he insists, nudging her with his elbow. "Go on. Get."

She relents with a smile. "Thank you. So much. I wouldn't have known what to do, and the whole house would have been flooded. I swear that I'm usually handier than this when I can consult the internet."

We share a laugh before I remember that I'm still supposed to be giving Mom the cold shoulder. I wait until she goes to bed before I retrieve the mop and dig out a bottle of all-natural cleaner from underneath the kitchen sink. "I can probably get the rest with the mop," I tell Cole.

He raises himself to his full height, which isn't much, and puts his hands on his hips. "Now, I'm not lettin' you touch this neither. You go on to bed. That plumber'll get in here eventually."

"I can't sleep anyway."

Cole pries the mop from my hands, flicks on the overhead fan, and shoves me out the door, saying, "Gosh damn, both of y'all are stubborn as anything."

The lock clicks.

Maybe I was wrong to doubt him after all.

The clamor of power tools rouses me shortly after dawn. I stretch, keeping one eye closed as I peer out into the living room. A team of plumbers is huddled in conference outside the bathroom, along with Mom, Sam, Venti, and a few of the miscellaneous staff whose exact functions I haven't quite determined yet.

I choose an outfit from my dresser, bundling each article of clothing in my arms as I select it. Since the bathroom is out of commission, I use my closet as a changing room to avoid the cameras. I dab on a bit of makeup and check my reflection in the mirrored door. I look awful, but that's okay. It's not like I'm going to be on national television or anything.

"Do they know how long it'll take to fix?" I ask as I emerge, pointedly speaking only to Sam. "It looked bad last night."

"It'll be a while, since the actual pipe broke. We've suspended any organized filming for the day. Sewage started bubbling up in the yard, too."

That explains the tube-shaped blue sandbags stacked on the far side of the swimming pool. "I guess I'll go hang out with Ella and Sabrina." I deliberately avoid mentioning Connor, since Mom hasn't seemed to pick up on whatever there is between us. "They won't have anything to do either."

"Uh-uh," Venti says, ticking his finger back and forth. "Just because they don't have anything to do doesn't mean *you two* don't have anything to do. This is a great time to shoot B-roll."

I look at Sam, horrified at having to spend an entire day alone with Mom when things are so awkward. "Please tell me that's a kind of sandwich."

"Sam, can you escort them off-site?" Venti asks. "I'm going to be busy dealing with the plumbing."

Sam's entire body jitters with such speed that it looks like he's about to enter another plane of existence. "Of course. That—that will not be a problem at all. I will, uh, we can make productive use! Of the day!"

Ian doesn't look nearly as enthused. "B-roll? We weren't supposed to do that until next week. My contract says that—"

Sam grabs Ian by both shoulders, putting his face so close to Ian's that they're one millimeter away from having their first kiss. "Mike. Wistrand. Asked. Me. To. Oversee. B-roll." He shakes Ian. "Let. Me. Have. This."

Ian bites his lip with his front teeth, and for a moment I think he's going to yell something obscene. "FFF-INE, you needy brat. It's easy for *you* to be excited about B-roll. You don't have to lug around the equipment for it and have a bunch of tourists mobbing the shit out of you."

"I'll run interference."

"Like you were supposed to in Denver?"

"What's B-roll?" Mom interjects before Sam and Ian's bickering can get any worse.

"It's stuff besides the main story," Ian explains. "The boss men will cut from that when they do stuff like opening scenes or finding the right clips for your voice-overs. Basically, we go film a bunch of random crap to give them a whole lot to choose from. Plus, since this is a vacation area, we can show a little of the beach, the highlights."

Maybe today's looking up. "We're going to the beach?"

"Near it," Ian says, cautious as always. "It's for B-roll, not for fun."

Angela helps us change into casual outfits before packing some spare clothes, travel makeup, and hair products to bring along. She passes the backpack to Sam, who leads us toward the front of the house. "It's a shame we can't walk," Sam muses. "It's such a nice day out."

"Nice day" is an understatement. The sky has a smattering of clouds to block the worst of the sun. I feel happier, more alert. It's so different from the dreary northern summers I'm accustomed to, where the sun is like an unreliable second cousin who only visits once a year and then asks to borrow money.

Even though our first stop is nearby, Sam insists that we drive to avoid looking flushed or sweaty. "This is awesome." I sigh as we cross the street, swinging my arms and throwing my head back in the tropical breeze. "No cameras except Ian's. I can pick my nose. Scratch my butt."

"I don't know how you stand it," Sam admits. "I know I'm on

the house cameras, but that's different than having Ian following my every move. They'll just cut me out."

Over the next couple of hours, we fall into a rhythm. Take dramatic walks on the beach or sit on benches beneath palm trees and look pensive. Sit in the air-conditioning for ten minutes. Change clothes. More dramatic walking.

But it's not all bad once Sam lets go of his nervousness and has a little fun with it. There's one point as we near the downtown that Sam has to hustle us back to the car to avoid onlookers who are a little too curious, but aside from that, it's nice to have a neutral day with a light emotional load.

I do wish Connor could have come and seen the water, though. I hate that it seems like it's feast or famine with the schedule. I hope he knows I'm not avoiding him.

On the way back, Sam chews the edge of his thumbnail, steering with his other hand. He abruptly pulls into a parking spot and turns to Ian in the passenger seat. "We're done a little early. If I take them to see the cemetery, are you going to throw a tantrum about it?"

Ian groans. "Man, why is there always a catch with you?"

"They're in Key West, and they haven't seen an inch of it except for where we went today. There's so much history. It'll only take twenty minutes. Think of it as your union break."

Ian checks the time on his phone. "You know, that's true. I was supposed to have my union break twenty-seven minutes ago per the original schedule for today."

"See? You could take a nap," Sam cajoles.

"Fine. But make it fifteen minutes."

I'm just as excited to get out and do something fun as Sam is, but I do need to confirm as we take off down the block. "You want us to go with you to a cemetery," I repeat back to him, just to make sure I didn't mishear. "With dead people."

"No, no, no, it's a *funny* cemetery."

"And you want us to laugh?" I protest. "That's how you get haunted."

Mom scoffs. "We're already haunted."

I break out ahead while she tells Sam about the broken stereo that keeps turning all our classes into Poltergeist Zumba. Even though I'm upset with her, I'm glad that Mom gets a day off without having to censor herself or consider how the contestants might interpret the glimpses she gives them of our lives back home.

"The cemetery is up here," Sam calls, turning left onto a strip of grass where the sidewalk crumbles to a finish.

We continue for a few more minutes before I spot an American flag waving in the distance and a black historical sign stuck in the grass at the corner. The nearest section of the cemetery is clearly the oldest, with weathered tombstones and moss-covered mausoleums. We pass through the gate, looking at the various grave markers. "You said this was supposed to be funny?" I prompt, confused.

"Look closer at the inscriptions," Sam replies. He points with his foot. "Like that one. 'So Long, and Thanks for All the Fish.' That's from—"

My mouth falls open. I've found a kindred spirit. Maybe literally a spirit. "THE HITCHHIKER'S GUIDE TO THE GALAXY!"

Sam is visibly taken aback. "I'm surprised you know the reference."

Mom lifts her chin. "I raised a science fiction nerd, just like me."

I meander through the disorganized rows, sidestepping aboveground burial vaults with mismatched lengths. The monuments are extraordinary. There's a conch shell at the end of the row and life-sized religious statues watching over individual plots.

I rejoin Sam as he finds another headstone worth reading. This one says, I TOLD YOU I WAS SICK. "I feel bad laughing," I admit, wondering what Connor would make of all this. "Isn't it disrespectful?"

His eyes twinkle. "I think these people would agree that sometimes a little self-deprecation is needed for the sake of humor."

I scream as a chicken dashes out of the bush an inch to my right. "I'm sorry," I say, squinting against the harsh sunlight at the fat bird scampering across an overgrown grave, its wings flailing for balance. "Is that a chicken?"

Mom bursts out laughing, pressing a hand against her chest. She throws her arms in the air and runs in circles, yelling, "The sky is falling! The sky is falling!"

But even the reference to *Chicken Little*, my favorite childhood story of all time, isn't enough to bridge the divide between us. I've let my guard down throughout the day, but I don't want Mom to think she can fix what's wrong by cracking a few jokes. I remain stone-faced, raising my eyebrows at Sam as I wait for the inevitable explanation.

He's quick to oblige, flushing as he absorbs my lack of amusement at Mom's antics. "There are wild chickens all over Key West. They escaped or were set free a long time ago, and now they're just another part of the island. Like feral cats."

"Do they have diseases?"

"I mean, I wouldn't recommend eating one." He pats his stomach. "Though speaking of eating, are you ladies hungry at all?"

I shrug. "I'm always hungry."

"Follow me. This is going to change your life." Sam exits the south side of the cemetery and crosses the street to a small gas station, the first I've seen on the island. I figure that he's going into the convenience store, but he rounds the corner after the pumps, waving us on.

I smell the taco truck before I see it. The sides are painted in bright yellows and oranges with a graffiti lizard on the bottom and a chicken holding a margarita alongside the pop-out veranda.

"I've eaten dinner here, like, eight times already," Sam confesses.

"I'll have to bring something back for Ian, or he'll hate me forever."

He places his order while I peruse the menu stuck to the inside of the window. There are so many choices, and I only have one stomach. I move out of the way as the employee returns with a heavy half-moon of fried dough, the rounded end sticking out past the wrapping.

Sam reaches up for his empanada like it's stuffed with ambrosia. He sinks his teeth into it, emitting a low groan. He chews with deliberateness, his eyelids heavy. "This . . . This is . . . oh my. It gets better every time."

"Give me a bite," I command, practically ripping it out of his hands. I'll take a taco truck empanada over Brad's hoity-toity French cuisine any day of the week.

Sam digs his fingertips into the tinfoil and covers it with the crook of his arm like a football. "You need to get your own." He shrieks a girlish giggle as I attempt to pry it away, singing the "Hot Potato" song. "One bite will not be enough!"

"If you insist," I say, sticking out my tongue. "Good defense."

"Um, we don't have any cash," Mom says, wincing. "I didn't bring my wallet. I figured we'd go back to the house for lunch."

"No worries." Sam is already heaping wadded fistfuls of small bills and coins on the counter. He starts wolfing down the empanada with quick, short bites. "Here. Here. You need to experience this."

"I'll have what he's having," I say. The worker shakes his head in amusement and passes a few napkins to Sam, whose lower lip is dripping grease as he hunches over his meal like a territorial dog.

Sam wipes his mouth, scrubbing at his patchy stubble.

"Excellent choice."

Much to my surprise, Mom pushes some of the change back across the counter and orders an empanada for herself. I expected her to get the taco salad with no cheese or a side of plain pinto beans. I almost drop dead when she adds on a churro.

When we've all been served, we walk back across the street to the cemetery, where an old bench with peeling white paint is tucked against the iron fencing. I pivot to face Sam. "I never thought I'd be able to say that I had a taco truck picnic in a cemetery."

"I told you it's a quirky little town. How's your food?"

"Life-changing," I reply, taking another bite. "Worth every one of your pennies. Thanks for lunch, by the way."

"Anytime."

Mom holds out her churro. The delectable smell of butter and cinnamon sugar fills my nostrils. I can almost feel the crunch of it between my teeth, the sweetness melting across my tongue. "Want some?" she asks.

"No," I snap, folding my arms. This is the longest I've ever stayed angry with Mom, but I will not be so easily bribed. My dignity is worth at least *three* churros, thank you very much.

Ian is so preoccupied with his food that we take a circuitous route home, stopping to view a lighthouse that I've seen in the distance throughout the day. It strikes me as strange that it's so far inland.

I find that I don't want this afternoon to end, this surprise reprieve from the drama of the show. There's no one vying for my attention or conspiring against me. I'm just an ordinary girl on vacation, who should stop being pigheaded and make up with her mom already. But I don't, because this freedom is fleeting. I'm not ordinary. Not anymore. Maybe not ever again once my face is known.

The plumber is waiting by the pool when we return. A pump hums from inside the living room, powered by the orange extension cord snaking through the doors. "We were able to find the source of the blockage. It was the toilet." He holds up a baby-blue knee sock patterned with ice-cream cones and cats in goofy sunglasses. "Is this yours?"

chapter twenty-three

*D*espite the occasional bout of homesickness, I do enjoy having a set routine. There's breakfast in the morning, then an activity in the early afternoon. On voting nights, Mom and I sequester ourselves in the guesthouse, debating who to send packing now that we're down to six pairs of contestants. The schedule takes the guesswork out of planning what to wear or what to do.

But I'm more than willing to make an exception to see Chelsea's face after Tall, Grande, and Venti call an emergency meeting the next morning to berate us all about the sock in the toilet. I can tell from the way Ella, Connor, and Madyson angle their bodies toward her that at least the kids know the culprit, even if their parents are clueless.

"We're guests here, and no matter what happens, we have to respect the property." Venti paces the foyer, his skin pallid except for the dark lines shadowing his eyes. "I think we all owe Cole Sherwin a big thank-you for intervening when he did. That saved us from even more extensive damage."

Little Grady leads the round of applause for his dad. Cole beams, giving a series of miniature bows.

I keep waiting for Venti to out Chelsea as the one who did it, but he holds back, probably because he knows I'm still fighting with Mom about it. *Even if she did put the sock in the toilet, I'm sure she didn't mean any harm by it,* Mom said, as though we weren't one half-drunk nuclear non-licensed operator away from flooding a million-dollar guesthouse.

When I catch up with Connor again at breakfast, even he seems frustrated by the situation. "You weren't kidding that she's in denial."

"It's like she's on another planet. Planet Brad, where everything is bespoke and God forbid your fucking underwear isn't made of hand-stitched llama butt fur."

Instead of sitting in our usual places by Brad and Chelsea, I ditch Mom to stay with Connor, which clearly isn't lost on her since she keeps looking over with this wounded puppy expression.

"Do you have an idea on how to get through to her? I could ask my dad to maybe mention a few things."

"That would be great," I say, noting that Charles and Mom are already in conversation anyway, though she might just be asking about me and Connor. "She seems to think your dad is a pretty sensible guy."

"He is. That just doesn't make him the most fun or involved. From what he's told me, your mom vents to him a lot about the others. He is a good listener, I guess."

It hurts a little to know that she's not coming to me anymore, even though I recognize that our relationship has taken a definite turn for the worse lately. I don't want to be replaced, but I can't listen to her when she's acting like there's nothing wrong with Chelsea's behavior.

Maybe there's something coming up that will help us reconnect. "What's on the agenda for today?" I ask Sam as I leave to grab a quick shower, still munching on bacon strips rolled up in a syrup-soaked pancake.

He checks his tablet, flicking his finger along the screen of his email inbox. He steals a blueberry muffin from the basket. "Looks like roller-skating."

I perk up. "How did that happen?"

"You sent us a list of your favorite hobbies and things to do for fun. The big shots try to incorporate them into the show. It gives us a little insight into your personality."

Up until now, we haven't left the grounds as a group. That must be the side benefit of having such drastically reduced numbers compared to the massive opening contingent of contestants. Still, it takes two enormous vans to shuttle all of us and the film equipment to the roller rink.

When I mention the hassle to Ian, he says, "Off-site activities are always a logistical nightmare. A year or so ago, I was working on this show about cake decorators, and one of the stars just vanished. We found him an hour later crashing the wedding." He leans forward and taps Sam on the shoulder. "Hey, Sam, do you remember the cake guy?"

"The one in Colorado who got drunk and spilled marinara all over himself?"

"That's the one."

"Do you think this will stain?" they quote in unison, chuckling.

The drive is short, ending in a rectangular, gravel-filled lot surrounded by palm trees. The metal siding is painted in primary colors with cartoonish animal figures cavorting along the length of the building. The contestants spill out behind us, watching Ian and Sam for cues like kids with a chaperone.

As soon as I step inside, I'm overcome by nostalgia. It's not so different from the rink I used to visit as a child. A glass display case of by-the-ticket prizes sits to our right alongside a tiny arcade with a pitiful selection of games. The concession counter is visibly sticky with spilled soda and covered in boxes of individually sold candies. I love it.

"There's no one else here," Madyson observes.

I exchange confused glances with her and Ella. "They must have bought out the rink. Even better."

I follow the strip of blue industrial carpet to the skate rental, reaching it before any of the others. The young man working the booth watches me approach, setting aside a pair of low-top skates with wheels decorated like eyeballs. "Hi," he says, staring at the camera without blinking. "Ticket?"

I frown, glancing over my shoulder to try to track down Sam. "We didn't get any."

"Right. Because you're the TV people. Um, what size?"

"Men's seven," I say. "In-line, if you have them."

He passes me a pair of scuffed black-and-red skates with fraying laces. As I'm turning around to sit, he blurts out, "Am I gonna be on TV?"

Ian lets out a long sigh that rustles my hair. "Yes, the Emmys are calling your name already."

I sit on one of the benches lining the wall, tightening the trio of buckles to a secure fit. Ella and Madyson join me shortly after, both clutching tan pairs of traditional quad skates. "I'm horrible at skating," Madyson admits. "I don't know how to stop."

"You can hang on to me," I promise. "I used to skate all the time growing up. My dad was in an indoor hockey league." My voice cracks on the last syllable as I remember the way he'd line me up with a stick twice my height and let me shoot penalty shots until there were blisters on my thumbs.

"Just don't run over any of the little kids," Ella says.

I realize that I've been spending so much time worrying about Chelsea that I haven't thought about leaving here with a new stepsibling since the opening night. It's felt more like I was making friends when really, one of these kids is probably going to be a part of my life forever.

It seems less daunting with Ella and Madyson since we're all older, or at least middle-school age in Madyson's case. But when I look at the younger kids like Sabrina, it's difficult not to panic. I've spent my whole life worrying about myself. I wouldn't even know what to do if I had a stepsibling ten years younger. What if they were bullied at school? What if they were unhappy and I couldn't figure out why? It's so much pressure.

Just thinking about it stresses me out, so I let everyone else go on ahead while I wait for Connor, who was stuck with the group in the second van. He grabs a pair of skates, exchanges them, then exchanges them back for the original pair. "I hate places that don't have half sizes."

"I just wear double socks."

He nods, impressed. "Smart idea."

I move over to give him room on the bench. He sticks his foot in a skate and wraps the laces around his fist, then kicks his leg out to tighten them. "Do you need help?" I ask.

"I've got it." He folds his leg in a figure-four until his skate is high enough to tie with both hands without having to move his bad shoulder.

"Are you going to be okay skating?" I eye his sling. "What if you fall?"

Connor puts his foot down and switches to his other skate. "I get that you're just trying to help, but this is what I meant about treating me differently just because you know." He smiles and spins one of the wheels with his fingers. "I promise I will not actually die from an hour and a half of roller-skating."

"I'm sorry." I wince, cringe, and shrink at the same time, as if my entire body is trying to condense into a literal ball of shame. "I'm so sorry. I didn't mean to, like, baby you."

"Really, it's fine. People do it constantly." He single-shoulder shrugs. "To be fair, my orthopedist would probably not be thrilled either, but I'll be careful. I'm decent on skates. I taped my knees and stuff too."

"What's that mean?"

"It's called KT Tape. Like duct tape to help support your joints. I'll show you sometime." He smiles and leans his good shoulder against mine as he finishes up tucking in his laces. "Wait! I didn't mean, like, *show you*. Fully unintentional creepiness."

I can feel the heat in my cheeks rise at the implication. As I watch those around us, I know that the odds of Connor staying around much longer are narrowing as we approach the final five. I hope Mom gives Ray a fair chance, but it's all Brad, Brad, Brad. And if things get too far with Charles, I'll have to come clean about my growing feelings for Connor.

Mom's unpredictable, and I have no idea what the producers have been whispering to her. The postponed-by-sewage Sweetheart Ceremony is tomorrow. This could be our last genuine time together without everyone else in our faces.

The real me in my real life would never do this, so there must be some kind of magic to this show. I turn to Connor, not caring that I'm wearing a microphone and they might blast this out to all of America at some point. This is my life, and it's not always going to be a production. "Listen, Connor. I like you. Like . . . I like-like you. I guess you must have figured that out by now, but I just . . . wanted to say it."

"That's so many likes," he says, pretending to swoon before growing serious again. "I'm just kidding around." He smiles. "I like you too."

"I might have, uh, had a crush on you from the first time you were introduced and spilled the beans to the producers."

"Is that why they've been obsessed with whether I think you're pretty? Which, not gonna lie, was a little creepy in the beginning when I was just looking at you as a potential stepsister."

I laugh, thinking back to my original reservations. "Yeah, I've already gone down that particular rabbit hole. Not to mention that my parents' divorce made me swear off relationships for all eternity." Okay, maybe not *eternity*. It's not so much that the magic of love is gone. It's just that after seeing Mom so devastated by Dad's affair, I know the difference between being enchanted and being bewitched. "But it must count as juicy drama because Venti was practically drooling over the idea that I might like you."

"We're the forbidden romance?"

I squeeze his hand. "Yes, but Dingeldein doesn't have the same ring to it as Montague, so don't get too full of yourself, Romeo."

"Should we tell our parents?" Connor asks.

"I don't think so. For all I know, Mom will have a meltdown over it and send you home in the next round."

"But we can't let them become a thing either. That would be too weird. Do you think my dad has a shot?"

I shake my head. "I don't know anymore. Things are still really awkward with my mom. So, we'll just have to play it cool until we can't anymore."

"You're the evil mastermind," he jokes. "I'll leave it up to you."

Together, we step over the rubber threshold onto the rink proper, attuning ourselves to our skates. Madyson teeters along a few feet in front of us, bending her knees and throwing her arms out at the first sign of danger. A sheen of sweat glistens on her forehead. "I can do this," she chants. "I can do this."

"We probably shouldn't spend too much longer together," Connor notes. "The others are going to wonder if you don't mingle. You're the star."

"That's a good point. I guess I'll start ignoring you now?"

"Sounds like a plan. I should go anyway. My dad is a disaster in regular shoes, never mind ones with wheels on them."

I skate away, annoyed that we have to sneak around to avoid

making everyone jealous or disrupting whatever social balance the producers are going for. The last thing I want to do is give them a reason to start turning Mom against Connor and Charles.

I try to stay visible and blend in, literally making rounds around the rink. After pacing me for a few minutes, Ella and her father, AJ, gravitate toward the wall. I stay in the center of the outer ring, watching the disco ball spin to life above us. Mom and a gaggle of suitors are clustered on the opposite side, poking fun at Cole and Charles, who can't skate more than three inches without face-planting or grabbing on to each other.

Connor is helping Grady, who is surprisingly steady for his age. Grady's laugh is pure joy as he watches Cole go sliding across the floor. "Daddy! You fell AGAIN!"

Much to my chagrin, Brad and Chelsea both know how to hold their own on skates, though they're nowhere near as proficient as I am. I smirk at them as I pass, skating backward or dancing in time with the flow of the music. There's an unusual concentration of slow songs and love ballads, but this *is* a show about romance.

"I think I'm getting it!" Madyson exclaims, clopping forward. She's stomping on the stationary wheels more than actually skating, but it's progress.

"Want me to spin you?"

"No! Yes! Just do it before I change my mind!"

I grab on to her hands and pull her into a tight spin. She howls and crushes my fingers, squeezing her eyes closed.

Meanwhile, Ian is attempting to capture our conversations without interrupting our movements. He relocates from the center of the rink to the carpeted area, popping up from behind the wall at random like a demented gopher.

Sabrina is probably the weakest skater and the youngest, so I snatch her up as I pass, whizzing her for half a lap before setting her back down. "I never did get to tell you that you're a genius for coming up with the hide-and-seek excuse when we got caught."

"I didn't want you to get in trouble with your mom."

I almost ask about hers before I recall Mom's first jog with Ray when he mentioned that he's a widower. "Thanks. You really saved my butt."

She nods, as though this is a very serious discussion. "I did. But only because you're nice."

I pick up the pace again as I follow Ella, who seems to have found her stride. I suppose it shouldn't surprise me that a gymnast has good balance. I try to avoid focusing directly on Connor in such a congested area where someone might notice.

Plus, I'm just enjoying the speed. I never realized how much I missed this. Dad's hockey team used to have a free skate after the matches were finished. We'd bat around the hockey ball, play tag, challenge each other to races. I watch Mom rounding the far corner with ease, her feet crossing at the apex. I wonder if she's thinking about those days too.

Suddenly, her right ankle catches on the front of her left skate, and she tumbles, slamming her knee down first, then her elbow. She rolls with the impact, landing on her side by the glass-enclosed announcer's booth in the corner. I'd feel better if she just cried, but she lets out a high-pitched, wounded mewling instead.

I rush over, afraid to touch her and make it worse. "What hurts the most?" She doesn't answer. "Mommy? Mommy?"

"I thought you were mad at me," she croaks, her throat bobbing as tears stream from her eyes. Her breath is shallow and rapid, her fingers bent into claws against the fabric of her jeans. "Is this karma?"

I manage to force out a laugh that sounds far too cheery for the circumstances. "I'm not mad at you anymore. I can't be mad at you when you're hurt." I crouch over her, absorbing her pale face, her lips drawn taut in pain.

Ian is the first member of the crew to reach us. He sets his camera on the ground—of course, it's still filming—and slides to his knees on the polished surface of the rink. "Should I call an ambulance?" He takes out his cell phone, his thumb hovering by the red emergency button.

"No!" Mom shouts, causing him to recoil. "No ambulance. No hospitals. I'm fine. I just need to get these skates off and take it easy for the rest of the day."

Sam's feet slap against the wooden floor as he sprints over, his arms pumping in uncoordinated swings. He hurls himself onto the ground beside Mom, bowling Ian over with his momentum. "Julia, my God, are you all right? You went down like a ton of bricks."

I lean in close for privacy, covering the side of my mouth with my hand. "Mom, if this is about not having insurance, the show will pay for it. Are you sure you don't need a doctor? That was a really hard fall."

"I'm fine," Mom insists, holding her hands aloft like a toddler. "I just need help getting . . . vertical."

I don't know where Tall and Grande are, but Venti hustles over—the only time I've ever seen him move at anyone else's pace—with his phone to his ear, finishing up the last of an address. "Excellent." To us, he adds, "There's an ambulance on the way."

Mom lets out a cry that might be for the ambulance or might be for the pain. "I don't need that. It's unnecessary."

"You're getting checked out," Venti says in a voice that's final. For once, we agree. "Can someone go outside to meet the ambulance?"

Madyson and Edgar volunteer to go while Ella and AJ help the rink staff secure the doors open in case a stretcher has to come in. Charles has the foresight to take off Mom's skates while Connor gets her shoes from the skate counter.

"I really just think I need to sit up," Mom repeats.

Connor sets her shoes down, locking eyes with me and leaving the offer open to come closer. I drift over inch by inch until we're almost touching again. I don't need to talk to him. I just need him to be here with me.

Ray is easily the largest of the remaining bunch. He scoops Mom into his arms, her head lolling against his chest as he adjusts her weight. She prods his arm. "If you wanted to snuggle, you didn't have to break my leg."

"It's broken?" I gasp, chewing on my knuckle. I think of all the autumn races she's going to miss. The annual Spooky Sprint Marathon and costume party. The Pumpkin Patch 10k. "Oh, man. This is bad. You *do* need a doctor."

"No, it's not really," Mom says, panting each word as Ray sets her down on the nearest bench. "I was exaggerating."

Sam, poor unathletic Sam, dashes to the concession stand, his arms lashing about like a scarecrow in a storm. He runs into the kitchen area and snatches a bag of cotton candy off the spinning rack, tearing the end apart with his teeth. Cotton candy explodes in a pinkish vortex as he empties the bag and fills it with ice from the drink dispenser.

"Here," Sam rasps, catching up to us and pressing the improvised ice pack into my hand. "And there's ibuprofen in the glove box of the van too!" He takes off out the front door, fumbling with the keys at his belt.

I watch this scene unfold with a mixture of fascination and pity. He reminds me a bit of the discombobulated chicken scampering across the cemetery. "I don't think Sam does well under pressure."

Mom snorts. "What would ever give you that idea?"

chapter twenty-four

Mom is a horrible patient. Whenever I'm sick or injured, she won't stop fussing, to the point that I took to calling her "Smother Mother" when I had the flu. But now, when her kneecap is purple and swollen to the size of a baseball, she accuses me of worrying too much.

"There's nothing that they'd do at the doctor's except for what I've already done," she says, jiggling her ice pack and nestling deeper into her pillows. "I have water. I have ibuprofen. The EMTs said I was fine."

I resist the urge to adjust her blankets or fiddle with the thermostat. I can't imagine that she isn't cold from all that ice. "On a scale of one to that time you stepped on a sewing needle, how much does it hurt?"

"Two point five," she replies. "I've been through childbirth, you know. I think I'll survive bumping my knee." A little more gently, she adds, "Go to bed. I'll yell if I need anything."

"Don't go anywhere without me," I command, rising to my feet as smoothly as I can to avoid jostling her leg. "I'll come help you if you need to go to the bathroom."

Mom gestures to the headless mop handle that she's been

using as a makeshift cane. "I'll manage. The farthest I'm going is to sit outside and get a little air. Maybe have a drink."

"Okay. Fine. Try to get some rest." I leave the door cracked to allow in some of the ambient light from the fixture by the pool.

Back in my room, I let down my hair and burrow into the covers. I'm comfortable enough to drift off into a half sleep, but not enough to prevent the occasional worry about Mom from filtering across my psyche.

What if her knee is seriously injured and we're not able to continue filming? What happens if filming is delayed and it's time to go back to school?

I groan and flip my pillow over to get to the cold side.

"What are you doing here?" I hear Mom ask from outside. "It's late."

I leap out of bed and rush to the window, nearly smacking my face against the glass in my haste. I scan the grass and the pool area, but I can't see anyone approaching. "If it's Brad, I swear I'm going to go off," I mutter, forgetting that my room is bugged. As soon as Mom fell, he vanished like a squeamish rubbernecker.

My shoulders relax as I recognize the low rumble of Sam's voice. "I had some last-minute stuff to wrap up for tomorrow. I saw you sitting out here. Figured I'd come check in on you. How's the leg?"

"I've been better," Mom admits. "Nothing a little ice won't fix."

"The ice on your knee or the ice in your bourbon?"

Mom giggles. "I think you know the answer to that."

I pad across the house in my bare socks and tuck my body into a corner of the kitchen where I can hear and see. Mom has dragged one of the pool chairs underneath the overhang, which she should *not* be doing with an injured leg. Sam is sitting beside her on the concrete, his knees pulled up to his chest.

They remind me a bit of me and Vanessa hanging out in the walkway outside of our apartments. No games or phones. Just the two of us, companionable and happy. "It's such a gorgeous night out," Sam observes. "I live in Pittsburgh, so I'm not used to it being so dark at night. It's amazing how much you can see."

Mom eases off her flip-flops and slides down in the chair to stare at the few stars that aren't washed out by the bright lights. "I wish I knew some of the constellations, but they all look the same to me. The only one I can pick out is the Big Dipper."

"The Big Dipper is actually part of another constellation," Sam says, sipping at a bottle of grape soda. "It's not one all by itself."

"Really? I never knew that."

Sam shrugs. "I like trivia. They have games every night at this café back home. I have no life, so I'm there all the time."

"Don't worry. My life is pretty boring too. Being on television is probably the most interesting thing to ever happen to me. Or Cara."

"Are you glad you came on the show?"

Mom swirls her drink, the ice clinking together in her glass. "I'm just here for the free booze." She takes a swig. "Just kidding. I'm having fun so far, but it's also been harder than I ever expected. What about you? What made you want to work on the show?"

"I don't have the credentials to be picky, honestly," Sam replies. "It was either this or a real estate show. I'm still making connections to get better gigs. Ian helped me with this one."

"He seems . . . very . . . angry."

"Yeah, he's like a moody teenager. He's a good guy, though. I knew that the first time I met him, even though he was yelling at me for moving his coat."

"I wish I had a better people instinct." Mom sighs. "My ex is a real winner. I'm terrified that I'm going to screw it up again this time."

Sam shakes his head. "I bet you my ex is worse than your ex. I got asked for a divorce via text message on our four-year wedding anniversary."

I bite my knuckle to keep from laughing out loud. Sam doesn't know what kind of contest he just created. A competition *and* bashing my dad? Mom won't be able to resist.

"No way is your ex worse than mine," Mom says. "Let me tell you about this time that we took Cara to Maine in the middle of winter. Rick is all 'We have an SUV, and we'll be fine in the snow,' but it was coming down like you wouldn't believe and . . ."

I creep back to my bed and close the window until all I hear is the faint murmur of their conversation. Just before I fall asleep, the sound of Mom's laughter filters through the window. It's genuine, and breathless, and bordering on hysterical.

I can't remember the last time I heard her laugh like that with anyone but me.

As soon as I hear Mom's alarm in the morning, I jump into bed with her, folding my legs beneath me. She sits back against the headboard, quirking a brow and stretching through a prolonged yawn. "You're up early." There's a note of suspicion in her voice.

"You have a crush on Sam," I gush. "I heard you out there last night giggling and talking about stars like the biggest dorks on Planet Dork."

Her face burns redder than a chameleon on a fire hydrant. She pinches the pudge at my waistline. "You little eavesdropper!"

I notice that she hasn't denied it yet.

I draw an invisible banner in the air with my hands. "I can see it now. 'Star of Dating Show Falls in Forbidden Love with Production Assistant.'"

"Stop," Mom wails, tossing a blanket over my head. "It's none of your business."

I fight my way free. "Oh, it is so my business. I flew across the country to be involved in your dating life. I reserve the right to make any and all jokes."

Normally, I'd be more cautious knowing that everyone is listening, but the producers have never seemed to care about my interactions with Connor, which is probably against some kind of rule.

"Even if I did theoretically have a crush on Sam, it would never work out. The people in charge of the show didn't waste all this time and effort to watch me pick a crew member." Mom massages her injured knee like a worry stone.

"Yeah, but you don't want to end up with some jerk like Brad for the rest of your life."

Mom pushes at her blankets with her good foot. "I don't want to talk about this anymore."

A sickened chill scrapes down my spine as the truth washes over me. I feel it in my gut, as heavy and wrong as a long-carried secret. I sit up straight and square myself in front of her. She won't meet my eyes. "Look at me," I whisper. "I don't want you to end up with someone awful just because you feel like you have to for viewers to like you."

"I wouldn't do something like that." She might be able to fool anyone else, but I can hear the hesitation lacing her words.

Anger surges through me when I realize that this was never a fair fight. Mom didn't care about the silly contests or group dates. The evidence against Chelsea might as well have not existed. "That's why you don't want to get rid of Brad." I think about his swagger, the possessive way he touches her. "You know that it's the most dramatic. The best show. Or that, I don't know, he's the . . ." I growl in frustration. "You're not doing it for love, Mom. You're not doing it for happiness."

Mom lurches forward and grabs my shoulders with such force that I yelp in surprise. My heart thrums in my chest, quick and wild. "Brad might not be the best of them, but there won't be any surprises with him. I know what kind of man he is. He's very supportive of expanding the gym into a chain."

"It's not worth the cost." I mean it. I don't care if I need to defer college for a couple of years or beg Vanessa to get me that job as a line cook.

"That's not just your call to make."

Time to try a different tack. "But then I'm stuck with Chelsea. You know she's horrible even if you won't admit it. She'll probably burn our house—apartment, whatever—to the ground."

"It won't be for that long," Mom insists. "She's almost eighteen. You're both seniors this year. Sure, in the beginning, I didn't understand why the producers were always asking me about Brad. But after we got to talking, there's more to him than meets the eye. You'll just have to trust me."

It's jarring to realize that I don't, not about this. I hate that she has an answer to all my protests. It means that during those quiet moments when I caught her staring off into space or fiddling with the catch of her bracelet, she was contemplating this moment, this unraveling of her intentional ignorance.

"Mom." I latch on to her with both arms, squeezing my hands against her shoulder blades, smelling the sweet florals of her perfume. "You're not for sale."

The warmth of her tears spreads across my skin.

And I hold her. I hold on for us.

chapter twenty-five

Before I can cajole Mom into fully admitting her feelings for Sam, he's standing in our kitchen with two brown paper bags and a jug of extra-pulp orange juice. I stifle a laugh at his off-white polo with the thick burgundy collar, the red-and-gray argyle socks peeking out above his dress shoes. As much as he fusses over our wardrobes with Angela, it appears he doesn't care much for the fashionableness of his own.

"Good morning," Mom says, rising up on her good leg to grab two cups from the shelf above the sink. The coffee grinder whirs to life, dumping the grounds into a special measuring device that Mom fits into the cappuccino machine. "Sam, do you want coffee? It took long enough, but I finally figured out how to use this thing without shooting espresso across the counter."

"Sure." He upends the paper bags, shaking out a selection of labeled breakfast sandwiches, fruit, and a container of hard-boiled eggs. "Breakfast is canceled because there's a special event tonight. You're quarantined to the house until one of us comes to fetch you."

"We're grounded," Mom jokes, passing me a cappuccino with extra cane sugar and an unsweetened one to Sam. He opens the silver sugar dish and spoons in a heaping lump. When he stirs, I can hear the granules scraping against the bottom of the cup.

"What kind of special event?" I ask, reaching for a bacon-egg-and-cheese sandwich.

"I can't tell you much, but suffice it to say that you might find the vote tonight to be a lot easier than expected."

"Good," Mom quips, tapping out a drumroll on the countertop. "Because . . . DUM DUM DUM DUM!" She throws her arms up in the air, tossing her head back dramatically. "The moment of truth is here."

"What moment is that?" I ask.

"We're down to our short list of favorites," she says, unclipping the photo sheet from the magnet on the fridge and sliding it toward me. It's been revised and changed and updated so many times that it's barely legible. "Cole and Grady. AJ and Ella. Brad and Chelsea. Edgar and Madyson. Ray and Sabrina. Connor and Charles."

"Tonight, you'll be picking who goes to the final five," Sam pronounces with reverence. "It's a significant landmark for the show, too. This is when things start to get serious. There could be a ring in your future, Julia."

I don't like the sound of that. Sam goes on to remind us about the possibility of an official televised wedding, all-expenses paid. I'm sure the branding opportunities from that alone would be ridiculous. I picture Dad and LeAnne having to come to Mom's celebrity wedding, and it almost makes it worth it.

After breakfast, Sam leaves us to enjoy a quiet afternoon away from mandatory activities and the wear of forced social interaction. Mom and I kick back on the couch, sharing a bag of white cheddar cauliflower chips that I consider to be the least offensive of her health food snacks. "It was so sweet of Sam to bring us breakfast," I prompt, winking at her. "Such a nice guy, am I right?"

"You're shameless," Mom says, taking the bag back and shaking the cheesy crumbs at the bottom into her mouth. "I never really connected much with Edgar or AJ. I think my first pick to go home is Edgar. But aren't you really hitting it off with Madyson?"

"Not really," I admit, especially if sending her home protects Connor. "I just took her side because Chelsea's horrible."

"Not this again." She groans. "The smartest thing to do is choose Brad. I know he'll propose, and he's so supportive of growing the business. He sees the value in me. He challenges me to be better. And looking at the others, I don't know. Ray is too caught up on his late wife. Cole is too . . . young for me. Or acts that way, anyway. Charles is nice, but there aren't exactly fireworks. Brad and I understand each other. We both want to succeed."

"You think you understand each other. What a glowing declaration of love, Mom. I mean, that's the stuff of Valentine's Day movies right there." I roll my eyes until my nerves burn from the strain. "How are you even so sure that Brad wants to marry you?"

"He told me so."

"He did?" I snap, gritting my teeth so hard that my ears hurt. "Ugh, I hate that guy!" I tuck my legs underneath me and pivot to face Mom. "Seriously, you deserve to be with someone who makes you happy. And I know you like Sam. He's considerate and funny and nice. I mean, he was so worried about you when you fell that I thought he was going to vomit everywhere."

"You know," Mom says, chewing on her lip, "I loved your dad like in those Valentine's Day movies. From the first time I met him, I just wanted us to be together, always. And we all know how that worked out. So maybe, instead of going after the handsome prince, it's time to take a good hard look at Gaston."

I stab a cheese-covered finger at her. "Don't let Dad ruin this for you. There's a reason this show is called *Second Chance Romance* and not *Second Chance I-Guess-You'll-Do*."

"That's the sequel," she says, chuckling.

"Would you just acknowledge that you like Sam?"

She sighs. "Fine. I do like Sam. You're right that he's kind and he makes me laugh. But that's not all there is to a marriage or being a parent. And that's not the point of this show. I'm supposed to be considering the contestants. *They've* been vetted as potential matches, not the staff."

It's a start. "But if you met them somewhere else, like just in town, would you pick Sam over Brad?"

"There's no point in talking about hypotheticals that will never happen."

One of Mom's favorite conversational strategies is deflection-and-avoidance, but I won't be deterred. Not about this. "If you could!" I insist.

She crumples the empty bag of chips into a ball of foil. "Yes. Is that what you want to hear? If I could, I would pick Sam. But I can't. And I don't want to discuss this again."

"Okay." I know when I've pushed hard enough. I kiss her on the forehead. "I'll give you some time to think about your actions, young lady," I say in my best imitation of her. "Don't forget that we're supposed to be ready by five o'clock."

While Mom is zoning out and breaking the world record for how long you can stare without blinking, I sort through my dresses and coordinating accessories to choose an outfit for Angela to approve later. I scurry between my room and the bathroom, modeling them in the mirror until I decide on a black cocktail dress with a beaded halter that crisscrosses in the front. It's versatile enough to blend into a myriad of environments, which I'll need given the mystery of our event this evening.

When I check the living room again, Mom is still hunched over the couch with her palms pressed to her eyes. Her shoulders tremble as she takes a shaking breath. I walk behind her, leaning over to rub the hard knots at the base of her neck. "It's going to work out," I tell her. "We'll land on our feet."

"Will we, though?" she mumbles. "What if I choose wrong?"

Her self-doubt is reassuring. Maybe she is hearing me after all.

"What do you always tell me when I'm upset about Dad?" I ask, thinking of all the days I came home from Dad and LeAnne's custody weekend with snotty tissues in my pockets.

Mom nods and takes another deep breath. "Don't ever let them see you cry."

chapter twenty-six

*A*lthough Sam warned us that selection for the final five is a big deal, I wasn't expecting to find such a commotion at the main house. When we enter, Danny Romano and the producers are chatting at the entrance to the hallway that leads to the library. That's the first clue that this isn't an ordinary activity. Aside from when he's hosting a Sweetheart Ceremony, Danny Romano is hardly ever here.

He falls into step beside us, herding us into the correct positions for Ian to film. It's easy to tell when Danny Romano is speaking to the audience through us because his voice deepens and slows as he enunciates each word. "This is a special event that we've been planning to help you pick the final five," he explains, gesturing to the foyer, where ten women wait in dresses varying from rigidly formal to cringeworthy in their casualness. "Tonight, instead of joining the contestants for dinner, you will be dining with their former spouses. This is your opportunity to find out more about their personal histories from the women who know them best."

I've developed a sixth sense for when Ian is filming just me, so I don't voice the questions pinballing around my brain. I know that Ray is a widower, so maybe they sent a friend instead. But that doesn't explain the fact that there are nine women and only five contestants.

I can tell from the set of Mom's eyebrows that she's confused as well.

"Stand here, and we'll send them in," Sam whispers, leading us to the dining room entryway. "Think receiving line."

Mom pats at her hair and brushes a stray piece of lint from the fabric of her gown. I'm so used to seeing her in stilettos that she seems short in the chunky, knee-friendly pumps Angela went into town to buy. I stand to Mom's right, salivating in secret at the smell of roast beef and potatoes wafting from the table. I know I ate two plates before we got dressed, but it still seems unfair that I can't eat any of this food on camera.

The first woman to approach is a petite brunette with doelike eyes and rosebud lips. The bow on the waist of her yellow sundress flops from side to side as she skips forward in brown leather cowboy boots. "Hi," she says, hugging each of us. "I'm Amelia. Cole's ex. It's so nice to meet y'all."

"Nice to meet you, too," I say, glancing down. "I love your boots."

"Aw." She presses a hand to her heart. "Aren't you sweet?"

I do a double take as the next woman steps up to replace her. For a split second, I wonder if they're twins. But upon closer inspection, Amelia's nose was less aquiline, her hair the slightest shade darker. "I'm Emily," the woman says, shaking Mom's hand. "Cole's second ex-wife. We'll be coming through in order to keep it simple for ya."

"There's more?" Mom asks, incredulous.

"Aw, honey." Emily nods. "There's five of us, and we all look like sisters. It's kind of a joke back home."

"Five wives?" Mom mutters through her teeth as she stands aside for Emily to pass and join the buffet line. "What is he, Henry the Eighth?"

I narrow my eyes, attempting to block out the procession of women before me and replace it with my world history classroom. "Does that make you Anne Boleyn?" I ask Mom. I used to know this. It was on a test. "No, wait. Anne of Cleves."

"I think his last wife was a Catherine."

"I'm pretty sure it was an Anne. That's going to drive me up the wall." Before the next woman can reach us, I sidle off camera and flag down Sam. "Hey, quick question. Who was Henry the Eighth's sixth wife?"

He looks to me and Mom, then Ian, bewildered. "Catherine Parr. Why?"

"Damn," I mumble. "She was right."

Mom gloats. "Told you so."

After three more of Cole's ex-wives, I can tell just from looking at the next woman that she isn't here for him. Between her riot of natural red hair and dark hazel eyes, she looks nothing like the others we've met so far. Her wrists and fingers are dripping with turquoise jewelry set in thick bands of silver. They complement the cerulean swirls on her long-sleeve bohemian dress. "I'm Lydia," she says, shaking our hands, her rings cold against my palm. "Ray's sister-in-law."

I can't think of an appropriate response. I'm too focused on reconciling the person in front of me with what I know of Ray and Sabrina. Lydia must interpret our silence as mistrust. "Don't worry. I was very close to my sister, and I know all the juicy gossip."

I have trouble making eye contact with Madyson's and Ella's mothers, knowing that they must be curious about how their daughters stack up in the rankings. But no matter what I think, Mom's obsession with Brad makes it impossible to know who else is actually at the top.

When I meet Connor's mom, Kathy, I have to acknowledge the hard truth that he could be leaving soon. Mom seems to get along with Charles, but I don't know what happens when she's on group dates or having a drink with a suitor. When I imagined being here, I thought she'd tell me everything.

With a slight gasp, I realize that I wouldn't even know how to get in touch with Connor if he disappeared right this moment. Would the producers tell me his phone number? Would an internet search suffice? How many Dingeldeins can there be?

The producers must have saved the worst for last because the final guest is Brad's ex-wife, the woman we met at the audition in Pittsburgh. "Julia," she says, the word clipped and precise. She makes no move to shake Mom's hand or give her a hug. Instead, she runs her eyes from Mom's neat chignon down to her simple shoes with a floral buckle across the toe.

"I'm sorry, I didn't get your name." Mom's voice pitches higher as a blush floods into her cheeks.

"I'm Margaret. Chelsea's mother." She's the first to introduce herself as a mother rather than as a former spouse. I don't blame her. I wouldn't want to be associated with Brad either.

I can tell where Chelsea gets her style from. Margaret looks stunning in a black-and-tan shift dress that would hang like an old sack on anyone else. A matching cashmere cape is draped over her shoulders, the tassels brushing against her wrists.

When she moves, her ice-blond hair remains frozen in place like the plastic wigs on Lego figurines. I stare at it in fascinated confusion. I know that physicists claim there are only three states of matter, but they've never seen this woman's hair before.

"It's a pleasure," Mom says.

Margaret ignores me entirely and picks up a dinner plate. She holds a piece of roast beef by a pair of tongs, watching the sauce drip back into the tray. "Is it?"

I resist the urge to drop a scoop of scalloped potatoes down the back of her dress as I join the line behind her. I almost make a snide comment to Mom about having Margaret in the extended family, but she looks traumatized enough as it is. "It's not you," I reassure her. "She's just jealous because she wanted to be the star, remember?"

Since we're the last to be seated, we don't have a choice except to sit in the open chairs at the center of the table. It's a tight fit thanks to Cole's ridiculous number of ex-wives.

It's basically an extremely uncomfortable, slightly murderous dinner party.

"This is some house." Amelia tips her head back to trace the supports of the pergola above us. She tuts and sends the whisper of a whistle through her teeth. "I'm surprised y'all let Cole live here. What a slob."

The rest of Cole's ex-wives giggle along in a knowing way. It's a strange effect, the five look-alikes all making the same merry, girlish laugh. I concentrate on my green beans to have somewhere else to focus my eyes.

Margaret props an elbow on the table and points at Mom with her fork. "So, Julia, how would you feel knowing that you're just the most recent girl in a long line of"—she swivels the fork to point at Cole's ex-wives—"that?"

I scoot my chair a few inches back in case any of them feel the need to start throwing food or utensils across the table. Amelia plasters a bright smile on her face and turns to address Margaret. "Well, bless your heart." She looks at the fellow exes seated on either side of her. "Do I detect a hint of jealousy, ladies?"

Lydia finishes chewing a mouthful of potatoes. "You know what my favorite part of being an aunt is? I take so much enjoyment in helping to raise my niece, Sabrina, that I don't have to be a shriveled-up, crotchety hag who puts others down to make me feel better about myself."

Sam attempts to step forward, probably to remind Lydia not to eat, but Venti stops him. The drama is too good.

"Isn't there some essential oil you should be mixing for your tie-dye tarot-reading party?" Margaret drawls.

Mom opens her mouth to defuse the situation, but I smack her thigh under the table and shake my head. I can't, in good conscience, let my sweet mother jump into the middle of this conversational bloodbath. Plus, Cole's ex-wives and Sabrina's aunt can clearly hold their own.

"Julia, what do you do for a living?" Emily asks. Or at least I think it's Emily. One of Cole's other ex-wives. That's safer. "We don't know anything about you."

Mom releases the breath she's been holding. "I'm a personal trainer. I own a little boutique gym up in Ohio."

"A gym?" Amelia nods appreciatively. "No wonder you look so fantastic. I should really exercise more."

Their conversation sparks a round of introductions and short biographies. I'm relieved to hear that Cole's ex-wives at least have different occupations. I sneak a peek at Connor's mom while mine is grilling Lydia about what it's like to be a professional glass-blower. I can see what Connor meant about both of his parents having an even keel to an almost annoying extent.

Before long, everyone is dishing out secrets and stories about the contestants. From what I can tell, Margaret is the only one holding a grudge about either her divorce or her rejection as the star of the show. "I hope you know that Brad will want a prenup," she sneers. "In case that affects your decision."

"Ray couldn't care less about money," Lydia says, dunking a

chunk of oversized cookie into her coffee. "But he also learned a hard lesson about appreciating what you have when you have it. And that you can't buy the things you really want the most."

"What was she like? Sabrina's mom." I ask just loud enough for her to hear. "I know Ray misses her a lot."

Lydia gives me an appraising look. "My sister loved those two. She thought the sun rose and set by Sabrina. She was all about family, all the time. Ray's the same way. That's part of the reason he's a teacher. He wanted the summers off to go on road trips."

"I'd love that." The words are out of my mouth before I can consider their weight. They're true, though. I picture myself in the back seat of Mom's car, Sabrina sitting on the far side behind Ray.

My mind takes the four of us on a nationwide tour, like changing the backdrops in a photo booth. I see us standing at the Grand Canyon. The Golden Gate Bridge. Niagara Falls.

I wait until the next lull in the conversation to turn to Connor's mom, Kathy. "Hi. Um, I just wanted to say hi because I've been hanging out with Connor a lot."

"That's wonderful," she replies, looking genuinely pleased. "I was curious to see how Connor would bond with a potential stepsister."

For just a moment, and that's all it takes, my face shifts out of its neutral, smiling expression to something approaching discomfort.

Kathy must have a good read because she lifts her chin slightly, saying, "Or is this something different?"

"We just get along really well," I say, trying and failing to deflect. I'm going to have to ask Mom for lessons.

I feel eyes on me and turn around to see Sam hovering in the doorway of the dining room. "I'm supposed to take you to your next activity," he explains when Mom waves him over.

We exchange puzzled glances. "But there's nothing on the schedule except for the Sweetheart Ceremony," Mom says. "I checked before we left." Conspiratorially, she adds in a whisper, "I wouldn't have had so much wine if I'd known I had to do something else besides the vote."

Sam shuffles his feet. "Sorry. Like I said, this is kind of a secret."

We say our goodbyes to the other women and follow Sam across the house to a nondescript door that I always thought led to a closet. I bark out a laugh as Sam opens it, and I realize that it *is* probably a closet. But like every other room in this house, it's about three times larger than it needs to be.

It's the Confessionals Room for the contestants. But instead of just the camera directly across from us on the wall, there's also a screen that, judging by the sawdust on the floor, is a new addition.

I fidget with the slippery fabric of my dress, which, combined with the plasticky surface of the sofa, makes it impossible to sit upright without sliding. "Don't hate me," Sam begs, his knuckles white around the remote in his fist. "I couldn't tell you. It's my job not to tell you."

Mom leans forward to rub his upper arm. "I couldn't hate you, Sam. I know that you can't tell us everything. We forgive you."

He looks at me next. "Do you?"

"I forgive you," I promise, even though I don't know what he's done.

Sam clicks the remote and watches as the screen displays a shaking camera feed that must belong to Ian. It stabilizes as he stops moving, focusing on the sprawl of the luxurious foyer. "It's your turn," Sam whispers.

I watch in muted horror as Dad and LeAnne walk through the front door.

Confessional: What. The. Actual. [BLEEP]. Is. Happening.

chapter twenty-seven

I can tell that Dad is unnerved by the cameras, but LeAnne is in her element. When they introduce her to the contestants, she flashes a coy grin at the assembled suitors and giggles her way down the line, planting little air-kisses next to each of their ears. I think she's had her teeth whitened for the show.

"Mom, she's drooling all over your boyfriends," I joke, attempting to lighten the mood.

Mom rolls her eyes. "Nothing she hasn't done before."

The contestants move through the buffet line and assemble on the patio where we usually eat our breakfast. The meal seems cozier with just the eight of them, instead of the twelve that we had at our farce of a dinner. LeAnne claps her hands together. "So, what do you guys want to know about Julia?"

I don't take it as a good sign that she's leaving me out of it. She wouldn't hesitate to sabotage Mom, but I know that Dad would stop her from maligning me too much.

Madyson's father, Edgar, is the first one to ask a question. "I feel like all of us are trying to put our best foot forward," he explains, earning nods from the others around the table. "But we all have our flaws. What would you say is Julia's worst trait?"

"Rude," I mutter. "No brownie points for you."

But Dad doesn't miss a beat, almost as though he's been waiting for this particular question. "She's so high-maintenance." He sighs, his face drooping into a long-suffering frown. "I just got tired of the constant stream of new clothes and designer shoes. I hope that all of you have fat salaries because she's not a cheap date by any stretch."

"That's crap!" I yell at the screen, recalling a particularly animated argument about a pair of high-dollar orthotic inserts for Mom's upcoming triathlon. "The only designer clothes Mom has are for races. You can't wear garbage to an ultra-marathon. It'll disintegrate!"

But the contestants have only ever seen us in our television wardrobes. They don't know that it's a lie. My eyes scrape over LeAnne's homely dress and Dad's plain button-down shirt. They look like they're going to get their taxes done. We look like Lady Gaga's backup dancers.

"And she takes forever to get ready to go anywhere," LeAnne adds. "Total princess."

Mom's hands bend in the air around an invisible neck. She grinds her teeth, fuming and spitting substitute profanities under her breath. "I can't believe that stuck-up flippin' witch has the nerve to call me a princess. Home-wrecking little . . . If I had a free pass from the cops on one fistfight . . . I swear . . ."

As the dinner draws on, I watch as Mom's fury morphs into despondency. She gnaws on the edge of her thumbnail, her eyebrows knitted together over the bridge of her nose.

"I love jogging with Julia," Ray gushes to Dad. "She says that you and your wife are runners too. It's nice to have something in common, isn't it?"

LeAnne looks at him like it isn't nice at all. "Yeah, we love working out." She rubs Dad's shoulder. "Rick and I met at the gym."

"'Rick and I met at the gym,'" I parrot, pretending to toss my hair around. "I love how she doesn't mention that it's our family gym and Dad was married. She makes it sound like they just bumped into each other and fell in love."

"Oh, I'm sure they bumped into each other," Mom mutters.

By the time the dinner is over, Mom has dissolved into a puddle of tears, tulle, and expensive mascara. I hand her off to Sam, who flashes me a guilty smile as he steers her toward the nearest bathroom.

I stalk across the house to the dining area, hoping to confront Dad before he can be whisked away to the airport. Two of the producers are lingering in the foyer watching the contestants ascend the stairs. Venti spots me and waves me over. "I just sent the guys to change for the Sweetheart Ceremony. How long do you think you'll need to get ready?"

I completely forgot about it. "Listen, we can't do a vote tonight. My mom is really upset. She needs to get some rest."

"That's the best time to do a vote!" he replies, grinning. "The tears. The drama."

I puff up to my full height of nothing-foot-nothing and plant both hands on my hips. "No. We're not doing it. You can't make us."

Confessional: My head is spinning with everything that happened tonight. I don't even know how I'm going to sort myself out for this Sweetheart Ceremony. I'll be heartbroken if Connor leaves, but I have to protect my mom, too.

As far as Sweetheart Ceremonies go, this one is over as soon as it starts. There's no fanfare or lengthy introduction. Even Danny Romano seems uncomfortable with the sheer level of Mom's distress. Her makeup has smeared across her face and the backs of her hands. She can't even speak to tell me who she wants to throw off.

I lock eyes with Connor, who holds my gaze for a moment before looking back at Mom, his jaw tight. I hold up the cheat sheet with the pictures, and she points to Cole and Grady. When it's time to close the locket, Mom pushes the doors with a little too much force, almost knocking their portrait off the wall entirely.

"Cole and Grady, you have been selected for elimination," Danny Romano intones. "Please say your goodbyes to Julia and Cara."

Cole's lip wobbles as he meets his son in the center of the room. They step toward us, Cole's face taut with a forced smile.

"Cole," Mom says, holding one of his hands in both of hers as she attempts to compose herself. "You are such a sweet soul. I love your energy and your sense of humor. But I have to admit that I was shocked when I found out you have five ex-wives. You've never shared that before, and sharing is important to me. That's why I decided to vote you off tonight."

"I'm sorry, Miss Julia." Cole blubbers through a verbose apology, dipping to plant a kiss across Mom's knuckles. He throws his arm around me next, almost knocking me into Grady, who gives me a hug around the waist. "It was so wonderful to meet y'all."

I wave goodbye, but my heart isn't in it. Cole was always entertaining, but I knew Mom wouldn't want to be with someone with his chaotic energy.

As the contestants begin to disperse, Venti sidles over in that slithery way of his when he has an agenda and he doesn't care if I know it. "What now?" I ask, a slight whine to my voice.

He points toward the door. "I just thought you might want to say goodbye to your father and stepmother before they leave."

"I can talk to them?" I say, incredulous.

Venti makes a shooing motion.

I shove past him and out the front door, Ian and his crew jogging after me. I catch up to Dad and LeAnne as they approach the same idling silver sedan that Sam used to pick us up from the airport.

Dad notices me first, slipping his hands free of his pockets to spread his arms wide. I don't hug him. He's lucky I don't take the free shot to clock him in the mouth. "Hey!" he says. "They told us we weren't allowed to see you. We just had dinner with the guys."

"I know," I whisper, clinging to the last vestiges of self-control I possess. "I was watching."

"I don't get a hug?" he asks, reaching for me.

I wrench my arm free of his grip, raking my nails across his skin. "Don't touch me. I don't want to hug you. I don't want anything to do with you. I just thought I'd tell you that face-to-face. You betrayed Mom. You made her look horrible."

"Come on, Cara," Dad admonishes. "Don't be like that."

As I stare at him, I feel the beginnings of true rage, an all-consuming ire and wrath that builds in me until my hands begin to shake with the effort of containing it. I want to hurt him like he's hurt us. I didn't know pain could feel like this. It splinters. It aches. It feels like grief.

"I never loved you as much as I love Mom," I spit at him, savoring the venom in my voice.

LeAnne steps forward to defend Dad, but he pushes in front of her. "We can talk about this when you come home. Maybe we should just leave it tonight before you say something you're going to regret."

Ian almost breaks his ankle trying to get in between us without literally getting in between us.

"Dad. Look at me, Dad." I slow my breathing, letting a cold

peace settle within. I want my next words to follow him forever. Everyone always says that the truth sets you free, but it makes cages, too. "When the judge asked me who I wanted to live with, I didn't even want you to have your crummy three weeks after Christmas. I was afraid I'd miss Mom too much."

I rip off my high heels and throw them into the bushes, tearing my hair loose with my other hand. The camera hovering in my peripheral vision hardly registers. For once, I want to look how I feel. Vengeful. Feral.

Dad picks up my shoes and tries to return them to me. "This is about me and your mother, not you."

I scoff at his weak apology. "You know what the best thing is about being on this show? I get to pick my own dad this time. Because I sure as hell wouldn't have ever picked you."

chapter twenty-eight

Mom falls through the doorway of the guesthouse and plops facedown on the couch with her feet dangling over the armrest. I run to her, cradling her against me and kissing the top of her head. "Mom. Mom. Don't cry."

"How could he do this to me?" she sobs against my stomach. "We were together for twenty years. And he leaves me for that vulture and then humiliates me like this."

"LeAnne's awful. She probably made him do it because she's jealous of you." When I don't get a response, I add, "She runs eighteen-minute miles."

Mom sniffles and opens one of her eyes. "You're just saying that because I'm upset."

"Mom, you're so beautiful and smart and funny that you've had over a dozen guys acting like complete jackasses trying to get your attention."

"I don't even want him back," she mumbles. "It's not like that. I just feel like he owes me more than cheating on me and then ruining my only prospect of taking care of you."

I groan. Not this again. "How many times do I have to tell you that you don't need to take care of me?"

She shakes her head as much as she can within the confines of the cushions. "I do. I'm your mom."

Before I can reply, Sam comes waddling through the door with an armful of plastic bags and sets them on the kitchenette counter. He starts trying to kick out Ian's crew. "You have your shots. Get lost."

"Dude, this is the good stuff," Ian hisses, swatting Sam away as he steadies the camera.

Sam walks over to stand behind the couch, his fingers digging into the back of it. "You can't film if I'm in the way."

Ian lets out an impressive slew of insults but eventually relents, leaving the three of us alone.

"I brought you something," Sam says, rattling around in the silverware drawer.

"Is it a time machine?" Mom asks. "I can go back in time and refuse to fall for my ex's bullshit."

I bop the top of her head, scowling at the crunch of hair spray beneath my palm. "Oh, thanks, way to un-birth me from existence."

"I didn't mean it like that."

"I know."

Sam appears in front of Mom with a pint of rocky road, a can of whipped cream, and a shaker of sprinkles balanced in the crook of his arm. "I got some chocolate and a frozen pizza, too. Oh, and I stole a bottle of cabernet from the lounge."

Mom sits up and pivots to face him, her cheeks mushed up to keep from crying. She eyes Ian's retreating form through the glass wall. "Aren't your bosses going to be mad that you threw out the big camera?"

Now it's Sam's turn to look pained. "I can, uh, look the other way. Just this once."

She doesn't argue. "How did you know that I love rocky road ice cream?"

He turns sideways to show the tablet stuffed into the waistband of his pants. "You wrote that it was your favorite junk food on the personality questionnaire. I just happened to remember because it was my grandfather's favorite."

Mom pounces on the ice cream, shoveling it into her mouth like a sweetened anesthetic. She grinds the cold almonds between her teeth, the tears streaming along the wet lines made by the melting ice cream at the corners of her mouth.

Sam offers her a napkin. "I don't know what to say. I'm so sorry."

Mom sets down the half-empty container, watching the condensation form a pool on the surface of the coffee table. Her hands are shaking as she rubs at her eyes. When she lowers them, they're smeared in makeup again, but she doesn't seem to mind. "I feel a little better now. Thank you."

"Good," Sam says, propping his tablet against the silver fruit bowl. "You need something to keep your mind off of it. How about a movie or an episode of something? I have a pretty decent collection of shows I've worked on."

Mom looks at me and shrugs. "Movie night, Cara?"

"As long as we won't get in trouble." The producers are pretty strict about the no-media thing, and I'm not sure that it's wise to push them this soon after the Great Sock Debacle. But if Sam says it's okay, then it must be. "Sure."

Mom sits up and draws the blanket from the back of the couch around her shoulders. "How long will it take to make the pizza?"

Two hours later, I look up from the latest episode of *High*

Steaks Chef to find Mom and Sam asleep beneath the blanket, their foreheads knocked against each other's. The bottle of wine beside Sam's tablet is mostly gone, along with the box of pecan turtles, the ice cream, and the meat lover's pizza.

I clean up as quietly as I can, tossing the leftovers in the fridge and the grease-stained napkins into the garbage. I turn off Sam's tablet to preserve the battery and tuck it into his messenger bag. I want so badly to send Vanessa an email, but I can't take advantage like that. Sighing, I figure that the dirty dishes can wait until tomorrow. I don't think there's a quiet way to wash them.

I change in my closet and snuggle into bed, hoping that Mom will come to her senses soon. Despite the calamity surrounding dinner, I could tell that we both enjoyed having a simple night at home with Sam, listening to him improvise a behind-the-scenes narration to the cooking show we chose from his library.

One of the pitfalls of living in a private Floridian mansion is that we can do things here that we wouldn't be able to afford back home. It's easy to make friends or fall in love in paradise. But the night we just had with Sam could be re-created anywhere, anytime, with any budget.

I cling to that optimism, using it to fight off the residual anger and disappointment that seeps into my mind every time I think of Dad. I stay awake for so long unraveling the knot of my emotions that I need to go to the bathroom again. It must be all the water I drank to balance the saltiness of the pepperoni.

I pad across the house, navigating by the thin strip of light filtering from beneath the bathroom door. I laugh under my breath. It seems that no matter where we go, we will always need to use the facilities at the same time.

I lean against the wall for a few minutes, but I don't hear the toilet flush or the low hum of her bizarre sonic toothbrush. I rap my knuckles against the door, assuming that she left the light on when she went to bed. "Mom?"

There's no answer, and the knob isn't locked, so I push inside, immediately regretting my decision. Mom and Sam, thankfully both dressed, are squashed inside the boxy shower stall, making out like two drunk suckerfish. I let out an appalled shriek of surprise before I remember the microphones in the rest of the house.

Mom throws Sam away from her. He stumbles through the glass door, catching himself against the counter. "Oh no," he gasps, smacking a hand over his mouth like it's something obscene. "We thought you were asleep."

"As happy as I am about this development," I say, gesturing between the two of them, "I really need to pee. If you could, you know, maybe get out."

They scurry into the living room like naughty teenagers caught upstairs at a house party. "Well, this is backward," I mutter to myself, laughing.

This time, when I go to bed, I fall asleep in seconds.

chapter twenty-nine

*T*he only thing more awkward than catching my mom making out with Sam is knowing that our dirty laundry has been aired, hung, and waved around on television. Breakfast at the house is especially odd because we're the only ones around. No Ian. No Sam. No contestants. No one to even tell us why.

"Should we talk about last night?" Mom asks. "Like, on a scale of one to that time 'Santa' forgot to fill up your stocking, how bad of a parent am I?"

I shrug. "Even though that was absolutely horrifying, I'm happy with the outcome. I like Sam. He's nice." I glance over my shoulder in time to see Venti cresting the hill with a couple of assistants. "Here comes trouble."

"Danny Romano is coming out to talk to you in a moment," he says to Mom as the assistants rearrange a table with two chairs at a more advantageous spot on the breakfast patio. "Would you mind moving over there?"

Mom hunches her back as she stands while trying to finish her coffee. "Sure. What's going on?"

I look around for Sam to clue me in, but he isn't anywhere in sight. Instead, Danny Romano emerges through the dining room, shedding his suit jacket and tie onto the back of a chair. Ian follows, actively filming and pawing the threshold with one foot to find the slight step down without tripping.

Venti holds out an arm to stop me as I try to move over toward Mom. Danny Romano takes a seat, pulling his chair a bit closer to adjust the angle. He sits forward, his emotionless mask morphing into concern with a flick of his eyebrows and a tug at his lips. "Julia, I have to be honest. This has been a tough morning for all of us."

"What do you mean? Is everything okay?" She picks at the decorative hole in the front of her distressed jeans, plucking apart the white, undyed strings. "I was worried when no one came out to eat breakfast."

"Well, the contestants are concerned about some recent developments."

"Like, because of the visit from Rick and LeAnne?" Mom asks.

I don't know if she's playing coy or she really doesn't see this torpedo coming at her. I knew things were too easy. Most people in the house believe Chelsea sabotaged Madyson and almost flooded the guesthouse. Connor and I admitted we like each other. There isn't enough drama anymore, so I get the impression they're about to make some.

"After the emotional night you had yesterday, Brad thought he would come check on you and offer a shoulder to cry on. But when he went down to the guesthouse, he saw something unexpected—you, the star of our show, spending time with a member of production instead of the contestants. According to Brad, the longer he watched, the worse it became.

"Obviously, we had to look into an allegation of that nature. That's when we discovered that there's also been fraternization between the two of you. The contestants are devastated."

"They know?" Mom's voice is small.

"Brad felt it was only fair to tell the others."

Of course he did. On the bright side, maybe this will finally convince Mom that Brad isn't all he makes himself out to be. "We've assembled everyone in the lobby. We think it would be a good idea for you to talk it out with them, maybe apologize," Danny Romano adds.

Mom sighs. "It's not like I planned it or anything."

"Don't tell me; tell them."

Danny Romano leads us into the lounge, where everyone is already assembled, clumped around the main seating area where there are enough brown leather couches to accommodate all of us. The contestants are dressed up too much to look completely casual, so it's clear that they were warned ahead of time.

Tall and Grande hover in the doorway to the galley kitchen. There's still no sign of Sam. Mom and I step closer together on instinct.

I look to Connor for some cue. He just stares at me, eyes bulging, as though he's straining to beam me a telepathic message. My heartbeat picks up when he starts shaking his head. This isn't going to be good.

Danny Romano takes both of us by the arm and directs us to a couch that someone pulled out to face the contestants. We sit on the end opposite Danny Romano as Ian's crew finds strategic places to film.

I glance down at my bland T-shirt and jeans. I never thought of my makeup and gowns as armor before, but in this moment, I miss them both.

"Julia, we asked you to come here for this unscheduled emergency meeting to let you talk through some recent developments with the contestants," Danny Romano says. "It's been incredible to see how your relationships have grown with these amazing men and their children. But we just learned that you were spotted socializing inappropriately with a member of our production team. There are a lot of hurt feelings in this room. Is there anything you'd like to say about that?"

Mom actually looks at the closest window like she might just pop it open and leap into the shrubbery outside.

"It was my fault," I blurt, earning a bewildered look from Venti and Danny Romano. It's taken this long, but I've finally caught them off guard. "Mom was so upset last night when she heard that Dad and LeAnne had been putting her down. She really cares about all of you, and she wasn't sure whether you believed it."

I scan their faces, wondering whether this is working. Connor nods in silent encouragement. I look only at him and pretend that this is just any other conversation.

"We know we're not supposed to hang out with Sam, but he's always been around helping us. He just seemed like the right person to turn to at the time."

Danny Romano fixates on Mom again. "Julia, does this sound like what happened? Why don't you tell us your side?"

"I was confused and upset," she says, her voice wobbling. "My ex turned all our friends against me after our divorce. He told the neighbors horrible things. They went to court and made me sound like an unfit mother." She breaks into tears, not even bothering to cover her face as she ugly-cries. "I'm sorry. I just couldn't stand feeling like it was happening again and you'd all think I'm this awful person."

Brad makes a cooing noise at Mom that is downright alarming, like a T. rex opening its mouth and having a cute puppy squeak come out. But his roar isn't far behind. He looks at Danny Romano. "What's being done about this staff member? Sam?"

"Well, first of all, Sam would also like to apologize for his behavior." Danny Romano makes a gesture at Tall and Grande, who disappear into the lobby for a moment, then return with an ashen-faced Sam. "Here he is."

Sam, unaccustomed to being in the spotlight as an on-camera figure, stammers through a short apology. The too-wide legs of his trousers ripple from the shaking of his knees. "I ab-abused my job to take advantage of J-Julia."

Mom gasps, her features contorting from compassion to indignation. "No, Sam, that's ridiculous. You didn't take advantage of anything."

Danny Romano continues on as if she'd never spoken. "Sam, we're going to give you a chance to say goodbye to Julia and Cara. Do you have any final words?"

Mom jolts. "Final words?"

"It's us or him," AJ calls out. I glance at Ella, who lifts her shoulders an inch in an apologetic shrug. Her father continues. "It's not fair if we don't even know who our competitors are. Even if it was a mistake, he shouldn't be allowed to stay."

"I agree," Chelsea says, folding her arms and sitting back, as though the decision has anything to do with her.

"Julia," Sam begins as he steps forward. His voice is hoarse and raw, his hair mussed as though he's been running his fingers through it at random angles. "Nothing should have happened between us in the first place. I mean, I don't know what I was thinking."

He gestures down at his baggy khakis and frayed cuffs, the scars across the tops of his shoes from standing on his toes so often to see around equipment. "I'm not right for you. It wasn't appropriate. You were upset, and I shouldn't have let you break the rules when you were in that state of mind."

"No, no, you didn't at all," Mom pleads, rising to her feet and ignoring Danny Romano's attempts to get her to sit back down.

She takes his hands in hers. "You can't go. I don't want you to lose your job because of my actions."

"Please don't feel sorry for me," Sam says. "I got to come to this beautiful town and meet such wonderful people and work at a job where every day felt like a dream. And that was before I saw you for the first time in that airport."

I try to herd them closer to each other, with logic, if not physically. I don't care if we incite a riot. I can't just let Sam walk out of here like he's nothing to us. "You guys can still be together! It's just a stupid show. You have your whole lives outside of here."

But they don't listen.

I watch as some semblance of acceptance bleeds across Mom's face. Her expression hardens into a familiar mask, the same poise that carried her through mediation, divorce court, and custody assessments.

Sam lets go of one of Mom's hands to grab one of mine. He squeezes it, his eyes misting over. "I'll watch the rest when it airs on television. Surprise me, okay?" His smile is small and sad and private. "Wherever I am, I'll be rooting for you. Bye, now."

There have only been a few moments in my life when I've been able to sense potential futures diverging before me, as though the Fates were dangling threads above my head like a child taunting a kitten. One was the day Dad left, hearing the *thump* of Mom's body hitting the floor as she fell to her knees in front of the picture window. Today is another.

"Why do I feel like we're always watching people leave?" I whisper, not really expecting an answer. My Belgian waffle from earlier is a concrete Frisbee in my stomach.

"It's not you." Mom dashes away a tear with the hem of her blouse. "It's me. I'm just leave-able, Cara. I'm like a temporary tattoo. A disposable fork." Although she remains rooted to the same

240

spot, there isn't a single static muscle in her body. The faint twitches become tremors, then trembles.

"This is outrageous," Madyson's father, Edgar, calls out. He steps around the couch to get closer to Danny Romano. "I didn't come all the way here to compete for a woman who isn't even available."

"We should let her speak," Charles interjects after conferring for a moment with Connor. "I think most of us can sympathize with having an ex that makes our emotions run a little high."

"That's an excellent suggestion." Danny Romano manages to get us all back in our seats. "Let's just talk this through one at a time, gentlemen. Edgar, do you want to go first?"

"Yeah, I do. I left my job to come here, and now I find out she's screwing around with some producer?"

"Dad!" Madyson whispers. "Stop it!"

AJ seizes the interruption to speak up again. "Julia was upset. Sam was the producer. He should have made the rules clear. That's not Julia's fault."

Danny Romano holds up a hand for silence. "Julia, there's a lot of tension right now, as we can all see. I'm sure you can understand why this must be frustrating for Edgar."

"I do, and I said I'm sorry, but that doesn't make it Sam's fault." Her chest heaves, both hands smacking against her thighs. "I thought of Sam just like I'd think of any other contestant. That was wrong of me. It was a poor decision in a moment of weakness."

But even with Danny Romano trying to tactfully referee, Edgar just keeps doubling down. "How am I supposed to believe anything you say? You're obviously not trustworthy. And your ex said that you're just here to marry for money anyway."

Mom huffs. "That's not fair at all. You've spent all this time with me, and you're still going to agree with my ex-husband without even thinking he might be a wee bit biased?" She pinches her thumb and index finger together in the air.

"Did you sleep with that guy?" Edgar demands.

"Whoa, whoa, whoa." Venti steps into view of the camera, hands waving. "We have minors in the room. If you want to go there, we can, but you have to let us get the kids out of here first."

Edgar rolls his eyes. "Sounds like Julia *already went there*."

You know what? The producers want drama? I'll give them drama.

I stomp out of the lounge and over to the wall of lockets, where I find Edgar and Madyson's heart hanging in the corner. I take the whole thing off the wall, waddle back into the lounge, and throw it on the floor. It barely splinters. I pick it up again—it's heavier than it looks—and hurl it toward the empty corner. It breaks against the wall and flops open, revealing half of Edgar's face. "YOU WANT TO CALL MY MOM A BAD PERSON AND A LIAR? WELL, THEN, CONSIDER THIS YOUR SWEETHEART CEREMONY AND GET THE FUCK OUT."

Confessional: Maybe I overreacted just a smidge.

The producers seem to know better than to try to get us to do much after that whole fiasco. The contestants haven't had breakfast, so they eat on the patio while Mom sits on the far side in a lone chair, drinking a mimosa and talking it over with Brad, who of course took the first opportunity to "comfort" Mom.

A bunch of us crowd around to eavesdrop. I grab a chair and sit just inside the dining room door, my presence obscured enough by the patio doors to be hidden without it seeming deliberate.

"I feel like you misrepresented things and misled me," Brad says. "I thought we had something. I'd shared with you about my dreams for the future. I thought you were on board with that. You never told me there was someone else."

"I just feel like that's implied in this kind of show. I'm supposed to have options, but you're putting all this pressure on me to choose you. And it's not like I meant for anything to happen with Sam. It just did."

Brad sighs. "It's not just that I want you to choose me. It's also that I want to know my competition. How was I to know that you were seeing a member of the production staff in an inappropriate way?"

"It wasn't ongoing. It was a spur-of-the-moment thing."

Chelsea arrives a moment later and gives Mom a hug, putting her face square into the camera. "I'm sorry you're sad, but we'll help make it better. We love you."

Since her villain routine isn't working, I guess Chelsea is going for honey now. I can't take any more of this.

I retreat to the lower level where Ella, Connor, and Sabrina have already commandeered the main seating area. I join Connor on the sofa, leaning against the armrest and staring at the floor. I'm still reeling from the suddenness and severity of Sam's dismissal, unable to talk about this morning and unwilling to talk about anything else.

After sitting in silence for almost ten minutes, Sabrina says, "Can I ask something?"

Ella sits up to hear her better.

I shrug. "Sure."

Sabrina points at the ceiling, her brows pressed together in that serious look young children often have when confronted with a complicated problem. "What happened with that man up there?"

I don't know if it's her phrasing or the tenor of her voice or the sheer innocence of the question, but the rest of us start giggling, our laughter building until I'm on my side, one hand clutching my stomach. Connor is bent over beside me, silently shaking, his hair flopping into his face.

"You don't have to laugh at me like that," Sabrina murmurs. "It was just a question."

Ella recovers first. "No, no, it's not like that. We just needed to let it out. We're not making fun of you."

It occurs to me then that I screamed the f-word and Hulk-smashed a gigantic gaudy locket against the floor of a mega mansion while a small child watched. I sit up and walk her through the whole thing in the simplest terms I can, ending with an apology if I scared her.

"It was a little scary."

"Do you want a hug?" I hold out my arms. "Would that make it better?"

She runs over and smacks against my chest, nodding. Ella and Connor lean over her, wrapping her up in love. Maybe, even without Sam here, I'll be okay after all.

chapter thirty

*T*he next morning, my arms are still sore from throwing that stupid heart locket. The producers wiped our schedule yesterday to get more one-on-one eavesdropping, as it seemed like every remaining suitor needed to have some extended dialogue with Mom in the lounge.

I didn't escape unscathed either. I went for a walk with Ray to talk about what had happened, then sat through hours of filming Confessionals that felt more like interrogations. By the time I managed to meet up with Connor at our late lunch, I was too exhausted to do more than pick at my fried chicken.

I thought today would be round two, so I'm especially excited to learn that we're going to spend the day out in town with the contestants in a less-structured group date. I was starting to feel like the spoiled house pet that digs under the fence and runs away anyway. Despite flying across the country to be here, I haven't experienced much of my surroundings besides the cemetery and the ill-fated excursion to the skating rink.

And it means more time with Connor, which is becoming more and more valuable as we near tonight's double elimination leading into the final two. I know Charles can't compete with Ray and

Brad. Our time together is coming to a close, and I'm still not sure how to feel about it.

"It would be nice to de-stress a little before we leave," Connor admits at breakfast. "The past few days have been ridiculous. Even my dad is tuned up, and that just . . . doesn't happen."

"At least he's not making a fool out of himself," I mutter, watching Ray and AJ grow progressively angrier that Brad and Chelsea are doing their best to hog Mom.

He shakes his head, mirroring my thoughts. "Do you think it's possible to really fall in love on a show like this?"

I keep waiting for someone to barge in and yell at us for referencing the show, but they must be too preoccupied watching AJ and Brad bicker in the corner. "I don't know. I'm sure it's possible. It just seems like the show makes it hard to get to know anyone." It's like with me and Connor. Some days, we feel so close. Others, it's like I have to fight to catch a glimpse of him on the way to makeup or a Confessional. I wish it didn't have to be this way.

Connor holds my hand under the table while he waits for me to finish my coffee. There's not a huge point in hiding our feelings anymore when he's on the verge of going home. Even if, by some miracle, Mom wanted to keep Charles around for the final two, we'd have to come clean and tell her about us. "I don't want you to go," I admit. "I've been dreading it."

"You'll still have your mom and Ray and Sabrina around."

"It won't be the same."

He wiggles his fingers in between mine. "Even if I end up getting sent home tonight, I'll be waiting for you on the other side."

"That makes it sound like you're going into some alternate dimension."

Connor snorts. "Yeah, it's called real life, and boy, do I miss it."

At least the producers are trying to give us a relief valve. I think this day trip is just the producers recognizing that we're

246

wiped. Without some actual fun, how are we supposed to connect after something as dramatic as Sam's departure?

I also realize in retrospect that I could have been kinder to Madyson. It wasn't her fault that her dad was being an asshole. Maybe we'll be able to get in touch somehow after I get home. If anyone knows to never underestimate the power of the internet, it's me.

Instead of donning formalwear, we choose from among our meager selection of casual clothes. I rip the tags off some new shorts and pair them with a sleeveless white blouse to keep me cool in the heat. I packed mostly heels for the show, but Mom has an extra pair of comfortable sandals that she lets me borrow. "Do you think we'll go to the beach?" I ask. "Should I bring a bathing suit?"

"I think we're just exploring downtown."

This is when I would usually pester Sam for extra details. I permit myself a single second to miss him, siphoning off my sadness in bite-sized pieces before it drowns me. It does little to alleviate the pressure throbbing behind my eyes, like attempting to drain a lake through a straw.

I'm not usually so fickle, but I know, with Sam out of the picture, that Ray is my last hope. He doesn't have the arresting beauty or physique of the other contestants, but he's kind and steady, the Honda Civic of eligible bachelors. Most importantly, he's not Brad.

"So, uh, are you looking forward to more time with Ray?" I ask Mom as we finish packing her purse full of toiletries. Sunblock, hand sanitizer. Her "mom swag," as she calls it.

She shrugs. "Yeah. We enjoy each other's company." Her tone suggests that she isn't in the mood for another anti-Brad campaign.

"I'm just excited to get out of the house. It's still a vacation, remember?"

But it doesn't feel like it anymore, and I know that Mom can sense it too. "I have to accept that Sam is gone," she says out of the blue. "I know you don't like Brad, but I do have feelings for him. It's not love, but there are feelings."

"Mom, he's never going to love you. He's only going to love the version of you that he makes for himself. Just promise me that you'll think really hard about that today."

"I will."

We meet the contestants on the front lawn when the worst heat of the day has passed. The downtown isn't terribly far, so we decide to walk rather than cram into the vans, where there's a nonzero possibility of being impaled by a piece of recording equipment.

It's evident from the offset that this is peak tourist season for the island. We turn onto the main street, where stores, restaurants, and bars line the curb across from the busy central square. "Are we going to eat while we're here?" Ella says, ignoring the stores and focusing on the menus posted on the walls outside the various eateries. "They have seafood!"

"I'll eat anything except perch," I reply. After seventeen years of living by Lake Erie, I have reached my lifetime quota of perch. And that's significant, since I'd probably eat a sneaker if it was dipped in batter and fried. At least with the sneaker, I wouldn't get stabbed in the mouth by fifty million microscopic fish bones.

Ray nods at the far end of the street. "It looks less crowded over there. We'll probably have better luck finding a table for"—he points his finger at each of us in turn—"ten, plus space for the crew."

"Wow, Ray, what a great idea." I nudge Mom. "Isn't Ray supersmart?"

She smacks my elbow. "Stop it."

"You're so subtle," Connor jokes, leaning over as we fall to the back of the group. He kisses my cheek. "It's adorable."

Confessional: CONNOR DINGELDEIN KISSED MY CHEEK. HE THINKS I'M ADORABLE. WHAT AM I GOING TO DO WHEN HE GOES HOME? CAN'T I JUST HIDE HIM SOMEWHERE IN THE MANSION?

Tall hurries over, his face obscured by the brim of a massive sun hat. "We've got reservations already in about half an hour."

"Are you guys going to eat too?" I ask Ian, glancing at his entourage of support staff.

He shakes his head, waving his hand in front of my face like a magician. "You don't see us. We do not exist."

While an assistant jogs ahead to verify that the restaurant has been set up appropriately, we kill time by popping into the few stores that aren't too overwhelmed by other patrons. There's one shop dedicated entirely to old-fashioned candy and specialty pop. Ray laughs and holds up a bottle with a pig on the front. "This one is supposed to taste like bacon." He spins it around to read the label. "I wonder what's in the ingredients."

Brad grimaces. "That's disgusting."

The rest of us aren't as discerning. Connor buys a miniature tin of sour candy in the shape of a nuclear waste barrel. He eats one and can't open his eyes for the next three minutes.

"Are you okay?" I ask, rubbing his shoulder as he presses his throat and gasps.

"That is . . . *sour.*"

It's fortunate that I don't have any money, or I'd be leaving with bags and bags of their peanut brittle. Ella and her father buy a container of saltwater taffy and offer to share. I've never had it before. I pick out a chocolate mint one that tastes like melted plastic mixed with used chewing gum.

"How is it?" Ella asks.

I force myself to swallow. "Interesting. Bad interesting."

Next, Chelsea drags us into a jewelry store, already badgering Brad about whether she's still accumulating her allowance during the show. Connor rolls his eyes and whispers, "My allowance is getting a place to live."

"Me too."

Mom is hunched over in the corner, her nose an inch away from the case. "What are you mooning over?" I ask, squatting to see the second row of jewelry.

She taps her nail above a tray of thin silver rings. "The one with the sand dollar. When I was a kid, we used to hunt for them when we went on vacation to Myrtle Beach. They're supposed to be good luck." She steps aside as Ian hefts the camera to capture the display. I watch him in alarm, wondering whether it's responsible to hold such a heavy object over glass.

"You should get it," I tell her. "We could use a little luck."

Mom laughs and waves away the store associate who is suddenly eyeing her with renewed interest. "I brought more than enough jewelry to wear for the rest of the show." She twists her finger where her wedding band used to sit. "Plus, it's pricey."

One of the assistants tracks us down to notify us that our tables are ready at the restaurant. We follow her as best we can, weaving around slower walkers and children clinging to their parents.

"'The Happy Hen,'" Mom reads from the giant wooden sign out front. "Seafood. Margaritas. Burgers. Sounds good to me."

"I swear to all that is holy, if they brought us to this restaurant and do not let us eat, I am going to throw a chair through a window," Connor mutters as we enter, echoing my own thoughts.

The hostess directs us to a smaller secondary dining area where two short tables have been pushed together to accommodate us. I rush to sit next to Mom before the contestants can fight over the seat, saving the one beside me for Connor. Brad moves toward the head of the table, but Ian pushes the extra chair aside to make more room for the camera.

All the adults order margaritas. The rest of us have a tropical punch that's featured on the specials board. I don't really want the drink; I'm just in it for the mini umbrella and pirate sword from the picture.

After some deliberation between the spicy chicken sandwich and the shrimp tacos, I decide on the latter, agreeing to split some with Connor in exchange for a piece of his crab cakes.

"I'll have a house salad with chicken and light ranch on the side," Mom says when it's her turn. "The grilled chicken, please. Not fried."

Brad smiles at the waitress. "Actually, we'll both have the seafood fra diavolo." He closes Mom's menu and pulls it away from her, adding, "You'll love it."

Mom hesitates. "I don't really like spicy food."

"You said yesterday that you were going to be open to my way of seeing things. Remember when we talked about being adventurous? That mindset could be life-changing for your business. Trying new food is a great way to start. If you don't like it, you don't have to order it ever again."

Ray reaches across Sabrina to try to snatch a menu back from the baffled server. "Hey, just let her order what she wants."

"The fra diavolo," Brad reiterates, shooing the waitress away with a pointed look.

Ray sucks in a deep breath and rises halfway out of his chair before Charles pushes him back down, whispering, "Just let it go. Don't make a scene."

Ian, meanwhile, is hopping around the edge of the table, giving directions to his crew with sharp nods of his head and quick hand signals. I slide over a few inches closer to the end of the table to give them space.

Over the course of the meal, the rest of us implement an unspoken strategy that involves loudly talking over Brad anytime he tries to contribute to the conversation.

I notice that Mom isn't thrilled with her seafood fra diavolo. She picks at the shrimp, rubbing it against the clean rim of her plate to scrape off the sauce. Ella must see it as well. She feigns fullness and offers Mom the remaining half of her Cobb salad wrap.

The waitress comes by with a dessert display, spinning the tray in a slow circle to showcase their extensive selection. "Are we thinking about dessert? The key lime pie is our feature. It's named for the islands, after all."

I wonder for a brief moment if Sam knows that. It sounds like a trivia question.

"Dad, can I have the brownie?" Sabrina indicates the brick-sized mass of chocolate nearest to her.

I raise my hand. "Make that two."

We corrupt Ray and Ella into joining us in our sugar binge. Chelsea follows suit. A few of the others settle for coffee or a second margarita. I catch Ian licking his lips and pass him my untouched water out of view of the camera.

Once everyone is finished eating and rotating through the restroom, we continue our aimless walk through the square. We keep a loose formation, allowing individual movement in case there's a bicyclist or a wild chicken crossing our path.

Ella finds the chickens hysterical. "I was wondering why I hear roosters all the time from my room! I thought I was imagining it. It's not like there are any farms around here."

As the sun sinks toward the horizon, more and more tourists pour from the various hotels lining the nearby blocks. The square is particularly packed, with pockets of bystanders surrounding different street performers. There's a sword-swallower standing on the steps of a gazebo, a contortionist using a bench as a prop.

"I'm in pain just watching that," Ray mutters.

I guffaw in Mom's ear. "That's so funny, Ray!"

I don't think my antics are having any effect.

"Look! An acrobat!" Sabrina shouts, pointing at another group. We cram against the outskirts of the assembled crowd, craning our necks to watch as he launches into his latest trick. Once the other tourists notice Ian's camera, they scatter to clear a path for us, some covering their faces. Ella wriggles in through a gap to reach the front row, towing her father, AJ, behind her.

The acrobat sprints toward a trash can and vaults over it just as his partner tosses two lit torches into the air from atop an enormous unicycle. He tucks his legs into a flip and catches one torch in either hand. He sticks the landing perfectly, allowing the momentum to carry him forward into a short bow.

"Dad," Ella says, mesmerized. "We should learn how to do that for competition!"

He laughs. "I don't think your coach is going to let you throw fire at each other. That sounds like a lawsuit waiting to happen."

An assistant approaches Mom, reading on a tablet that I'm fairly certain belonged to Sam. "We have to start heading back now to get ready for the Sweetheart Ceremony," she says. "The stylists will be ready in about twenty minutes."

Mom relays the message to the contestants and sets a quick pace toward the house. I hang at the back of the group with Connor. "I think maybe Mom is starting to change her tune on Brad."

"It has to help that the rest of us think he's an asshole."

"I hope you're right. I really do."

I try not to think that the next time I see Connor, I could be saying goodbye.

chapter thirty-one

*T*he makeup artist heaves the sigh of a long-suffering eaves-dropper as Mom and I bicker through our entire preparation period before the vote. I'm so flustered that the dusting of pale blush on my cheeks doesn't make a discernible difference. "I know you haven't connected with AJ and Ella as much, but at least AJ sticks up for you. Brad doesn't treat you with any respect at all. He wouldn't even let you order your own food."

Mom scowls, making eye contact in the opposing mirrors of our cosmetic stations. She turns her head to project her voice over her shoulder, earning an irritated rebuke from the stylist. "Okay. You have a point. Maybe the food thing was a little over the top."

I talk faster as I sense her resistance waning. "Can you imagine how he'd be if you were married? He'd take over. If you can't get him to listen to what you want to eat, what makes you think he'll care about your opinion when it's important?"

"It'll be different when it's just the two of us," she insists. "Competition brings out the worst in people.

"You also have to remember that there's no guarantee anyone else wants to be with me. I know with one-hundred-percent certainty that Brad will propose if he's the final contestant. AJ and

Charles and Ray are wild cards. Isn't it better to take a sure thing over a gamble?"

"No, not when it comes to this. God, it's so stupid that you can't propose. That would make this so much easier."

Mom shrugs. "Tradition."

We only have a few minutes before we're due up at the main house. I spring out of my chair the moment my makeup is done and fling both of our dresses over the portable privacy screen. Mom follows with our shoes and accessories. "You have to understand that choosing a lifelong partner is a bigger decision than having to tolerate less than a year of living with a stepsister, depending on when we set the wedding." She shimmies out of her casualwear and into her gown. "My vote should carry more weight."

In my anger, I practically leap into my dress and jam it over my chest. Mom helps me with my zipper and waits for me to reciprocate. She sucks in a breath as I cinch the ribbon of her decorative corset. She spins for Angela's approval.

I can tell from Mom's tortured expression that she isn't going to budge easily, but it's not impossible. It's time to tote out the big guns. "I need you to do this for me, Mom. I don't want Brad and Chelsea in our lives. All through the divorce, I stuck by you. I supported you. I need you to support me now and believe me when I say that they're dangerous."

Mom groans. "How can I argue when you put it like that?"

"You can't. You're defenseless." I slide my lower lip into a pout, blinking at her innocently. "Please, Mommy. For me. I won't interfere with the final vote if you get rid of Brad. That can be all your decision. *Please*." Even if she picks Charles, we could sort it out. But I can't sort this, handing so much sway over our lives to Brad.

She toys with a stray piece of hair, scowling when she realizes it's an inch too short to tuck behind her ear. "I don't know. I'm just so convinced that Brad is going to be the best choice for us."

"And I'm so convinced he's not! You have to get rid of him. I haven't groveled like this since I wanted you to let me go to the midnight showing of *Endgame*."

"Let me think about it while we head up," she says, turning toward the door. "We should go. You know how cranky they get when we're late."

I sense that more pleading isn't going to have an effect, so I remain silent for the short trek up the hill. Mom's hand rises to her mouth and falls away as she resists gnawing on her nails. "On a scale of one to LeAnne, how much do you dislike Brad?" she asks as we enter the foyer and take our position across from the contestants.

"LEANNE TIMES A THOUSAND," I shout with enough volume to make Ian jump. I guess that's a side benefit of the show. I have newfound appreciation for the fact that LeAnne is only the third most horrible *Homo sapiens* on the planet.

"Okay, so, let's say we do it your way. Who do we bring to the final two?"

"Ray and Sabrina, Charles and Connor." Because then I can tell Mom about my budding relationship with Connor, and she'll be forced to choose Ray. It's manipulative, sure, but to be fair, she hasn't made it easy to outmaneuver Brad.

"And you really, really feel strongly about this?"

I don't know how many more ways I can say *Brad sucks* unless I start learning foreign languages. "Yes. Please. Mom, I don't know what our relationship is going to look like if you marry Brad, but I promise it's not going to be good. I'm sorry. That's just how it is."

Danny Romano strides across the room, flipping his tie into a knot. "Have you settled on who you're voting off?"

Mom squeezes her eyes closed. "Brad and AJ. We're getting rid of Brad and AJ."

I throw my arms around her, hugging her as hard as I dare with her boobs already dangerously close to exploding out of her dress.

"Don't get too excited," she warns. "Danny Romano is talking to the producers, and they don't look happy."

"I don't care."

Grande and Venti return with Danny Romano, keeping their backs to the contestants as they drift into the room. Venti explains their concerns about eliminating Brad and Chelsea. "We all think that the very clear conflict between the four of you makes great television. I'd love to see that tension continue until the final vote."

I scoff. "Are you telling us that we're not allowed to vote him off?"

"We're not telling you what to do," Grande clarifies. "We just wanted to make our thoughts known while you still have time to reconsider your options."

Forget about my options. I'm reconsidering my life choices. I could have refused to participate in the show in the first place. I'd be at home right now in my lazy pants, probably lamenting Mom's latest tofu casserole as my worst problem.

I watch Mom as the crew runs through their last-minute checks. She taps one heel against the ground like a metronome. "Are you chickening out?" I ask.

She shakes her head, but I'm not sure whether to interpret that as an answer or as a general sign of her indecision. Before I can pry further into her thoughts, Danny Romano clears his throat, and the room quiets.

I fake a smile, my top lip curling a bit as I show my teeth. I'm suddenly aware of how much my muscles ache from the stress of parading around on a constant stage. I haven't relaxed in weeks knowing that there's a camera watching me even when I'm asleep.

I grab Mom's hand as we near the end of Danny Romano's introduction. I try to convey all my emotions through that fleeting touch.

Danny Romano's giddiness is evident in his voice, the excited way he asks, "Julia and Cara, who have you chosen for tonight's elimination?" He squares off on Ian's camera. "And remember, folks, that the two remaining contestants will proceed to the final, where Julia will choose her *Second Chance* sweetheart."

Mom's fingers ghost along the edge of Brad and Chelsea's locket. A vindictive, sour joy slices through me as Chelsea meets my eyes across the room. I mentally parse the right words for when we hug goodbye, something pithy that still manages to convey my eternal loathing for her constant passive-aggression, the Nair, the lying. She didn't win. Mom came through for me.

Chelsea's head jerks back, tilting to the right, then the left.

I lift my gaze to the Wall of Hearts just as Danny Romano announces, "AJ and Ella, you have been selected for elimination. Please say your goodbyes to Julia and Cara."

Okay. Starting off easy. I get it.

I give Ella a long parting hug, promising to look her up online. "I'm really sorry that you have to go."

She sniffles against my hair. "That's all right. I didn't want to come on the show in the first place, remember?" Her laugh is a humorless rasp. "I hope you don't end up with Chelsea. You're an awesome person. You deserve better than that."

AJ opts for a handshake that becomes a hug anyway.

And then it's the moment of truth. I can't wait to catch up with Connor after this and get a better play-by-play of Brad's reaction.

"Julia, who have you chosen to follow AJ and Ella?" Danny Romano asks. Even though there are only three sets of contestants left, he doesn't need to work too hard to keep the tension up. Chelsea actually looks worried, for once.

Mom returns to the wall. She pauses, her head hanging low. MOTHER, DON'T YOU EVEN—

Both of her hands dart out simultaneously and close the locket for Charles and Connor. Her palms linger against the wood.

It would take a frame-by-frame replay to determine which of us reacts first.

"I veto!" I yell in the producers' general direction. "I veto! That's not what we decided!"

"Ah, it looks like there was some disagreement on this decision," Danny Romano remarks. "Unfortunately, these selections are final. That's why it's so important for Julia and Cara to trust each other, and it matters who is actually closing the lockets during the Sweetheart Ceremony."

Connor rushes past Charles. I run to him and hold him close, wondering whether I will ever see him again. "I didn't know," I whisper. "I'm sorry. It was supposed to be Brad."

"There's nothing you can do about it now." Connor smiles past the tears welling in his eyes, like an errant streak of sun shining through a storm. He speaks faster and faster, clearly unsure whether they're going to pull us apart. "I think we both knew I couldn't win. I'll see you again. We'll talk as soon as you're out of here, okay? Just remember that the rules aren't as strict as you think they are. Brad and Chelsea don't color inside the lines. Why should you?"

I nod repeatedly, not trusting myself to speak. Mom and Charles wait off to our left, both clearly perplexed.

"I'm not a contestant anymore, right?" Connor asks Danny Romano.

"You are no longer in the running."

Connor raises a hand to cradle my cheek. "Before I go, do you think I could get a dramatic reality TV kiss? Just one?"

I would normally balk at kissing in front of my mother, a bunch of relative strangers, and dozens of cameras. But seeing Connor standing there, and not knowing how long it could be until I see him again, if ever . . . I don't care about propriety anymore. It isn't a peck. It isn't a kiss. It isn't even a French kiss.

It's a goodbye kiss. And I kiss him with all of that hope, and longing, and wishing, and wanting. I kiss him for the days we might have had and the ones we may yet have together. My kiss is half of a promise that our next one will be hello.

Confessional: [Muffled, unintelligible sobbing]

I never paid attention before, but it takes longer than I thought for Connor and Charles to exit the house when the ceremony is over. I continue watching through the lounge window long after the assistants escort them outside. I don't turn away until I hear the rattle of the front gate closing and the bump of a car driving over the lip at the end of the driveway. "I knew it," I mutter to Mom. "I just knew you weren't going to get rid of Brad that easily. After I begged you."

"I'm sorry," she says, wringing her hands. "Once the producers got involved, I just panicked. I couldn't do it. I didn't know that you had a thing for Connor. God, I feel so clueless that I missed it. Do you hate me? Is it serious? Why didn't you tell me?"

I sigh, knowing that she only wants the best for me, but sometimes, that isn't what I need. "No, I don't hate you." I don't know what to say to her other questions. More than anything, I'm just worn out. This weariness transcends the physical, the slow thudding of my heart like the tenuous knock of an unannounced visitor. For a moment, I trace the innumerable choices that led to this present and wonder whether I ever had more than just the illusion of control over my own life. "I wish that this had all gone differently."

And part of it was my fault. I thought that I was just having fun, that Connor could be a silly summer fling. I never imagined that I might want to know more, that I'd begin to see the possibility of us. When we agreed to come on the show, all I cared about was getting enough money to start a new life. Connor made me think about what that life might actually be like. And now he's just. . . gone.

"I feel so trapped," Mom says, pinching the bridge of her nose. "I ruin everything. You're upset with me. It was my fault Sam got fired. I didn't know that apparently you had a romantic relationship with this kid. And I still don't know what I'm doing. I don't know what's wrong with me. I'm sorry."

I nod. "I know you are."

As I trudge back to the guesthouse and the allure of my bed, I'm relieved that she didn't ask me to forgive her. I don't think I have the strength to lie.

chapter thirty-two

*T*he next morning, one of the production assistants fetches us after breakfast, leading us into the lounge and closing the ornate double doors. An elderly man swimming in a double-breasted jacket watches us enter from his perch on the nearest barstool. Between his overlarge horn-rimmed glasses and the smattering of wispy fuzz around the crown of his bald head, his spindly appearance gives the impression of a newborn bird.

"Hi. I'm Julia, and this is my daughter, Cara," Mom says, stepping forward to shake his hand as he hops down from the stool. "Are you a last-minute contestant?"

He laughs and angles his head back to compensate for the humorous discrepancy between their heights. Being generous, he must be five feet tall. "Hardly. My name is Gary. I'm the jeweler."

"The jeweler?" Mom asks, stooping her shoulders and bending her knees, maybe unconsciously, as she addresses him.

"For your engagement ring," he clarifies. "Instead of designing a single ring for the show, I have several available for you to choose from. They're all in your size, but now is also a good time to ensure that the one you want fits comfortably."

I nudge Mom. "What about Mommom's diamond?"

"I gave it to LeAnne," she mutters.

"You did what?"

She shrugs. "Your dad asked for it back, and I didn't have a reason to keep it anymore. Don't worry. Part of the bargain was that you'll inherit the ring no matter what."

"I'm not sure I want it," I grumble. "It's been contaminated with LeAnne cooties."

Gary hefts an exquisite hardwood jewelry case and sets it on the antique card table by the window. He reaches into his pocket and holds up a teardrop-shaped device. "This is a loupe," he explains, flipping the magnified lens free of its cover. "Feel free to use it to take a closer look at any of the rings."

He unlatches the jewelry case and eases the hinged lid open. Mom and I almost knock our skulls together leaning over it at the same time. There are rings of every style, some plain, some adorned with colored gemstones. "I didn't expect there to be so many," Mom comments.

I bend to inspect a monstrous ring with two rows of small diamonds that wrap around the one in the center. "Do we have to decide today?"

"Yes," Gary answers, pushing the case closer. "But please, take your time. Touch them. Try them on. You won't hurt anything."

He doesn't have to tell me twice. Within seconds, I have a ring on each finger as I prance around the lounge like Marie Antoinette.

Mom giggles and picks up a round solitaire in rose gold. "The prongs on this one look like little fangs." She tilts it toward me. "Check it out."

"I see what you mean." I laugh, not because I've forgotten our quarrel, but because I don't want us to spend our last free days together in an argument. If Brad and Chelsea become part of our family, I don't know how mother-daughter time will rank in Mom's new priorities.

"That's called a double claw," Gary interjects. "I personally think that prong style looks better on the squarish shapes." He points out a few. "Princess. Radiant."

"What about this other square diamond over here?" Mom asks, resting the nail of her index finger beside a wide band covered on all sides in tiny diamonds. "It looks different from the others you just mentioned. I like it. It's unique."

The jeweler picks it up and smiles down at the center stone like it might be his favorite. "That's called an asscher. It has a different kind of faceting. You can see how it has long lines and a windmill pattern. Would you like to set that one aside?"

"Yeah, I think I would."

I step forward because I feel the need to warn this poor innocent man about my mother. "Mom takes half an hour to choose the scent of her laundry detergent. You might want to get a chair or a find a snack."

"Hey!" Mom says. "I'm not that bad."

"On a scale of one to Goldilocks, you are a nine and a half."

Over the next few minutes, she manages to accumulate seven other potential rings. The diamonds themselves are similar, at least to my untrained eye, but the settings vary from plain and petite to downright garish. She compares two of the white metals. "What's the difference between platinum and palladium?"

I waggle a finger at Gary, smiling. "I warned you. You should have gotten a snack when you had the chance."

While Mom debates between the asscher and the princess cut, I take advantage of the relative quiet in the house to meander through the halls alone. Since there are no organized activities, I assume the contestants are upstairs until I pass a rear-facing window and spot Ray in the swimming pool. They must have free time too.

I pass into the makeshift work area for the crew and production staff. Plastic folding tables dot the room, laden with laptops, paperwork, and used coffee cups. I flip through glossy, high-definition photographs of the opening ceremony, pondering why a television show needs still shots.

A cheery jingle draws my attention to the far side of the room where a small tablet is propped up on a kickstand, the screen displaying a report of some kind. I don't know what gives me the courage to do it, but before I can make a conscious decision, I've already snatched the tablet and stuffed it into my waistband.

I scamper out of the room, acting nonchalant as I parade past the stationary cameras. I hook a left into the hallway, seeking out the cramped restroom across from the library.

I check behind me before locking the door and sitting on the toilet seat cover. My hands shake with excitement as I figure out how to place a call and dial Vanessa. I never would have bothered to memorize her number, but the cell reception at the gym is so poor that I've had to call her from the landline a thousand times. Through the static, I hear, "The voice mail box of the subscriber you have reached is full. Please hang up and dial again."

I dial again. And again. And again. And again. And again. And again.

Finally, on the eighth call, she picks up. "Hello?"

"Don't hang up! It's Cara."

"What?" she shrieks. "Cara? My bad! I thought you were a telemarketer. I didn't recognize your area code. Are you okay? Didn't they take your phone?"

"They did." I turn down the volume and giggle away the lingering fear of getting in trouble. "I stole a tablet from one of the guys on the set. I miss you, Va-Ness Monster."

"I miss you too. What's wrong? You sound upset."

"Kind of," I explain. "I'm having a moral dilemma, and I need you to tell me whether or not I'm making a huge mistake."

"Okay." I hear the door of her refrigerator close, then the *crack* of a can opening. Knowing Vanessa, it's probably her second energy drink of the day. At least Mom convinced her to switch to the sugar-free version. "Shoot."

I fill her in on the game so far, along with most of the major players. "Brad and Ray are the last two left." I leave out the stuff about Connor, knowing that she'll get too distracted by my romance to worry about my life getting lit on fire by Mom marrying Brad.

"Ray doesn't sound so bad."

"He's not. But Mom's not going to pick him. She basically admitted that she's going to choose Brad no matter what because she knows that he'll want to get married, and he's supposedly supportive of her making her own business separate from Dad."

"But that isn't what you want." It's a statement, not a question. Vanessa's tone suggests that at least part of her analytical side agrees with Mom. "You'd rather have Ray."

"I'd rather have Sam, but that's never going to happen."

"Why not?"

If there's one attribute that has served Brad well, it's his boldness, his willingness to flaunt social conventions. He was the first to touch Mom, to kiss her cheek, to have a private dinner. Sam is too meek to compete. "Sam is gone already. It's not like I can hunt him down and force him to change Mom's mind."

"Not with that attitude, you won't," Vanessa points out.

"I don't even know if he's still on the island."

"Did Princess Leia say, 'Aw shucks,' and give up when the Death Star blew up Alderaan? No. Did River quit running from the government just because she had a meltdown in a bar and beat up a bunch of strangers? Also no." It isn't hard to believe that Vanessa is the debate team captain. She's really speaking my language here. "You've got to fight for the life you want."

"But I'm not Princess Leia," I protest. Still, her words remind me of Connor's parting advice. *Brad and Chelsea don't color inside the lines. Why should you?*

"That's not a very Leia thing to say. Show me your princess face."

I laugh, the sound echoing in the strange acoustics of the bathroom. "You can't even see me. How will you judge my princess face?"

"Through the Force. Obviously."

Somehow, I doubt that Princess Leia ever held war conferences from a toilet seat. I growl into the phone, setting my face into a determined snarl. "There. Happy?"

"That's my girl," Vanessa says. "Now go get 'em."

chapter thirty-three

I mull things over as I go to return the stolen tablet. I wish Connor's departure hadn't been so rushed. We could have talked over a plan together. Alone, I'm just not sure what to do. I pace along the hallway, replaying the past few weeks in my mind.

Maybe I did care too much about being safe. Anytime I've felt like I had any control, I looked back on the path only to realize I'd ended up right where the producers wanted. It's time to be unpredictable. And just like that, it clicks.

I rush around the ground floor until I finally find Venti in the lounge. "Your whole job is to put on a great show, right?"

He narrows his eyes at me. "Yes. Why?"

"Hear me out. This is the first season of *Second Chance Romance*, and odds are that my mom is going to choose Brad, who is an unlikable asshole. No one is going to buy that or be happy about it. Or, you could have Sam, the normal, relatable, funny guy with the heart of gold."

Venti waves me off. "Sam Whitley is not a contestant on this show."

"But he could be." I gesture to the cameras. "He's on all this footage. Hanging out with Mom. Walking with Mom. I'm not saying put him in the main show. But make it about him. The unexpected

grand love that resulted from the first season." Venti doesn't interrupt me, which I take to be a good sign. "Catastrophic divorce with Brad, or heart-melting, goo-goo forbidden romance with Sam that's saved by Julia's daughter, who was so devastated over Sam's departure that she fought for him to come back." I make jazz hands. "Based on a true story."

Venti holds up a finger as he types something into his phone. A minute later, the doors open behind me, and Tall and Grande stride into the room. Venti returns his attention to me. "Tell them what you just told me."

I search half the house before I locate Ian on the patio, slouched in a chair and eating a sandwich. "Did surmfing happen?" he garbles, half rising and setting his hand on the camera sitting at his side like a dog begging for scraps.

"Yes, there's something new going on." I pull up a chair and lean forward, setting my forearms across my knees. "Do you know how to get to Sam's place?"

"Why do you wurna know?"

"It's rude to talk with your mouth full."

He swallows and swishes a bit of peach iced tea around his mouth. "It's also rude to bother people on their contractually negotiated, collectively bargained, absolutely sacred union break. Plus, I was really enjoying this sandwich, and now it's getting soggy."

"I need you to drive me to Sam's place and film us without anyone else knowing," I whisper, unsure of who else might be lurking around.

Ian tears open his bag of chips and crushes a handful between his teeth. "Look, I'm pretty pissed off at him right now, so I'm not exactly up for some scheme. I vouched for him to get this job, and then he got fired. That makes me look like crap too."

"You're not getting it." I waggle the piece of paper with Sam's address in front of Ian's face. "Production wants us to do this. They signed off on it."

"Sure, they did."

I grab hold of Ian's camera. "I will throw this thing down the hill if you don't get up right now and help me. The producers want us to leave now to catch Sam before he skips town."

For once, I'm happy to see Venti appear. He leans down to confer with Ian, whose eyes get steadily wider. "Oh. Kay." Ian sits up straighter. "Yeah, I got it. My bad. Misunderstood the situation."

"Do you need to, like, pack anything?" I ask.

"Nope," Ian says, jangling his keys at me. I follow him over to the parking lot and climb into one of the vans. Before we leave, he glares at me. "By the way, if you ever, ever touch my camera again, there's going to be another crew down here filming the news story about the cameraman who murdered a teenage girl and threw her body off the Seven Mile Bridge. Got it?"

I rub my chin. "Wow, Ian. That's awfully specific."

"No one would blame me. I'll just tell them that you interrupted my union break while I was having an out-of-body experience with a meatball sub and some jalapeño chips. No one could argue with that. *Nolle pros.*"

The Sun and Sands Motel is a two-story motor lodge sprawled half the length of a dead-end street like a lounging cat. Sam's room is on the second floor in the northern corner. I run my hand along the railing, the chipping paint rough against the skin of my palm. It reminds me of my apartment building. Home.

I knock on the door with the side of my fist, standing on my tiptoes to position my face in front of the peephole. "Sam, it's Cara. Open up."

I hear a faint banging from inside, then the murmur of the television cutting out. If he wanted to hide, he would have been better off ignoring me. Now I know for sure that it's him. "I can hear you! I know you're in there!"

I take a step back as the dead bolt snaps open. Sam sticks his head over the threshold to look past me at the empty walkway. "Did you come here by yourself?"

"Look both ways," Ian drawls.

Sam startles at the sight of him. "What are you doing here? Why are you filming?"

I kick my foot across the jamb, rendering my next question moot: "Can we come in and talk?"

"Yes?" He steps back. "Sorry about the mess. I wasn't expecting any company."

I linger to the side of the room while Sam clears the two-person table of empty beer bottles and individual-sized cereal boxes that look like they were pilfered from the motel breakfast. Ian comes in after, throwing open the curtains and turning on the lights. "Would it have killed you to grab my lighting guy on the way out?" he grumbles, stepping over a pair of Sam's dirty socks with a frown.

"Well, might as well get to the point," I tell Sam, ignoring Ian entirely. "You should come back and convince my mom not to marry Brad because he is the biggest turd on the planet. And then you guys can go out and it'll be adorable and I will never have to see Brad and Chelsea ever again. The end."

Sam doesn't even smile. "I can't. Your mom is a wonderful, amazing, beautiful person. But she deserves a life that I can't give her. If she wanted us to be together, she would have said so."

"She didn't have the chance. One day you were there, and then you were gone. If she sees you again, she'll change her mind. I just know it."

"I'm sorry," Sam says, sighing. "It's just not my place. There's a reason she went on that show. The contestants are always a certain caliber of"—he waves a hand the length of his body—"man. And that's not me."

"But what about what *you* want? Is this it?" I ask, gesturing to his mountain of dirty laundry and the ten-year-old boxy television. "Motel rooms and trivia night and getting dumped by a text message on your fourth wedding anniversary? Come on!"

Scarlet splotches burst over Sam's cheeks. His thumb punches through the Styrofoam of his coffee cup. "You act like I don't want to be rich and successful and married to the love of my life! But I'm not ever going to get those things." He presses harder against the cup until it disintegrates in his hand. "I'm middle-aged and unemployed, and it's a contest to see whether my gut or my bald spot is growing faster. I'm going to die alone with six cats in my crappy basement apartment. That is my life."

"It is if you don't take any risks."

"I did take a risk!" His skin flushes again beneath the smattering of freckles across his nose. "I took a risk on your mom. And then I got fired for it!"

"Don't blame this on her," I warn, holding up a finger.

"I'm not!" Sam shouts, then quietly adds, "I'm blaming myself for thinking anyone that good could ever happen to a loser like me."

I slap a copy of the schedule onto the table, even though Sam probably still has it memorized, and point to one square with the cheap motel pen. I try to circle it, but the ink doesn't run, so I scar it into the paper instead. "Would it change your mind if the producers wanted you to do this because they agree with me?"

His face scrunches together into a tight mess of confusion and wrinkles. "I don't understand." He turns to Ian. "Mike Wistrand authorized this?"

"Please don't speak to or look directly at the camera," Ian deadpans.

Sam holds up his coffee-splattered dirty thumb. "I will rub this all over your lens if you don't answer me."

"She's telling the truth. Somehow, she convinced Wistrand."

"I don't believe this," Sam says, but it's more incredulity than a literal statement. "And you really think that, that, Julia would be interested in me?"

"Yes. That's why *she was making out with you in our shower*. And this is the last date we're going to have before Mom picks a winner. It's a combination Sweetheart Ceremony and Engagement Ceremony. If you ever cared about her at all, if what you felt was real, you'll call the producers, and you'll be there." I search his eyes, finding only doubt and heartache. I leave him with the wisdom of Connor and Vanessa: "Everyone else gets ahead by coloring outside the lines. You have to fight for the life you want, Sam."

chapter thirty-four

I spend most of the next afternoon packing up the guesthouse and making lists of items to remember before we depart for the airport. I must check the schedule five times before I truly believe that it's almost over. In two days, we'll be on our way home. I will be shamelessly scouring the internet for any mention of Connor Dingeldein.

While I clean, I avoid the subject of Mom's potential engagement. We're deadlocked and we know it. My only hope is to play the wild card—Sam.

Unfortunately, Venti says that Sam hasn't called. I'd assume that the producers are just messing with me again, but Ian has no evidence to the contrary.

I panic when Angela informs us that we'll be wearing casual clothing—"chic casual, not lazy Saturday on the couch casual"— since we'll be filming the finale on the beach. I told Sam the time and the day, but the copy of the schedule I gave to him doesn't have the location. I can only hope that he did the smart thing and called Venti.

Once we're dressed, we climb into the silver sedan usually reserved for transporting the losing contestants after an elimination vote. "Where's everyone else?" Mom asks.

Our driver points south. "They're already at the beach."

We park at the edge of an overlook with views of the water and a sun-bleached wooden pier. Mom and I kick off our sandals, carrying them by their straps as we follow a narrow path outlined by lit torches stuck in the sand. At the end, we find a pavilion draped in sheer white curtains and a round table set for six.

Confessional: I miss Connor.

On the far side, closest to the water, there are three low pedestals painted to resemble natural stone. Two of them display the remaining lockets from the Wall of Hearts, the wooden doors open to show the pictures of Brad and Chelsea, Ray and Sabrina. The center pedestal showcases Mom's engagement ring, encased in a polished cherry ring box that gleams in the torchlight.

"Welcome to your surprise dinner," Danny Romano says in his officious host voice, gesturing to the charcoal grill and a prep table covered in ingredients, spices, and plastic shopping bags. "The contestants have spent the past hour making a variety of dishes for you to enjoy."

"That's so sweet," Mom says, smiling as Ray turns on a playlist of classical music.

I'm not particularly enthused about the making-a-meal concept until the producers add that we're allowed to eat, as long as it's not limiting conversation.

We take our seats, leaning back as Sabrina delivers a pale orange drink and a glass of water to each of us. "That's a mango-and-squash smoothie," Ray explains. "I tried to come up with a recipe that was sweet without having to add sugar."

"I helped!" Sabrina chirps.

Mom and I hesitate for a split second before taking a sip. We've both been burned by Dad's experimental tendencies at the juice

275

bar. Ray and Sabrina are far more gifted, however, because even I enjoy the taste and consistency. "This is really good," I tell Sabrina. "And I usually don't like smoothies."

Sabrina smiles and sits across from us. "Thanks. My job was drinks and setting the table."

As if on cue, Ray appears next with an oblong platter that he sets in the center of the table. He hands Mom a pair of tongs. "We don't have an oven, so I had to get a little creative." He picks up a fork and uses it as a pointer. "This is a peanut curry dip with grilled sweet potato fries. Bacon-wrapped figs in a maple glaze. Deviled eggs with avocado. And my personal favorite—what I call 'Lunchables for grown-ups'—the crostini topped with prosciutto and fresh mozzarella."

"I don't know what to eat first," Mom says, laughing. "It all sounds delicious."

"I'll take one of everything." I reach out and start piling food onto my plate, not caring about the tongs. Anything is finger food if you try hard enough. "How'd you learn to make all this? I thought you were an English teacher, not a chef."

Ray flushes a bright pink. "When my wife passed, I could barely figure out how to make mac and cheese out of a box. I signed up for a couple of cooking classes at the community college. It was a bit more advanced than I expected."

Sabrina taps her spoon against the side of her plate to shake off a dollop of peanut dip. "They flipped a coin to see who gets to make the steak."

"Who won?" Mom asks.

"Brad."

My mouth is full of bacon, so I just roll my eyes.

Whenever the producers or Ian are within view, I search their mannerisms or body language for some indication of what to expect. But to no avail.

Brad and Chelsea stop over periodically for a sip of smoothie or to pick at the hors d'oeuvres. It's clear from Brad's uncharacteristic silence that he's nervous. He opens the lid of the grill too often, flinging bits of meat onto the sand as he fidgets with the spatula. I don't think he anticipated Ray's obvious prowess at this particular skill.

"Filet mignon," Brad announces as he delivers the main course. "Cooked medium with a light char." He takes his seat beside Chelsea, serving himself first.

I don't need to cut into the filet to know that it's overdone by any standard. The outer edge looks like it was cooked by fire-breathing dragon. When I poke it with my fork, it takes considerable force to sink the tines into the meat.

"Thank you all so much," Mom gushes, cutting off a sliver of filet and chewing it for a full thirty seconds before swallowing. "This is so amazing. What a wonderful way to have our final evening together."

Without saying a word, Ray returns to the makeshift cooking area and searches in the cooler at his feet. He throws a few ingredients into a metal mixing bowl, sets it on the grill, and then carries it over. "Would anyone like a topping for your filet?" he asks, spooning the concoction over his meal. "It's just butter, garlic, and parsley."

"Sure," I say, holding out my plate next. Hopefully it'll make the dry meat palatable. Otherwise, I'm going to have to saw off the crust on the outside.

My mind drifts to eating grilled cheese sandwiches on the floor with Connor.

Confessional: I *really* miss Connor.

Brad scowls when he notices that no one finishes the main course, but all of Ray's appetizers are gone, down to the last drop of dip.

"Hope you aren't too full for dessert," Chelsea says. She retrieves a tray of marshmallows on skewers, each accompanied by a pair of graham crackers and a generous square of chocolate. "I thought we could use the Tiki torches to melt the marshmallows."

"Man, that's a great idea," I mutter, hating that she thought of it.

Chelsea looks equally surprised by my compliment. She offers me the first skewer. "I'm addicted to s'mores. I even have s'mores cereal at home."

"They make s'mores cereal?" I look at Mom. "Can we get that?"

She huffs a laugh. "Why? Sick of my organic flaxseed already?"

In a way, I'm happy that we're not all bickering with each other. It's the final vote. We should be able to spend at least one pleasant hour together. Brad even lightens up a bit and shares in a laugh when he accidentally liquifies his marshmallow in the fire and drips it onto his own toe.

The camaraderie ebbs as Danny Romano announces that it's time to begin the Sweetheart Ceremony. My *actual* heart sputters and jumps like an old truck starting on a winter morning. It's too late. Sam isn't coming. I give a confused look to Venti, who only shrugs.

As a group, we move closer to the three pedestals as someone cuts the music. I stare at Mom's engagement ring, noting that she ended up with the princess cut. It's funny for there to be so much meaning assigned to such a small object. I could toss it in the ocean right now, and we'd never find it in a million years of searching.

I know that Danny Romano is talking, but I can't hear beyond the rush of blood in my ears, the roar of my own thoughts. In spite of the food, I feel suddenly faint. Cold. I swear that the world turns for a moment before Danny Romano asks, for the last time, "Julia and Cara, who have you chosen for tonight's elimination?"

chapter thirty-five

*M*om moves in slow motion toward the pedestals and inspects the pictures in both lockets. I can't tell if she's pretending to deliberate to draw out the tension or if she's legitimately unsure of her decision. All I know is that I can't sway her because she's right. A spouse is the bigger decision.

Finally, she reaches out and closes Ray and Sabrina's locket, just like I suspected.

Danny Romano nods. "Ray and Sabrina, you have been selected for elimination. Please say your goodbyes to Julia and Cara."

Brad clenches his hand into a fist and pumps it at his side. Chelsea doesn't react at all beyond a slight shifting of her posture.

"I'm sorry that things didn't work out for us." Ray spreads his arms wide, kissing Mom's cheek as she meets him halfway in a quick embrace. Beneath his disappointed expression and the dejected tone of his words, I detect acceptance. I don't think he believed he could win.

I step forward to hug Sabrina. "I'm sorry too. I had a lot of fun hanging out with you."

"It was a tough choice," Mom says.

Ray nods and takes a deep breath. "You've given me the

courage and the confidence to start dating again. I can't thank you enough for that. Bye, Julia."

I crush him in a hug before he can say anything, pulling Sabrina against my side with my other arm. "I'm so happy I got to meet you two. Stay in touch with us, okay?"

"We will," Ray promises.

"I'll miss you!" Sabrina mumbles against my shirt.

We stand as a group and watch them depart. Danny Romano breaks the solemnity once they're clear of the beach. "Congratulations, Brad and Chelsea!" he exclaims a moment later, smushing in between them. "You are this season's winners. Now, Brad, you have a big decision to make. Will you choose to remain friends, continue dating, or ask Julia to marry you?"

Danny Romano pivots to deliver a monologue straight at the camera. "Now, Julia and Brad, we have a bit of a surprise for you as well. If you choose to tie the knot, we'll be thrilled to have you back for an all-expenses paid special feature of your wedding."

Mom gasps and presses a hand to her lips. It's surprisingly convincing, given that they've told us about this prize multiple times already.

Confessional: There is no way I'm doing this shit again. Come on, Sam. Come on.

Danny Romano takes a step back to let Ian move in for a closer shot. "So, what will it be, Brad?"

I suspect that there will be a commercial break at this exact moment when the show airs.

Brad smirks, pinching the band of the engagement ring between his fingers. He brushes an errant shell out of the way before bending to one knee. "Julia, I truly believe that we are made for each other. I can't wait to help make you into the best possible woman you can be. We'll see the world together, try new things. Will you accept this ring as a symbol of my love and commitment?"

Before Mom can respond, Danny Romano cuts in. "This is such an intense moment, but there's more here than what meets the eye."

Brad mashes the ring onto her finger. *"Will you accept—"*

If there's one thing I can trust Danny Romano to do, it's talk louder. He raises his voice to drown out Brad. "Julia, we at *Second Chance Romance* felt that we couldn't rightfully deny you the second chance that your heart yearned for. With that in mind, Julia, we're giving you . . . a second chance . . . at Sam."

All our heads whip around as Sam strides into view in a mismatched suit with an ill-fitting jacket. "Julia, I'm so sorry about everything."

"Sam," Mom gasps, reaching for him involuntarily. "You're still here. You haven't gone home yet?"

Brad rises to his feet and puts a hand on Sam's chest, giving him a light shove. "What's your problem? You're not a part of this. She doesn't want to talk to you."

I inadvertently make eye contact with Venti. With a smug smile, I sweep my arm over the scene, from Brad's purpling face to Mom's complete shock. *I give you drama à la teenage girl.*

"Is that true?" Sam asks.

Mom, speechless, shakes her head.

Sam uncrumples a piece of notebook paper, holding it an inch away from his glasses in the low light. His shoulders are rigid and tight, his elbows tucked against his sides. He turns to Mom. "J-Julia, I couldn't let you go without telling you my feelings. Ever since our first video conference, I've felt drawn to your energy and your drive. There were a few times that I even made up reasons to call you. You are so smart and funny, and I would lose my job fifty more times to get fifty more date nights with you."

He looks up from his paper, locking eyes with her.

"I can't swear that I will marry or fall madly in love with you, but by God, I would love the chance to try." He struggles to kneel and holds up a black velvet ring box. "Will you accept this promise ring as a symbol of my affection?"

Ian kicks him on the bottom of his shoe, hissing, "Open the box, you dolt."

Sam pries open the top to reveal the silver sand dollar ring.

Brad scoffs. "A promise ring? What are you, fourteen years old?" While Brad's natural inclination seems to be to get louder, Chelsea shrinks back. If she's such a television insider like she claims to be after her commercials, she can probably tell this isn't a flattering look for them.

The relief on Mom's face is tangible, but I'm still not leaving this up to her judgment alone. "Do it, Mom! Say yes!"

"I accept," Mom blurts, still in a daze as she pries Brad's ring off her finger. I lurch forward to take it from her before she drops it into the sand. I have a feeling that the show will need to exercise its return policy.

"This is ridiculous!" Brad shouts. "He's not even part of the show. I'm the last man standing. That means I win."

Chelsea holds up a hand. "Dad, may—"

"Shut up, Chelsea!" he snaps.

Mom turns to him. "I'm so sorry. I didn't know they were planning this. I just . . . I should explain how I've been feeling and why I was a little nervous to pick you."

"There's nothing to explain," Brad says, grabbing her arm and tugging her off-balance. "We just need to talk away from everyone else."

Mom twists free of his grip, pressing her bare foot against his stomach and shoving him with a move straight out of her Kickboxing 101 class. She rubs her wrist. "I'm trying to talk to you right now, but you're not listening to me. If you touch me again, I'm calling security."

Brad fixes his shirt. "How is this legal? I signed a contract when I came on this show."

Mom barks a laugh. "Go ahead. Sue." She waves a hand at him. "You can go now. Thanks for playing."

Two of the larger crew members intercept Brad and steer him away from the beach. Chelsea follows at a distance, her head hanging low. It's a beautiful sight.

Mom holds out her hand to Sam, and he slides the sand dollar ring onto her finger. The design is tiny compared to the bulk of the diamond solitaire, but I can tell from the shy grin on her face that she loves it. She never wore her original engagement ring, anyway.

"Will you just kiss me already?" she says, breathless and blushing.

"I would," Sam croaks, "but I have really bad knees, and I honestly don't think I can get up with all this sand."

Without jostling the camera, Ian smacks his hand against his forehead, chuckling. He motions to an assistant to help Sam, but Mom hauls him to his feet with ease. She gets her kiss, swaying in his arms.

"How did you know?" Mom whispers, admiring the sand dollar ring on her finger.

Sam and Ian exchange conspiratorial glances. "Let's just say that I had a little help."

I turn the music back on, increasing the volume until it's loud enough for Mom and Sam to hear as they drift closer to the surf.

"This is going to be an editing nightmare," Ian mumbles, watching as Sam twirls Mom through an impromptu dance. "He just wrecked the entire story line. I've never been so happy to be just a camera guy."

"You're not just a camera guy," I say, throwing my arms around him and squeezing. "You're a good friend, too. Thank you, Ian. Thank you so much."

He pats me on the back. "You're welcome. Take care of Sam for me, okay?"

"We will."

I pluck a paring knife off the prep table and use the point to dig out the glossy photographs from Brad and Chelsea's locket.

In their stead, I carve two names: Julia and Sam.

epilogue

I'm exhausted from the three-hour drive to Pittsburgh, even though Connor stayed on the phone with me for most of it. It's soothing to hear his voice and feel like he's with me.

When I first called him after nagging Venti half to death to give me his number, I was afraid he'd tell me the whole thing was an act or that keeping a long-distance relationship going was too much work. It was hard to believe that in the beginning, I'd only let our relationship play out *because* it would end. I'd never hoped so much to be wrong.

But instead of hanging up, he just asked me which airport is closest to my house. It would have been easier to answer if we hadn't immediately ditched Dad and LeAnne the moment Mom got her check for appearing on the show.

I thought I'd stop visiting them so often once I turned eighteen, but guilt always seems to compel me back to Ohio. At least I also got to catch up with Vanessa and make plans for me to crash the Spring Fling. I can't wait for her to meet Connor. She insists that they've already met from our video chats, but it's just not the same. At least for me.

I check my watch, grimacing at the time. At this rate, I'll barely be able to eat breakfast before Mom is rushing me out the door again.

Thankfully, Sam already has a pot of coffee brewing in the kitchen of our little town house. "Hit traffic?" he asks, pouring me a cup and passing over a box of donuts. "I got you a bear claw."

"Thanks," I mumble, dunking my donut into the black coffee. "Traffic was okay. I just had trouble getting on the road because Dad wouldn't stop talking about how he's carrying the whole gym by himself and Mom's not doing anything."

Mom sweeps into the room in a pair of black leggings and a hot-pink racerback tank top. She groans, stealing a bite of my bear claw. "Not that argument again."

"He's still so salty. He can't even help it."

Sam chuckles. "As the two of you would say, on a scale of one to Cinderella's stepsisters, how salty?"

"Ten," I reply, draining my mug and setting it in the sink. "Absolutely a ten. He might as well start jamming his feet into other people's shoes."

We pile into Sam's SUV and drive across town to the industrial district. The warehouse is so large that it peeks above the surrounding buildings, dwarfing a nearby auto shop on the corner. Sam parks by the side door and swipes us inside with his security badge.

"That was a good idea," I admit, eyeing the cameras directed at the entrance from the inside. "We won't have to worry about any weirdos showing up again. Or if they do, we'll know who they are right away."

Mom nods with fervor. "Anything to help with this paparazzi problem."

She's been a little sour ever since we found a photographer hiding in the bathroom. She can't complain too much, though. Despite the show's ridiculous marketing of the first season of

Second Chance Romance as a whirlwind romance, they didn't offer Mom and Sam the luxury wedding, claiming Sam wasn't really a contestant.

It didn't matter. So many people were obsessed with them after the premiere that Mom and Sam can afford whatever they want with their own money. Sure, we sometimes find photographers standing on the toilets. It still seems like a small price to pay for the opportunities that have come out of appearing on the show—like Mom's new job.

The main floor of the warehouse is already prepped, smelling of lemon cleaner and the rubber of exercise mats. Mom checks her hair and confers with her two exercise demonstrators, whose jobs, as far as I can tell, are to work out in the background of Mom's videos and look like it's harder for them than it is for her. I lounge in a nearby chair, watching as everyone dashes around making their last-minute adjustments.

"Are we ready?" Mom asks, moving to the center of the room.

Sam cups his hands around his mouth and shouts, "Ready when you are!"

Mom waits a few beats before breaking into her opening greeting. "Thanks for tuning in to this episode of *Celebrity Fitness*," she says. "Today, we have three very special guests. The first, you might recognize from his cutthroat battle to become the king of swordfish: Brian Foster from *High Steaks Chef.*"

Mom and her demonstrators clap as Brian emerges onto the exercise floor, his fingers pulling at the spandex of his skintight compression shirt. He shakes Mom's hand. "Julia, thank you so much for having me on the show. You know what a fan I am."

Mom waits for him to get into position before she returns to the camera. "Our next guests are dear friends and the newest stars of *Second Chance Romance*, season two." She gestures off-screen. "Please welcome Ray and Sabrina Ortega."

Ray and Sabrina sandwich Mom in a double hug, bowling her over onto the floor. She stumbles to her feet, laughing, and uses Ray's shoulder for balance as she puts her sneaker back on. "You've only been here five seconds, and you're already knocking me over! What's going to happen when we start exercising near each other?"

"Cut!" Sam steps forward, grinning. "Let's try that again. We'll start from after Brian."

"Uh-oh," Ian mutters, leaning back from his camera and waving his arms in the air. "Everybody, watch out! Sam is using his producer voice."

"You can't make fun of me too much. I control whether or not you get a raise."

Ian scoffs. "I can just blackmail you by threatening to release those pictures from your bachelor party. Then you'll pay up."

I haven't seen these infamous pictures, but I know that they involve a distillery tour, a full-size chicken costume, and finding Sam passed out on our front step the next morning with a note that said *Julia's Problem* pinned to his shirt.

"You wouldn't dare," Sam says, narrowing his eyes.

"Try me." Ian jerks his thumb at me. "It's like she said back in Florida. All's fair in love and television."

I cup my hands around my mouth and shout back. "Except union breaks, right?"

Ian laughs. "See? She's a pro!"

Bethany Mangle's Recipe for All the Right Reasons:

✓ 2 amazing agents, the Jennifer Wills and Nicole Resciniti limited edition combo set: Jen, you go above and beyond in every way. When I first signed with you, I couldn't believe that I finally had an agent! Now, I value you much more as a friend. I feel so fortunate to have you, Nicole Resciniti, and The Seymour Agency cheering me on.

✓ 1 tireless editor with a love of reality TV: Cue Nicole Fiorica, who championed this project from the beginning and helped with all of the reality TV facts I would need to bring Cara's experiences to life. Thank you for making this baby author feel like a pro, even when I am a constant stream of technical malfunctions and ridiculous questions.

✓ 1 dramatic animal, collie mix: Mr. Dog, you will never read this because you are dog. But I want to say it anyway. I love you, my little bug.

✓ 1 husband, complete nerd, mildly radioactive: Thank you for all the behind-the-scenes work you do to make my writing career a success. Between driving me to bookstores and reminding me to keep receipts, it's never a slow day for you either. (Oh, and you forgive me for putting the dog first in my acknowledgments.)

✓ 2 parents, 1 brother, 1 sister-in-law-to-be (Mia, you better say yes because I'm writing this before he's asked you, and this will be awkward if you say no), 1 grandmother: The secret ingredient, obviously. Thank you for my daily pep talks, game nights, and book swaps.

✓ 4 full-size Mangles, 2 little Mangles, Barnetts to taste: I wish we didn't live so far away, but I love our visits and rubber chicken–flinging battles.

✓ A generous amount of Bethanys: To Bethany Ruccolo, the original Bethany in my life, I love you to bits and pieces. And to The Real B Hive, for the endless support—Bethany Baptiste, Bethany Bennett, Bethany Bliss, B.S. Casey, Bethany Hensel, Bethany Lauren James, Bethany Lord, Bethany Maines, Bethany Martin, Bethany C. Morrow, and Bethany Perry.

✓ 1 Stephanie and 1 Stéphanie: Stephanie Downey, I owe you for all of the support and the endless supply of adorable goat pictures. Stéphanie Sauvinet, thank you for coffee shop writer days and reminding me to get back to my favorite TV shows.

✓ 2 talented mentees: Kylie Jackson and Christina Schmidt, thank you for trusting me with your work and letting me help with your incredible stories.

✓ 1 Simon & Schuster–Books Forward variety pack: Thank you to everyone behind the scenes who brought this book to life and supported my career thus far—Bridget Madsen, Eugene Lee, Rebecca Syracuse, Isa Indra Permana, Tatyana Rosalia, Rebecca Vitkus, Mandy Veloso, Cassie Malmo, and Ellen Whitfield.

✓ 4 incredible, inimitable, extraordinary author friends who deserve all the adjectives: To Caitlin Colvin, for late-night talks and huge plates of nachos. To Laura Genn, for taking care of Sir Forehead Sloth and making me burn my toast. To Michelle Mohrweis, for cute bird videos and the best darn turnip run in history. To Melissa See, for laughing at my corniest jokes when no one else will, and, of course, for being so inspirationally inspirational.

Bethany Mangle is the author of *Prepped* and *All the Right Reasons*. She was born in Korea and raised in New Jersey in a household full of books, sheet music, and dog hair. She currently lives and writes in Mississippi. Visit her at BethanyMangle.com.